Joanna Bolouri worked in sales before she began writing professionally at the age of thirty. Winning a BBC comedy script competition allowed her to work and write with stand-up comedians, comedy scriptwriters and actors from across the UK. She's had articles and reviews published in the *Scotsman*, *The Skinny*, the *Scottish Sun* and the *Huffington Post*.

Also by Joanna Bolouri

The List
I Followed the Rules
The Most Wonderful Time of the Year

Relight my Fire

JOANNA BOLOURI

Quercus

First published in Great Britain in 2018 by

Quercus Editions Ltd
Carmelite House
50 Victoria Embankment
London EC4Y 0DZ

An Hachette UK company

A CIP catalogue record for this book is available
from the British Library.

PB ISBN 978 1 78648 858 9
Ebook ISBN 978 1 78648 857 2

10 9 8 7 6 5 4 3

Typeset by Jouve (UK), Milton Keynes

Printed and bound in Great Britain by Clays Ltd, Elcograf S.p.A.

To the love of my life.

Where are you?

Hurry the hell up.

JANUARY

Sunday January 1st

New Year's Day began with the sound of a ranting Irishman. Actually, this is how most of my days have begun recently.

'Phoebe, did you purposefully buy the ugliest potatoes you could find or were these all the shop had yesterday?'

I heard the blinds being sharply pulled open as I drowsily checked the clock radio on my bedside table.

09.17 – Jesus, even the winter sun has only just surfaced. Why did I have to?

'Potatoes?' I enquired, watching little specks of dust caught in the daylight float past the clock display. 'Oliver, what are you talking about?' I rubbed my right eye which refused to open fully and tried to sit up, but he was waving a huge bag of spuds in front of me, unintentionally blocking my attempt.

'These, Phoebe!' he said, holding them aloft. '*Po-ta-toes*. I specifically said I wanted baby potatoes for the meal today. These are clearly fucking elderly.'

'It was all they had!' I exclaimed. 'It *was* five minutes before closing on New Year's Eve, Oliver. It was them, a box of Smash or frozen chips. I'm pretty sure your family won't give a shit what form their potatoes take. *Because they're potatoes.*'

Tutting, he examined the bag again, before sitting on the edge of the bed, defeated. I've had many, many absurd conversations with Oliver but this was just silly. I started to giggle.

'What's so funny?! Just because I—'

'Oliver, you're Irish and you're ranting about *potatoes*! *Come on!* Even you must—'

'Forget it.'

'What, you're in a huff now? Really?'

He stood up and stomped towards the bedroom door, leaving me half laughing, half wondering what the hell just happened. As he pulled open the door, grumbling about having to make 'bastard mash', a second voice bellowed from the direction of the bathroom.

'I NEED TOILET ROLL!'

Oliver carried on walking towards the kitchen. 'Ask your mum, Molly. I'm carrying really heavy, really *ugly* potatoes.'

I rolled my eyes. 'If you say potatoes *one more time* I'm—'

'MUM . . . MUUUMMMMMMYY!'

I threw back the covers and grabbed for my dressing gown. Gone were the days when New Year's morning was spent nursing a gruesome hangover in a hotel room with my best mates Lucy and Hazel before travelling home to lie in bed for the rest of the day, hoping for some hangover sex when the nausea subsided. It appeared that this particular New Year's morning would be spent arguing about potatoes, pacifying my noticeably stressed boyfriend and assisting my pooing daughter.

Wearing the green, fluffy M&S dressing gown I got for Christmas, I grabbed a toilet roll from the hall cupboard and threw it to Molly who caught it triumphantly from her porcelain throne.

'Is Auntie Megan coming today?' she asked, placing the new roll on top of the holder. 'What about Granny and Grandpa?'

Louise and Brendan (Oliver's quiet, moderately religious parents), moved to Glasgow in 1993 for Brendan's job but returned to Ireland in 2006 to retire. And they retired hard. Pottering around the house soon turned into never leaving the house, separate beds and an in-depth knowledge of every person seen coming and going from their neighbours' houses. They had flown into Glasgow yesterday and it was only the second time they've stepped back on Scottish soil since Molly was born. We've always had to go to Dublin. Oliver calls them *the recluses* and although he's not particularly close to them, I can tell that their unwillingness to make more of an effort with Molly, or anyone else, troubles him. On the other hand, Megan, his older sister, is besotted with Molly – perhaps partly because she's Oliver's double, down to the curly brown hair and wrinkled-brow scowl. *'She has a much better nature, though. Oliver was a little smart arse. He still is to be fair.'* Megan shares the curly hair gene and looks like she was made in the same factory as The Corrs. I'm very fond of her and her stupid beautiful face.

'Yes, Granny and Grandpa are coming; they'll all be here at two,' I replied, admiring her cute pyjamas. 'You should wear the puppy t-shirt Auntie Megan bought you! She'll be thrilled to see you in it.'

She frowned. 'I hate puppies.'

'Just for today, Cruella,' I responded, laughing. Molly

hates a different thing each week. Last week she announced her loathing of books, yet she appeared to have two on her lap at that very moment. 'Um, are you finished? Do you need any help?'

'No. I'm almost five, Mum. I'm not a baby.'

'You're not five until July . . . and you're *my* baby.'

'Ugh, you *always* say that.'

'Sure do,' I replied. 'And please swap over the old toilet roll because it will drive me mad otherwise.' Closing the bathroom door, I stopped for a moment and listened as she fiddled with the toilet roll holder, muttering 'kittens are much better' under her breath. Even on the toilet she's the sweetest thing I've ever seen in my life.

Smiling to myself, I strolled into the kitchen to put the kettle on, only to discover that Oliver had obviously been up and at 'em for quite a while.

'Oliver, it's a family lunch, not a state dinner for two hundred people!' I exclaimed, gazing at the flour-covered worktops almost completely hidden by umpteen bowls and kitchen utensils. I moved a bag of carrots to get access to the kettle and he gave a little yelp.

'Don't touch anything! I have a system going here.'

'A system? But I need coffee . . . what the hell . . . is that a power drill?!'

He placed his hands on my shoulders and turned me 180 degrees, pushing me back towards the hall. 'I'll bring you a coffee, go and shower or something. I'm busy. I'm creating.'

'Damn, you're bossy today,' I replied, promptly turning myself back around. He looked flustered. He looked fucking sexy; his dark curly hair dishevelled, his t-shirt clinging to his chest and stomach. Even after all these years, he still does it for me. Big time. 'Are you stressed? I mean, I could help with that . . .'

I opened my dressing gown and pushed my body against his, slowly moving a hand down towards his crotch. A hand that Oliver quickly stopped in its tracks. He shook his head. 'I don't have time, Phoebe. We don't have time. Please just get dressed. Anyway, Molly will be through in a minute.'

'Fuckssake Oliver, I wasn't going to wank you off in the kitchen, I was just being affectionate.'

I took myself off to the bedroom before he could say anything else, but there was no response anyway. He continued chopping and peeling vegetables while I made our bed. Christ, I know we're not love's young dream anymore but I thought I might at least get felt up.

By half past twelve the kitchen was in better shape and lunch was cooking, filling the house with steak pie aroma. Molly had helped set the table, before announcing how boring it was and leaving us to get on with it. I was still peeved with Oliver but I understood his anxiety. When my parents came over from Canada in August, I took them out for dinner every night so they wouldn't question why none of our cutlery or plates matched. However parents might claim not to judge us, they absolutely do. Luckily, my best mate Lucy had bought us new cutlery for Christmas, albeit reluctantly (*'Boo, you fucking bores. Take it quickly before I dismember you with it'*) so at least that's been rectified.

'I need to go and pick everyone up from the hotel soon!' Oliver called from the kitchen. 'Can you keep an eye on the veg? It'll only need another ten minutes.'

'Yup,' I replied, sticking my head around the kitchen door. I watched Oliver dry his hands on a tea towel.

'Cheers,' he replied, grabbing his car keys off the hook. 'You look pretty, by the way.'

'Pretty enough to ravage me later?'

'God, what's gotten into you?'

'Well not you, for, oh, *four weeks now*! Maybe longer . . .'

He frowned. 'It hasn't been that long. Has it?'

I nodded while he racked his brains, trying to remember the last time we'd had sex before snapping himself out of it. 'Look, we'll talk later, I need to get going. Tell Molly not to demolish the chocolates on the coffee table before I get back.' And with that he was off, leaving me wondering how we went from shagging ourselves senseless to only vaguely remembering what the other looks like naked. I think he might have gone off me.

Monday January 2nd

Yesterday's lunch went well, I think, given that no one ended up in tears or being punched repeatedly in the face, which is the benchmark by which I measure most things.

I had just drained the carrots when Oliver arrived back with his family in tow. Megan was brushing down her back-side, having just slipped and fallen on the ice.

'Phoebe!' she cried, stomping her boots on the doormat, 'Happy New Year! I've just done myself an injury. Where is my beautiful niece then?' She followed the sound of Molly's voice into the living room while Louise and Brendan made their way up the stairs and into the flat.

'I thought you'd have moved into a proper house by now,' I heard Louise mumble to Oliver. 'That wee girl should have a garden.' Brendan silently followed behind like an undertaker.

Oliver sighed. 'We live close to a huge park, Mam. It's Glasgow, not the Sahara. She's not grass-deprived.'

I smiled to myself, feeling somewhat vindicated. I had wanted to buy somewhere new with a garden when Molly was born, but Oliver convinced me that it'd be easier and cheaper if we all just lived in his flat. Although spacious, it still doesn't exactly feel like a family home and having to ask his landlord for permission every time we want to paint a room is getting on my nerves.

I kissed Oliver's parents hello, taking their jackets and inviting them to go on through to the living room. Throwing me a 'Here we go' look, Oliver shuffled behind them, like a seven-year-old who'd been bribed to attend his own party.

'Haven't you grown!' I heard Brendan say to Molly, while Oliver proudly boasted that she was only four years old and already four feet five inches tall, 'well above the national average', like he had personally been cultivating her in his greenhouse. I returned to the kitchen and pretended to be busy, staring through the oven door at Oliver's steak pie. Our shitty oven is capable of burning food that's not even inside it and if the pie went wrong I feared Oliver would never recover. He appeared moments later with the same concerns.

'Did the timer go off yet?' he asked, bending down beside me.

I nodded. 'Yeah, it went off ages ago. I'm just interested to see how long it'll take to catch fire and kill us all.'

He scowled. 'I hope you go up in flames first. Go and visit with my family. It's my turn to hide.'

Brendan and Louise sat side by side on the couch, while Megan played with Molly on the living room floor, already surrounded by chocolate wrappers. 'Lunch won't be long, everyone,' I announced cheerily. 'Molly, can you stop eating junk for five minutes?'

'Sorry,' Megan said, laughing. 'That was me. I skipped the hotel breakfast. I don't trust buffets – some fecker could have sneezed all over it. Or worse . . .'

'Megan!' Louise exclaimed. 'Watch what you say in front of the child.'

Megan rolled her eyes and carried on playing with Molly, who was now asking, 'What's worse than sneezing on food?' It's amazing to watch how Oliver and his sister, both grown-ass, greying adults, still get treated like kids by their parents and don't call them out on it. Family dynamics are so weird.

Two hours and three wrong-potato-themed comments from Louise later, lunch was over. Oliver and his throbbing forehead vein were stacking the dishwasher while I sat chatting with everyone else in the living room.

'Two food shopping deliveries a week!' Louise exclaimed, almost spilling her cup of tea. 'She lives alone with her dog! I said to Brendan, how on earth can one tiny woman eat so much? She'd be better off spending her money on fixing up her front garden. What a pigsty it is.'

'Mam, you really need to get a hobby or something,' Megan

sighed. 'I'm sure Mrs Finnegan can do without you spying on her.'

'Nonsense,' Louise replied indignantly, fluffing up her short grey hair. 'Since her husband died, she needs someone to look out for her. I'm doing her a kindness.'

Brendan sat quietly, neither confirming nor denying that his wife was a nosy bastard, while Molly scribbled away in the new farmyard colouring book Megan had picked up for her at the airport.

'Are you back to work next week, Phoebe?' Megan asked, changing the subject. 'I've taken the first two weeks off to move house. I can't be coping with work and all that shi— *nonsense* at the same time.'

'I am,' I replied. 'Molly will be back at nursery too. What's the new place like?'

Megan took a sip from her tea. 'It's deadly. Not too far from where I am now. Bigger flat though. Older. I'm sick of all the new builds with their low ceilings and open plan bathrooms. And it's closer to work. I can run there and back every day. Suits me better.'

She runs to work. There's nothing remotely average about this woman.

While I gaped at her in awe, Oliver appeared, drying his hands on a kitchen towel. 'Anybody need anything? I think we have some leftover Christmas cake.'

'It's leftover because it's vile,' I said. 'Don't we have any cheese and crackers?'

Brendan made a noise that sounded like a disapproving horse, stating that he couldn't manage another bite. 'Sit down, Oliver,' he insisted. 'Take a load off. We're all grand here.'

'I will,' Oliver replied. 'But first I just need to borrow you for two minutes, Phoebe, so you can show me where you've hidden the lemon and ginger tea bags.'

'They're where they always are. Beside the regular ones.'

'If they were, I wouldn't be asking,' he responded. 'Just come and help, will you?'

I tutted quietly and unfolded myself from my comfortable post-lunch position, then marched through to the kitchen with Oliver following behind, closing the kitchen door behind him.

'They're right here—' I began, opening the pantry door, but before I got the chance to wave some teabags in his face, he had pushed me into the pantry, pressed himself against my arse and slid his hand inside my bra.

'Sorry about earlier,' he whispered in my ear, 'I was distracted.'

'And now?' I enquired, my hand reaching around behind me.

He breathed heavily. 'Now it's all I can think about.'

I could feel him getting harder by the second. 'Once Molly is in bed,' he continued, 'we are going to shag until one of us passes out. Just thought you should know.'

'Oh, you fucker,' I murmured, almost giddy at the thought. I could feel his breath on my neck as he squeezed my breasts. If it wasn't for his parents, sister and our daughter fifteen feet away in the other room, my knickers would have been round my ankles. He really picks his moments. Nothing for weeks and now he was two seconds away from fingering me next to some out-of-date stock cubes. Classy.

Sadly, our kitchen rendezvous was cut short by the

appearance of Molly at the door asking for milk, while Oliver scrambled to pull his hand out of my large bra. My boobs never really disappeared after breastfeeding. Now it just looks like they have gigantism.

I grabbed the lemon and ginger teabags with one hand and straightened my top with the other, knowing that Oliver would have to give himself a moment to adjust before getting some milk for Molly. I was excited, his words *until one of us passes out* swirling around in my head for the rest of the afternoon.

At half past eight, Oliver drove the Webb clan back to their hotel as their flight was early the next morning. They seemed merry enough; Megan making us promise to visit soon and Louise telling Oliver to get his hair cut for the seventeenth time as she climbed into the front seat of the car. As soon as they drove off, I sprang into action. I allowed Molly to skip her evening bath and gave her a quick wash, brushed her teeth and put her promptly into her jammies. I let her read in bed while I swiftly ran an electric razor over my legs and armpits, choosing to ignore the fact that my knicker whiskers were running fucking riot. If Oliver calls my bush Phil Spector again, I'm going to batter him. Throwing on a random, mismatched black underwear set, I covered myself up in my dressing gown, just in time to hear him return.

By 9.45 p.m. one of us had indeed passed out ... it was Oliver, while reading Molly a story in her bed. I SHAVED FOR NOTHING.

Today he hasn't even mentioned it, busying himself with a work project while Molly and I had a *Despicable Me* movie marathon. I just don't get it. I remember the days when his penis made 99% of his decisions, including waking him up specifically to bang me. I miss those days. Maybe my New Year's resolution should be to go back in time. I'm as likely to fulfil that as I am to lose weight.

Tuesday January 3rd

God, today was boring. The weather was still cold and miserable so we all sat inside and annoyed each other to the point of murder. However, as we're all back to normality next week (thank God), I suggested we get out of the house and go for a family dinner somewhere. To be honest, I just wanted a cocktail. A big one. I'm not proud. After telling Molly seventeen thousand times that McDonald's wasn't an option, we finally decided on TGI Fridays in the shopping mall where she could get a burger, Oliver could get a parking space and I could get something made with Jack Daniels. It didn't have to be solid food.

The restaurant was full of weary-looking families who had had just about enough of the holidays. We had to wait a few minutes for a table, so we sat at the bar, giving me a chance to responsibly choose something from the cocktail menu and not just grab the barman by the lapels and yell 'JUST. NUMB. ME' into his face. We sat near the back of the restaurant, Molly beside her Dad and me beside the Lynchburg Lemonade I'd ordered.

'Mum, how come we had to come here and not McDonald's?' Molly asked, her swinging legs thumping the table as she opened her kid's activity pack.

'Because McDonald's doesn't sell this kind of lemonade,' Oliver replied on my behalf. He lifted my glass and took a swig. 'Damn, that's nice. I wish you'd driven now.'

I smirked. 'The burgers are bigger here anyway, honey. And we can share those chicken strips you like?'

'OK.' She shrugged and began colouring, just as another little girl three tables away started to lose her shit over ice cream. I took another gulp of my drink, feeling grateful that we've managed to raise such an easy-going child. No, not grateful . . . *smug.*

We got home around nine and Oliver put Molly to bed, while I opened a bottle of wine for us to share. It's not often we do this. Usually one of us will stay completely sober in case we need to drive in a 'Molly emergency'. My good friend Hazel says this kind of responsible behaviour is apparently very common for your first kid but after you've popped out a few more, you're both drunk by 8 p.m., thinking *Fuck it. We'll call a taxi.*

'She went out like a light,' Oliver remarked as he came into the living room. 'I think she had fun.'

'Come sit with me, handsome face,' I said, already half-way through my glass of wine. 'You know, this wine isn't as vile as the cheap price-tag suggests.'

He slumped down beside me, putting his feet up on the coffee table. 'I've eaten too much. I can't move.'

'Same. I'm down to one bar of health. You could rob me right now, I'd be unable to defend myself.'

'I'm unlikely to rob someone who had to borrow twenty quid off me last week.'

'Fair point.'

He laughed and gently nudged me. 'You know, you could totally take advantage of me, right now. I'd be powerless.' He started to run his finger over my thigh and towards my stomach. 'I might even let you off with that twenty quid.'

'You know that person you adore so much?' I replied, gesturing towards Molly's bedroom. 'I pushed her out of my vagina. You should be throwing money at me on a daily basis. You should be makin' it rain!'

He smirked at my attempt to palm imaginary money into the air. 'It's true. You did birth our lovely child. But to be fair, she was a lot smaller then . . .'

'Yeah, so was my vagina . . .'

He snorted and took a swig of his wine. 'Well, if we're not going to ruin each other, I might put a film on?'

I nodded for him to go ahead but his words made my heart sink a little. When did we stop wanting to ruin each other? Why didn't he defend my vagina? When did we let overeating interfere with sex? I've been overeating my entire life and it's never stopped me shagging.

Thursday January 5th

Mum and Dad called from Canada this afternoon, placing me on speakerphone from what sounded like the middle of a dog shelter. Which, as it turns out, is EXACTLY where they were calling from.

'Why are you getting a dog?' I exclaimed. 'You're always pissing off on holiday!'

'Oh relax, we're not getting a dog. We're just visiting them. I thought Molly might like to say hello.'

Jesus Christ. Everything I said about Oliver's parents – I take it back. Compared to mine, they are normal and reasonable. Louise and Brendan didn't sell everything they owned and emigrate to Canada, giving their only child two weeks' notice. They don't go skinny-dipping in their sixties or attend rock concerts or call their granddaughter to speak to random dogs. They didn't bring me a set of Kegel balls for Christmas. Still, they do come over every year for ten days and spoil the shit out of Molly. I think they're pleased to see me too. I hope so, anyway.

I called for Molly to come to the phone and watched her say hello to some dogs three thousand miles away. I could picture my mum: her blonde hair tied up in a bun, jacket hood up, holding the phone towards the cages, while my dad, head to toe in winter gear, would be telling her to hurry up so he could go home and knit a flaxseed cake or something. I was grateful that Molly was in her 'I hate dogs' phase. If she'd been listening to cats, she'd have been begging for one the minute she hung up.

After a minute or two Molly said bye, handed me the phone and went back to the living room while I had a quick chat with my parents. They think I'm daft. Not once have they ever just casually popped by a shelter to visit stray dogs. They're totally adopting one.

Monday January 9th

After Molly was born, I fully intended to go back to work full-time, even though the thought of going back to *The Post* for any length of time filled me with utter dread. However, after looking into the horrendous cost of private nursery, we decided that I'd go back part-time and look after her on my days off. Oliver did offer to go part-time instead of me but he earns more than I do and actually enjoys his job. So now I work Monday, Tuesday and Thursday while Molly splits her time between the council-run nursery and childminder extraordinaire Maggie Wilcox.

Despite having a new position as Entertainments sales rep at *The Post* and cutting my hours down to three days a week, I still hate selling advertising space and I'm still angry at myself for being here. Actually, I'm more angry at myself for being thirty-nine this year and still not feeling satisfied with my work life. How do these smug 'I love my job' fuckers do it?

Lucy has the right idea. She's completely nonchalant about her job. She found the least taxing, best paid job she could find and doesn't give it another thought when the clock strikes 5.30 p.m. We've worked together in the same office for seven years but she views it with amusement rather than the contempt I feel. She can afford to be indifferent though – her outgoings are minimal given that she's child free and rent free (she owns her granny's old house outright). All my granny left me was a purple cloth bag which contained some dress jewellery and what looked like an adult human tooth wrapped in a hanky.

I waved over to her as I entered the office, throwing my bag under my desk with a soft thud. I hadn't spoken to her since New Year's Eve, when she called me from Loch Fyne, so pissed I could smell tequila fumes down the other end of the phone.

'I think I found Nessie!' she yelled over what sounded like a mariachi band. 'Fucking Nessie! I mean, it's dark outside but there's something going on in that ... underwater ...'

'That's nice,' I replied, feeling a little jealous that I wasn't there in person to tell her that Nessie lives in Loch Ness and also that she's a maniac. 'Where's Kyle?'

'Who?'

'Your boyfriend.' I laughed. 'Remember him? Tree surgeon. Dark hair. Does occasional weird poetry. Pretty sure he drove you up there.'

'Oh yeah, him. He's lovely, right? Oh. Wait ... here, fishy fishy ...'

'Lucy, where are you? Have you wandered off?' I asked, feeling anxious that she was about to Jacques Cousteau herself into the loch, towards whatever the hell she thought she was seeing under the water. 'Go and find Kyle, please,' I insisted.

'He's here, *Mum*,' she snickered. 'Stop panicking. I can see him walking. He might be drunk. He has new glasses, you know – black rimmed. Like Huddy Bolly.'

The rest of the sentence was just a drunken slur but I heard Kyle's voice so was able to hang up knowing that she wasn't on her own. Unless he was equally pissed ... and they both end up in the loch ... ugh, I *am* such a mum. When did I become the intoxication police? Ten years ago I'd have been police-cautioned before the bells chimed midnight. Oh dear God, please don't let Molly grow up to be anything like me.

Anyway, my boss Dorothy wasn't back 'til Thursday which meant less pressure to sit at my desk and look like I gave a shit, so I started my day making coffee for everyone, except for office annoyance Kelly, who was already balls deep into her New Year detox.

'Hot water with lemon – every morning.' She sniffed loudly, holding up a flask. 'If it's not natural, I'm not interested.'

I could see Lucy biting her tongue as she listened to this streaky fake-tanned woman with drawn-on eyebrows and twenty menthols protruding from her handbag lecture the room on her new natural lifestyle. I knew that by lunchtime, there would be a sweepstake about how long it would last. (The pub downstairs are starting a 'buy one get one free' pizza on a Monday. I'm totally winning this.)

'You brought your own hot water?' Brian asked without looking up from his phone. 'Is it special hot wa—'

'Filtered . . . and smart.' She looked at her flask like she expected it to take a bow.

Brian chuckled. 'Your water is smart or it makes you smart? Will it make *me* smarter?'

'It doesn't fucking perform brain transplants,' Lucy hollered from her desk.

Kelly smiled, grateful that Lucy had stepped in. Lucy isn't particularly a fan of Kelly but she dislikes Brian even more.

We'd been in the office for fifteen minutes and already these two were ready to battle. They've hated each other for years. Brian is still the cock he's always been and Kelly is just, well, Kelly. Nothing ever changes around here. Actually, that's a lie – handsome Stuart, the man I once let shag me up against a jaggy fence, left before Christmas to move to Finland with his new wife, leaving us wondering who the hell Dorothy would hire in his place. Fucking Finland! The lengths men will go to avoid me.

I sat at my desk and logged in, allowing emails to start trickling through. Of course the most recent was from Lucy.

From: Lucy Jacobs
To: Phoebe Henderson
Subject: New Year

So? How was New Year? How was the Irish invasion? I feel like I haven't seen you in ages. Did Molly stay up for the bells or were you and Oliver snorting champagne and shagging in front of the telly?

From: Phoebe Henderson
To: Lucy Jacobs
Subject: Re: New Year

It went well, I think! I hope they had a nice time but his parents just give off a vibe of being uncomfortable everywhere except in their own home. It's weird. Yes, Molly did stay up for the bells – we watched Jools Holland. She spilled Ribena on the floor. It was thrilling. Oliver woke me up in the morning to moan about potatoes. I know, I'm boring myself now. Let's have lunch. You can tell me all about Nessie, you drunken arse.

From: Lucy Jacobs
To: Phoebe Henderson
Subject: Re: New Year

No can do – I'm meeting Kyle. Tomorrow though! We'll go to Max's bar and get those hotdogs with all the weird shit on them.

I looked through my work diary to discover that I had a grand total of zero appointments booked for next week, not great when my boss also has access to it so I can't bullshit her. Still, it's New Year. People are on holiday. I can't work miracles and even if I could, those miracles wouldn't be wasted on this fucking job; I'd save them for gravity-defying tits, world peace and turning wine into more wine.

Tuesday January 10th

Oliver dropped Molly off at nursery so I got into work pretty early this morning, which gave me time to grab some breakfast before starting the morning ritual of calling people who didn't want to speak to me.

Lunch at Max's Bar was fun; massive hotdogs, fries and a catch up session in which Lucy recounted what she could remember about New Year, including the sex they'd had in a four poster bed. And in the car. And against the window with the curtains open. Beasts.

'Ugh. Enough,' I said, scraping some onions off my hotdog. 'I'm beginning to hate you.'

She stared suspiciously at me. 'What's up?'

'Let's just say this hotdog is the only phallic-shaped thing that's been near my face recently.' I bit into it aggressively, continuing to speak with my mouth full. 'I think Oliver is finally fed up shagging me.'

'Nonsense,' she replied, politely ignoring the fact that I'd just sprayed food on to the table. 'Oliver is nuts about you.'

'He was,' I said, using a napkin to brush away the accidental food spray, 'and I'm sure he still is. But we're not the same. We haven't had sex since November and it was a quick spoon. We discussed painting Molly's room and didn't even make eye contact. Even before then, it's been really sporadic and not remotely noteworthy.'

Lucy shrugged, picking at my unwanted onions. 'So you're in a slump. You still fancy each other, right? No one is shagging anyone else?'

I could feel the colour drain from my face. I hadn't even considered this as a possibility. 'NO! Wait . . . do you think he could be shagging someone else?!'

She shook her head. 'I doubt it. He has a kid now. When the fuck would he have the time? Then again, you'd make time to shag, wouldn't you?'

My heart rate was increasing with every word that left her mouth. 'Well, not with me obviously!'

'I'm not helping, am I?' she replied. 'Is it both of you or just him?'

I thought for a moment. 'We're both a bit guilty. But it seems to be bothering me more than him. He's barely mentioned it.'

Lucy gulped down some of her beer and shook her head. 'What does Hazel think about it? She has a kid – maybe this is how it goes.'

Hazel is the adult of our group. Her life is in order, her shit is together and when I grow up, I hope to be just like her.

'I haven't spoken to her. She's still at Disneyland Paris.'

Lucy smirked. 'Then she won't be shagging either.'

I giggled. It's true. Hazel, Kevin and their seven-year-old daughter Grace will be sharing the same room; it'll be out of the question. I shoved some fries into my mouth and sighed.

'We're just not synched. And then stuff gets in the way. And before you know it, you're being felt up in a pantry.'

'A what now?'

'Never mind.'

As we headed back to the office, I vowed to speak to Oliver about this. Properly. We're going to pull out of this rut before one of us foolishly considers looking elsewhere.

Wednesday January 11th

Day off today! Morning was spent tidying and sorting Molly's old clothes into piles for the charity shop. Then off to nursery in the afternoon, where I bumped into Sarah Ward-Wilson by the gates, a woman who clearly cannot believe that despite her best efforts to marry well (and Botox poorly), she's a mother of four, still living in Glasgow.

'I cannot stand this weather, Phoebe. It doesn't matter how expensive your car is, when it's icy, these roads are a death trap to us all. Is that woman wearing a tracksuit? Oh dear Lord . . .'

I smirked, watching her pull her grey fur hat down over her ears, while simultaneously pushing her daughter Ruby towards the nursery entrance. Ruby is a sweetheart. A small ginger girl who looks exactly like her small ginger dad. If Molly wasn't so fond of her, I'd have no reason to speak to this awful woman. She's a mixture of aloof and sneaky, like a dastardly villain from a black and white movie. Most of the mums call her Lord Wilson because of her superiority complex. Including me.

Oliver arrived home late, moaning about his workload

and annoyed that he'd missed saying goodnight to Molly. He came into the kitchen where I stood washing the dinner plates.

'Did she have a good day?' he asked, picking at the left-over chicken on the worktop. 'I can't believe she'll be starting school this year. How the hell did that happen?'

'I know,' I replied, accidentally knocking a glass against the mixer taps. 'It's like she's getting older but I haven't aged at all. It doesn't make sense.'

'I'm bushed,' he said, completely ignoring my joke. 'I'm going to get my head down.'

'It's only half nine!' I protested. I reached into the fridge to get the two custard doughnuts that I'd bought earlier. 'Have some tea with me first! I bought those dough—'

But he was already halfway up the hall before I could fin-ish my sentence. It was then that I decided things really had to change. And that I'd eat his fucking doughnut, too.

Thursday January 12th

Dropped Molly with Maggie at a quarter past eight, accom-panied by my usual pang of guilt whenever I have to leave her to go to work. It's fucking ridiculous. How long will this last? Until she's a teenager? I mean, I'm not leaving her to waltz off and enjoy myself for the day, I'm doing it so we can eat, but fuck me, I still have that little voice saying *'She'd rather be with you. She should be with you. Hideous parenting. 1/10. Should not breed again.'*

Maggie pulled open the door and Molly shouted 'Hi!' as she ran towards the sounds of the other two kids that had been forced to come by their parents who probably feel as guilty as I do. Maybe not. I even feel guilty when I leave Molly at Hazel's house, and she's one of my closest mates. I think there's just a part of me that's scared that – even for a second – Molly won't feel wanted.

'Busy day ahead?' Maggie asked, wiping her hands on her apron. She wore an apron. I looked at her in admiration. She is a proper house-person. She has a tidy blonde hairdo, her tops always match her trousers, she bakes, and even with three kids to look after, her house is always more orderly than mine will ever be. Here is another woman who has her shit together; maybe I'm just scared that one day Molly will start to question why I don't.

'Oh, you know; same old!' I politely replied. I waved bye to Molly but she didn't notice. It looked like she was either cuddling a small boy or she had him in a headlock. 'Her dad will collect her at four, if that's OK?'

Maggie's eyes light up at the sheer mention of Oliver. It's obvious she fancies him. It used to bother me slightly – not enough to make a fuss but enough to neurotically make me wonder if the feeling was mutual.

Work wasn't horrendous. I managed to arrange a few appointments for next week, dealt with old emails and listened politely to my boss Dorothy's holiday woes when the romantic all-inclusive couples break she'd booked for her and her boyfriend in Gran Canaria turned out to be the package holiday from hell.

'They had bingo one night, Phoebe. BINGO. And several children pissed on the floor during the kid's disco. Honestly, I didn't sit on a plane for five hours to slip on piss in my Choos.'

Friday January 13th

Day #fuckknows in the Webb/Henderson household.

I tried to gauge whether Oliver might be feeling amorous this evening but as soon as I said, 'Shall we have an early night?' I felt like a 1950s housewife and cringed. His response was, 'Nah, there's a documentary on Netflix I've been meaning to watch.'

I used to be good at demanding sex but, bloody hell, I'm out of practice. Fuckssake, this man has been inside every one of my holes and yet I'm finding it difficult to talk to him about sex! Maybe I'm just scared there's something else going on . . . what if he's had enough of my holes?

Saturday January 14th

Hazel texted me this morning to let me know they were all back from their New Year trip to Disneyland Paris.

> Finally home. Grace has a present for Molly. When are you free for coffee?

I arranged to take Molly over tomorrow to catch up. Hazel's daughter is two years older than Molly but they get on like a house on fire, even calling each other 'sister' in a slightly creepy way. It's handy though since Molly is happy to sleep over when Oliver and I have plans.

The rest of the day was spent doing bugger all. I had a nap while Oliver played Pie Face with Molly and I yelled at them both when whipped cream got on the rug. Fucking hell, I'm becoming a bore. If this continues, they'll need to stage an arsehole intervention and force-feed joy into me intravenously.

Sunday January 15th

I took Molly over to Hazel's house, where she was presented with a Disneyland mug and a tiny Jungle Book elephant plush toy. Delighted, she went off to play with Grace while Hazel pointed me in the direction of the kitchen, pushing the door closed behind her.

'So how was—' I began, but Hazel quickly interrupted me.

'Never again,' she blurted out, whacking the kettle switch on. 'Overpriced, freezing and mobbed. Kevin wasn't keen either. He said that Gaston "sighed" at him. Tea or coffee?'

'Tea, thanks,' I replied. 'Gaston's an arsehole. I bet Grace enjoyed it though.'

Hazel shrugged. 'She announced on the second day that she was a bit old for Disney. We're standing in the middle of the fucking Magic Kingdom, up to our arse in Disney and she's all "whatever". She enjoyed the New Year fireworks though.'

I started to laugh. 'At least you got away for a few days. I'd kill for a holiday.'

She shook her head. 'This wasn't a holiday. This was an exercise in not losing your shit when you have to queue for an hour to sit on a twirling teacup in sub-zero temperatures.'

She filled up the teapot and placed it down on the table before rummaging around for biscuits, while I filled her in on my incredibly dull New Year, including my current predicament.

'Am I being unreasonable?' I asked, hoping not only that she'd have some wisdom to impart but also that she had something other than custard creams. The smell of them made me sick during my pregnancy and I've never fully recovered.

'You know, Kevin and I went through something similar, when Grace was two,' she began, retrieving some cleverly hidden, single-finger Twix from the back of a cupboard. 'We actually went to counselling.'

'WHAT?!' I replied. 'You never told me any of this!'

'Yeah, Kevin made me promise not to discuss it . . . so you cannot say a word! But it helped us. We'd lost the passion. It happens.'

'And now?'

She grinned. 'Let's just say we're back on track and it's easier for us to talk about it when we're not. I'd give you the name of our therapist but he retired a year or so ago.'

'That's OK,' I replied, pouring some tea. 'I think I know someone who could help.'

Monday January 16th

I watched a couple of strangers flirt on the tube this morning. In fact, I think the whole carriage was aware of the spark between them. I don't think anyone would have been surprised if they just mounted each other there and then. I won't lie, it made me pine for something. For that feeling of lust that makes you repeatedly stare at someone until they stare back or have you arrested.

The snow has finally fucked off which made my walk to

the office slightly less treacherous. It never fails to amaze me, the women I see in heels trying to negotiate ice and slush, like having sexy shoes makes you immune from sliding in public. Or from the effects of gravity.

Kelly was already in the office, eating something that definitely wasn't made by nature. It looked like it was made by Greggs. Her face went into full panic mode when she saw me.

'Do not tell anyone you saw this,' she begged, wiping the crumbs off her shirt. 'I was starving.'

'My lips are sealed,' I reassured her. 'But seriously. Fuck what anyone else thinks. You enjoy that . . . is that a pie?!'

She nodded, stuffing the last piece into her mouth.

I wish I had a pie.

Ten minutes later, Lucy and Brian appeared, quickly followed by Dorothy who was keen to start the morning meeting and make us all feel embarrassed that we were behind target for the month.

'We need to work on new business, people! And don't tell me that you can't just magic it out of thin air because it already exists; I've just torn it out of our competitors' publications and placed it on your desk. I will be adding incentives to the board for anyone who brings in new business.'

This meant wine. It always meant wine.

With Brian first on the phones to claim his weekend 'carry out', I decided to quiz Lucy on my conversation with Hazel.

From: Phoebe Henderson
To: Lucy Jacobs
Subject: Idea

Hazel suggested Oliver and I go for some couples therapy. Was going to call Pam Potter. What do you think?

x

From: Lucy Jacobs
To: Phoebe Henderson
Subject: Re: Idea

If you think it'll help you get back on top (pun intended) then it can't hurt to ask.

But I think Oliver will tell you to shove it up your arse. Soz.

From: Phoebe Henderson
To: Lucy Jacobs
Subject: Re: Idea

Ugh. You might be right. Still, nothing ventured.

Wednesday January 18th

Parents emailed photos of their new dog, Daphne. I FUCKING KNEW IT. Daphne is a mongrel with half an ear missing and Dad is convinced she understands French. Apparently, Daphne enjoys long walks, her new heated bed and barking at the wall for no reason. I think Daphne and I would get along famously.

Thursday January 19th

It occurred to me earlier that not only have I not been having sex but I haven't been masturbating either. Not for weeks. This is more than just a dry spell, it's a fucking drought.

I know I've been busy (and there's little to no privacy in our place) but I just haven't felt that turned on. I used to be this ball of sexual energy and now I just feel invisible. I'm the Invisible Mum. Soon my vagina will be writing its own monologue on how it's been forsaken by its terrible owner. I thought about mentioning this to Lucy over lunch but she'd immediately stop eating and declare a state of emergency. Instead we discussed her current living situation.

'Kyle wants to move in,' she revealed. 'I know it makes sense – he's paying rent on a place when he spends most of his time at mine, but I just don't see myself living with any-one. Like, ever. I think it's a bit soon anyway.'

I chuckled. 'Lucy, you've been seeing Kyle longer than I've been dating Oliver. And we live together. And have a child. I think it's probably time to take the next step . . .'

'Yeah, but you guys aren't even shagging anymore. What if that happens to us?'

'Um . . . ouch!'

Realising her unintentional insult, she desperately tried to backtrack. 'No! I didn't mean it like that! I meant that everything is great the way it is. I'm scared that will change.'

'It's fine,' I replied. 'I understand what you mean. You'd need to actually live with a boy. You've never lived with a boy. They're really fucking annoying – more so than children.'

I envy Lucy having her own space. There are moments when I'd kill to have an entire house to myself for weeks at a time, but to be honest those moments are fleeting; shar-ing my space with my little family is the only normal I know now. I wouldn't have it any other way.

Friday January 20th

Still annoyed about my lack of self diddling, I took Molly to nursery and came back to address the matter head on . . . well, vag on. I've had nearly thirty years' practise, so I was smugly confident that I could overcome any hurdles . . . but it just wasn't happening. Every time I tried to think dirty thoughts, I'd remember all the things I should have been doing in the three hours of nursery time, like mopping floors and sorting washing. Eventually I just gave up and did them. By the time Oliver got home, the place was sparkling and I was exasperated.

'What's up with you?' he asked, watching me mooch around my impressively clean living room after Molly went to bed. He looked around. 'Hang on. Did you get cleaners in?'

'No! I bloody did this!' I snarled unfairly. 'And do you know why? Because I have all of this extra energy – energy saved from not having wanked in an eternity!'

He snorted. 'Fucking hell, Phoebe.'

'Well, it's true. And I cooked for tomorrow night. AND I started teaching Molly how to play chess!'

He pursed his lips while I sorted the magazines on the bottom shelf of the coffee table for the tenth time before finally saying, 'The place looks great, though. Maybe this is a good thing. I mean, look how much you can get done when you're not busy putting things up yourself.'

'Oh fuck off,' I replied, laughing. He's so infuriating.

He grabbed the remote and turned the telly on. 'You should just knock one out in the shower, like I do.'

'How often do you do that?!'

'Most days,' he replied, without looking away from the television. 'Fancy watching a bit of *Parks and Recreation*?'

'Nope. Why don't you ask Pam and her five sisters to join you?'

He stared at me blankly.

'Your palm!' I replied, waving my open hand at him. 'And your five fingers. Pam and her – oh, forget it.'

Even as I flounced out the room, I knew that this was the most childish fucking thing I'd ever said. I'm cringing as I write this.

Sunday January 22nd

Exhausted today. There are dead people with more energy than I have. Oliver took Molly out to the TokyoToys shop while I tidied up and went food shopping. I warned them both not to come back with anything weird. I've seen those body pillows used by grown men for dry-humping anime characters. It's fucking disturbing. Luckily all Molly got were some Pokémon cards.

It's now 8.50 p.m., I have a glass of awful red wine, Molly is asleep and Oliver is snoozing on the couch. I don't have the heart to wake him up – or the energy. Ugh, maybe it's not just him who's not making the effort here. I should totally wake him up! I should wake him up with my mouth.

9.35 p.m. I'm in bed. He scowled at me for waking him up.

Whatever. I give up. ENJOY THE FUCKING COUCH, DICKHEAD.

Monday January 23rd

Oliver had indoor football this evening, so I picked Molly up from Maggie's after work before popping to the supermarket to buy dinner. I told Molly that we didn't have money for toys but of course bought her something anyway because I have no discipline whatsoever. I ate a giant bag of Maltesers on my way round the store and they were totally worth the judgemental look the checkout woman gave me while she scanned the empty wrapper. I did see a blonde woman with a wonky trolley trying to catch the attention of a guy in the cheese aisle, though. Thank fuck I'm not single anymore. Looking for love is grim. Even if I'm not shagging Oliver, he's still the love of my life.

Wednesday January 25th

Highlights today were:
1. Twenty-seven minute power nap.
2. Unashamedly hoover-dancing to Bruno Mars.
3. The pasta I cooked for dinner was the food equivalent of being wrestled to the floor by Tom Hardy; it was messy and I wanted it in me.

Unfortunately the low points included:
1. Molly being pushed over by a little shitbag at nursery.
2. Pulling a muscle in my back because of the hoover-dancing.
3. Being told in no uncertain terms that Oliver will not consider couples therapy with Pam Potter.

'I'm not discussing our sex life with your weirdo therapist!' he fumed in bed beside me. 'So we haven't had sex in a while; it's not the fucking end of the world. We could do it right now. Problem solved.'

'She's not a weirdo!' I insisted. 'She's a smart, insightful woman who—'

'You told me she once conducted an entire session wearing earmuffs shaped like a monkey.'

I paused and smiled. The heating in her office had packed up that day. It was actually a really productive session, even with the earmuffs.

'Well ... I don't remember telling you that. So she's a little offbeat – who cares? She's still wonderful. I told you she looks like Tina Fey, right? You like Tina Fey.'

'Not in earmuffs.'

'Forget the fucking earmuffs. This is about sex and the problem isn't just the lack of it – it's the reason why we're not doing it!' I protested. 'I could count on one hand the number of times we shagged last year!'

'Y'know, the more you keep going on about it, the less I want to shag you.' He turned over on to his side, letting me know the discussion was over. But I wasn't finished.

'Why won't you discuss this with me? Why is this not bothering you?'

He turned around to face me. 'Look, I'll shag you if you want me to. If not, I'm going to sleep, alright?'

'Oh, fuck you. I wouldn't let you near me now.'

Teary-eyed, I got out of bed and went and sat in the living room. That was an hour ago. So I guess we're still fighting.

Thursday January 26th

Dorothy announced that due to the *current climate* we won't be replacing Stuart, which is kind of a relief. The last thing I need is another attractive man in the office to distract me; I've had enough office indiscretions to last me a lifetime. She did however hint that there might be scope for me to come back full-time with Molly starting school this year. I told her I'd need to discuss it with Oliver, which I do . . . Of course the extra money would come in handy but my immediate thoughts are 'No' and 'Fuck No.'

When I picked Molly up from Maggie's, she informed me that there had been an outbreak of nits at nursery and Molly's head was crawling. Fear not though, she'd already washed Molly's hair in medicated shampoo and deloused every inch of her head. I'm so grateful. By the time I'd finished hand-wringing and attempting to look through her hair from 15 feet away, she'd have been old enough to treat it herself. God, how do some women just find this so easy? Being a parent is gross.

Saturday January 28th

'Hazel has offered to take Molly tonight!' I excitedly announced while Oliver was in the shower. 'We could go out! We could catch a film or go for a meal or—'

'I said I'd meet the footie lads for a drink,' he replied before I could list endless couple possibilities. 'Sorry. Didn't I tell you? Big Paul just had a son. We're going to wet the baby's head.'

'No, you didn't,' I replied, trying to hide my disappointment. 'Can't you go for a couple and meet me after?'

'No, we've got a late one planned. Ask Hazel if she'll do it next week instead.'

'She's not our fucking hired help, Oliver. She's doing us a favour.' My disappointment was well and truly showing. Along with annoyance. 'Look, forget it.'

He drew back the shower curtain just in time to see me storm out of the bathroom. 'What's wrong with you? I had plans. I wouldn't ask you to change your plans. Can you hand me that towel?'

I returned to the bathroom, grabbing a towel and throwing it at him. 'The difference between you and me is that I WOULD change my plans. When was the last time we spent some time together?'

'We fucking live together, Phoebe, so EVERY. BLOODY. DAY.'

Now *he* was annoyed. He wrapped his towel around his waist, stepped out of the shower and over the pile of his dirty clothes that had been lying there since Thursday.

'Are you bored of me, Oliver?' I snapped. 'Because I feel as invisible as these fucking clothes you've been ignoring for two days.' I picked up the offending items and threw them at him.

'You're being ridiculous. I'm not dropping everything at your whim,' he mumbled, drying his hair. 'You never used to be so high maintenance.'

'High maintenance?' I laughed but now I was in full rage mode. Aware that Molly might hear us, I closed the bathroom door, my voice lowered to a snarling whisper. 'That would fucking imply that there had been ANY kind of maintenance going on to begin with! You barely touch me. We never just sit and enjoy each other's company anymore. I've been back at work all month and not ONCE have you asked me how it's going or what I'm up to. When did we become this couple? What next? Shagging other people? Separate beds?'

He stopped drying his hair. 'You want to shag other people?' The colour in his face began to drain.

'NO!' I insisted. 'Do you?'

'No, and don't ever do that,' he said, softly. The pink hue began to slowly return to his cheeks. 'I couldn't bear that.' Without warning, he pulled me into him and hugged me.

'I have no intentions of doing that,' I said, taken aback by his sudden need for security. 'I love you, Webb. I just need to know we're OK. You need to start talking to me.'

'We'll sort this,' he mumbled into my hair. 'Whatever it takes – even your weird therapist . . .'

I hugged him back so tightly he yelped.

Monday January 30th

Productive day today. I finally managed to get an appointment with the manager of Downtime Bar near the station. Judging from the advertising they do elsewhere, they obviously have a decent budget. I'm going in to see him next month and if I can swing this, I'll win mega brownie points at work. The guy sounds like a bit of a prick to be honest but we'll see how it goes.

I also called Pam today and she can see Oliver and me on Wednesday at 2 p.m., so Oliver has arranged to work late tonight so he can get away early. He's definitely making the effort. Let's hope he doesn't freak out before then.

FEBRUARY

Wednesday February 1st

As we pulled up outside Pam's office, I was hit by a tidal wave of nostalgia. I'd spent hours of my life in that office, trying to understand myself, crying over old boyfriends, admitting my mistakes and forgiving myself for making them. And now here I am again.

Oliver stared solemnly out of the window. I still half-expected him to make a run for it.

'Don't look so scared, Oliver, she doesn't bite.'

'I'm not scared!' he responded a little too quickly. 'I'm just . . . wondering how we got here.'

'We drove, Oliver,' I replied flippantly, turning off the engine. 'Let's just go up.' I grabbed my bag and exited the car, knowing full well what he had meant. I've wondered that too. The great Oliver and Phoebe who once couldn't keep their clothes on have now gone back to being mates who occasionally think about shagging each other but never get around to it. We've been friends for over twenty years and I'm scared that falling in love has turned us into something that might not last for twenty more.

The betting shop that once stood underneath Pam's consulting room is now a Pound Shop, so long gone are the desperate-looking punters, smoking furiously outside between bets. As we pass, I notice that they carry my favourite conditioner and make a mental note to stock up after our appointment. My relationship may be in trouble but there's no excuse not to have tangle-free, shiny hair at a discounted price.

We made it up to the first floor and sat in the waiting area, Oliver perched on the edge of a plastic chair while I turned off my mobile phone. The reception area always reminded me of sitting outside the head teacher's office in high school, a place which, if I remember correctly, Oliver frequented often.

'You're making me nervous, man!' I whispered, gently placing my hand on his arm. 'It's not a police interview. Relax.'

'She's not going to make me lie down on a big couch, is she?' he asked, tapping his foot on the tiled floor. 'Or make me talk about my mother . . .'

'No, Norman Bates, it's just a chat. You're not—'

We were interrupted by the sound of Pam's door opening. A man in his twenties wearing a brown leather jacket emerged, chuckling loudly. I felt grateful for the happy vibes. He was followed by Pam, who told him she'd see him next week and asked us to come in.

Pam Potter hadn't changed a bit. Her hair was a bit longer but she still wore the same hippy shit she always did and had the same big Cheshire Cat smile. She welcomed us in.

'Very nice to see you, Phoebe,' she remarked as we walked past her and into the room. 'And Oliver. Nice to meet you. Please. Have a seat.'

Oliver smiled but his eyes were darting everywhere, taking everything in; the odd ornaments, the purple seat covers, the small kitchen with a bear-shaped tea caddy on full display. I warned him that she was a tad unconventional but I don't think he fully believed me. We sat down on the couch while she filled up a jug of water from the kitchen.

'She *does* look like Tina Fey!' Oliver whispered from the corner of his mouth.

'So what brings you both here today?' she asked, placing the water jug and two glasses on the table. Oliver crossed his arms in a manner that can only be described as 'fuck off'.

'Why don't you start, Phoebe?'

'Right. Um, sure.' I began, positioning myself further forward on the couch. I could sense Oliver tensing up beside me. 'I think we're here because we're stuck in a rut.' I continued. 'We're not connecting the way we used to. I know it's probably normal; kids come along, your sex life dwindles . . . work stress . . .'

She nodded. 'Are you still intimate with each other? I'm not exclusively referring to sex, it can also include cuddling, talking, date nights. Do you make time for each other?'

Oliver was still mute. Jesus, I might as well have come alone.

'I don't think we do,' I replied. 'I can't remember the last time we went out together. It's always separately. But someone has to stay with Molly. And it's not appropriate to be slobbering over each other in front of her, is it?'

Pam smiled. 'Slobbering no, but it's actually very healthy for your child to see you display affection for each other in front of her. Age-appropriate displays, of course, but seeing your parents secure in their relationship is never a bad thing. How is your relationship in general? Do you still—'

'We don't laugh as much as we used to.'

He speaks! I turned to look at Oliver but he avoided my gaze. 'Our lives aren't as fun as they used to be,' he confessed. 'Things got very serious, very quickly; the pregnancy, moving in together, becoming parents . . .'

Fucking hell, Oliver, divulge much?

'This was a difficult transition for you?' Pam asked.

Oliver shrugged. 'Not difficult as such . . . but when I stop and think about it, I realise how much we both had to change to make it work.'

Pam nodded as she scribbled in her little book while I listened to the once-reluctant Oliver convey just how much he missed the old us. The silly us. The carefree, funny, unburdened us.

'But most of all,' he continued, 'I miss our sex life. That year when you had your "list" and you were so open to new things and we . . .'

I saw his face tinge pink as he remembered that year. I felt myself blush too. That was the year I created my sexual bucket list and he volunteered to help me out. The year I finally told my ex-boyfriend Alex to get the fuck out of my life. That was the year we fell in love. God, that year not only changed our lives but created a brand new one.

He cleared his throat. 'I guess what I'm saying is, I miss that time. I know we have Molly and I love her to death but I want to feel like *us* again. I want to feel as wanted as I did back then.'

'Wanted? I come on to you all the time!' I exclaimed,

feeling more than a little defensive. I moved away towards the arm of the couch. 'You're never in the mood ... well, there was that time at New Year ... but usually you're tired or busy or—'

'We're not here to assign blame, Phoebe,' Pam interrupted. 'Oliver's just expressing how he feels.'

I retreated back to my side of the couch, fuming that she'd taken his side over mine. I am so not ready to be a grown up.

She put down her little notebook. 'Do you still love each other?'

'Yes!' we replied in unison. No hesitation, no thought required. Just a very firm, definitive 'yes'. I felt a warm tingle wash over me as Oliver squeezed my hand. All I could think was – *he still loves me.* I will never get tired of hearing that.

Pam saw my face and laughed. 'Then that's a very, *very* good starting point. From what I've heard, it sounds like you're both willing to put the work in, to reconnect not only physically but emotionally too. So, if you're both ready, I have some ideas that I think might help you.'

Friday February 3rd

First step for next week – individually, think of three songs which describe your relationship right now.

Molly is in bed and Oliver is glued to some Silk Road documentary so I've hidden myself away in the bedroom to work on Pam's music idea. Essentially it's a mixtape. A fucking mixtape. What are we? Fourteen? I remember making a mixtape for my high school boyfriend Chris Dolan, spending hours choosing a playlist that I hoped would accurately convey my teenage feelings of love and lust (neither of which I was well-versed in), but I made sure he knew I wanted to both shag him and marry him, possibly at the same time. He, in turn, handed me a tape which accurately conveyed his feelings . . . for Weezer and Oasis. What a fucking knob.

Anyway, yesterday – after the music assignment – we worked through Pam's plan: 'Relight My Fire'. Seriously, she named the process after a Take That song and now I can't get it out of my head. From what I understand, it's a series of different exercises that will help us reconnect as a couple. She hasn't told us what they are though – I presume so we don't start writing it off before we've even begun.

I'm looking through my Spotify tracks but it's harder than I anticipated. God, I listen to some amount of shite. Anyway, so far the contenders are:

- 'Romance is Dead' by Paloma Faith – Could work! Quirky, shows I still care.
- ~~'Heaven Knows I'm Miserable Now' by The Smiths~~. No. Behave.
- 'Need You Tonight' by INXS – Corny but true.
- 'I Touch Myself' by The Divinyls – Maybe not *entirely* true at the moment but I need to ensure he knows that he still turns me on.
- ~~'Bloody Mother Fucking Asshole' by Martha Wainwright~~. Hmm . . . maybe not.

I have until Thursday to finalise it. Ugh, I swear if Oliver hands me an entire fucking Radiohead album, I'll scream.

Monday February 6th

Oliver dropped Molly at the childminder this morning, which meant I wasn't in a massive rush. If I don't have appointments, there's no need to bring my car, so today I had the pleasure of standing on the underground from the West End to the city centre, trying desperately not to smell the female armpit that was directly in front of my face for the entire journey. It's still bloody Baltic outside though – really looking forward to the three days of sunshine we're expecting in June.

Work was pretty uneventful; Brian was off sick and Kelly moaned every time she had to put a booking through in his name. She's not big on team spirit; I'm pretty sure she'd prefer everyone starve to death rather than be paid for having the audacity to be ill.

There was a new email from Lucy waiting the moment I logged in.

From: Lucy Jacobs
To: Phoebe Henderson
Subject: So??

How did your couple's session go? Are you both on sex meds now? Do you have to feed each other oysters and do sensual massage once a week?

From: Phoebe Henderson
To: Lucy Jacobs
Subject: Re: So??

We have a list to work through, can you believe it? ANOTHER FUCKING LIST. Why is this my life? She gives us something new every week – this week we've each to make a CD with three songs that describe our relationship. Oliver doesn't seem too engaged with the whole thing but at least he's trying.

From: Lucy Jacobs
To: Phoebe Henderson
Subject: Re: So??

Well, that's different. Whatever will you choose? You should just take three random, 'I'm going to boot his truck to fuck' country songs and make him listen to them on repeat until death.

Wednesday February 8th

I took Molly to nursery this afternoon, trying my best not to make eye contact with Lord Wilson but she cornered me as I was making small talk with Lena and Judith (who also cannot stand her).

'Ruby was talking about coming to play at your house, Phoebe,' she began, without an apology for interrupting. 'Which is fine, in theory, but I just wanted to check where you live exactly before we take this any further.'

Lena and Judith slipped quietly away, making it clear that I'm on my own here. Rotten bastards. 'West End,' I responded. 'You know Dowanhill?'

'Of course!' she replied. The mere mention of an upmarket address brought a smile to her pointy face.

'Well, not there,' I continued. 'We're much closer to Maryhill . . . or should I say *Scaryhill*?'

Her smile changed first to a look of confusion and then annoyance when she realised that I was messing with her. Still, she put on her fake laugh and slapped me on the shoulder with her leather-gloved hand. 'You almost had me there,' she snorted. 'You wouldn't be in the catchment area for this nursery if you lived there! Anyway, we'll arrange a play date – yes?'

And with that, she about-turned and teetered out of the building, heels clipping loudly against the floor like a Shire horse. I finished putting Molly's trainers in her gym bag, wondering why the fuck Sarah Ward-Wilson had taken a shine to me, out of all the mums here.

Thursday February 9th

Back to Pam's today for the big playlist reveal, with a still-unconvinced Oliver who sighed as he sat down, clutching his CD. Apparently just Bluetoothing over a playlist wasn't ceremonial enough or something; physically making and handing over a CD was a far more personal way to reveal our feelings.

'How did you get on this week?' she asked, watching Oliver fiddle with his CD case. 'Any problems?'

'I'm not entirely sure how effective this will be,' Oliver blurted out. 'Like, men and women view music very differently, especially romantic music or touchy-feely shit. We just don't do it very often.'

'But some of the most romantic lyrics ever written were by men,' Pam interjected. 'Our society favours romanticism so our philosophies with regards to love are very evident in a lot of music ... regardless, this isn't an exercise in romantic music per se, this is an opportunity to express your feelings in a way that's perhaps less confrontational to begin with. There's a communication breakdown somewhere and sometimes letting a song speak for you can be very useful.'

To be honest, I also thought the idea was a little batshit crazy but the more she explained it, the more it made sense.

'If you'd both like to exchange your CDs,' she continued. 'Oliver. Can you read out Phoebe's choices and tell us what you think she's trying to say?'

We swapped CDs and I watched Oliver read down the list.

' "Romance is Dead" by Paloma Faith, "Need You Tonight" by INXS and . . . oh wow! "Closer" by Nine Inch Nails.'

I felt my cheeks start to burn. I hadn't considered that Pam would be privy to our choices. I'm hoping she isn't familiar with the song.

Smiling, Oliver continued. 'I guess Phoebe is trying to say that she'd like more romance in our relationship, as well as informing me that she's filthy as hell.'

Pam smirked and I died.

'I just want us to be close again. Erm, physically. OK, my turn,' I interjected, moving the focus away from my list. 'Oliver's choices are: "In My Life" by The Beatles, "Losing My Edge" by LCD Soundsystem and "Suddenly Everything Has Changed" by The Flaming Lips.'

'And what do you think Oliver's trying to say?' Pam enquired as I glanced at Oliver but Oliver stared straight ahead.

'I think,' I replied, 'that Oliver is a lot more romantic than he thinks! Also that he thinks he's getting old and . . . I'm not sure. That he's scared of how things have changed?'

Oliver put his hand on my knee and shook his head. 'I'm not scared. It's just . . . life is moving so quickly. Molly is constantly changing and growing, and us! Our identities have changed. We're no longer Phoebe and Oliver; we're mum and dad. It's a head-fuck when you think about it.'

'Do you think your new role has changed how you feel about Phoebe?' Pam asked. I took a deep breath, unsure of whether I wanted to hear his response.

'God no, I love Phoebe just as much as I always have. I think it's changed the way I think about myself. What if I'm a shit dad? What if I'm not good enough? What if she eventually decides she can do better? Christ, I just don't want to end up like my parents.'

I sat there stunned. Suddenly the most self-assured man I've ever known was worried that he wasn't good enough and his hands were trembling. He was also sharing more here than he had with me since Molly was born. Pam kept quiet as I took Oliver's hand in mine. I had zero idea he felt like this. I felt my voice start to wobble.

'I fucking love the bones of you, Webb. I always have. You and Molly – you're the reason I breathe. I didn't know you were that worried. You never—'

'Course I'm worried!' he snapped. 'We're in bloody therapy! What if we never get back what we once had? God, my mouth is dry. Is it warm in here?'

Pam poured Oliver some water. 'The fact that you're here is one of the healthiest decisions you could make for your relationship,' she said calmly. 'However, getting back *what you once had* is unrealistic. You are different people now. You know more. You've experienced more. What you can bring to your relationship now is far more valuable than what you could, say, five or ten years ago. If you're ready for the next step, I think you'll find it very useful.'

Oliver sipped his water and nodded at her.

She smiled. 'Great. The next step is to do nothing at all because the next step is abstinence . . .'

Saturday February 11th

Drinks with the girls last night; our first night out in ages and fucking hell, how I've missed it. Oliver had agreed to stay in with Molly, giving me the chance to run Pam's next idea past Hazel and Lucy. We started off in a pub near Central Station before moving on to Merchant City, planning to stay until closing, but under no circumstances end up leathered in a club at 3 a.m.

'Abstinence? I thought you went to therapy to get your sex life back, not remove it entirely!'

Lucy took her wine from Hazel, who'd just got our third round in at the increasingly noisy bar. 'What did I miss?' she asked, handing me my Jack and Coke.

'Abstinence.'

'What? You wanted absinthe?'

'No! Abstinence! Phoebe's therapist has told them not to go near each other for two weeks!' Lucy exclaimed. 'TWO. WHOLE. WEEKS.'

Hazel looked surprised. 'But you weren't shagging

anyway. How does that help?' The wine spilling all over her hand let me know that she had definitely arrived in tipsy-town.

'Seemingly, there's a huge difference from not having sex to not being *allowed* to have sex,' I replied, stirring my drink with my straw. 'It's all to do with wanting what you can't have.'

'So you can't do ANYTHING?!' Hazel seemed more horrified than Lucy. 'Damn. I'm kind of sorry I suggested you see her in the first place.'

'Oh, we're allowed to flirt!' I responded. 'We're allowed to be verbally sexual, make lingering eye contact, exchange photos . . . basically wind each other up. But no physical contact, regardless of how much we want to. And masturbation is also discouraged.'

'YASS! I love that idea.'

We both stared blankly at Lucy. 'You're kidding. Right?'

'Come on! It's genius!' she insisted. 'By the end of the week, Oliver is going to be so wound up, he'll last about three strokes! You'll both be gagging for it. Your therapist is a mastermi—CAN I HELP YOU?'

It took me a second to realise that Lucy wasn't offering her services, but was directing her question towards two men in their twenties at the next table who were listening in to our conversation. Red-faced, they both turned away and began to chat.

'I suppose she's right,' Hazel agreed. 'You need to make Oliver remember just how seductive you can be.'

I took a big swig of my drink. 'I'm just not sure Oliver is into the idea. I mean, he's been opening up a bit more but he hasn't mentioned this since we left Pam's office. I don't want to send him pictures of my boobs if he's going to be less than receptive . . . SERIOUSLY, BOYS. WE'RE NOT THAT INTERESTING. BUGGER OFF.'

They started laughing but Hazel leaned across towards them and in a sinister tone said, 'If you don't stop being a nuisance, I will pretend to be your very loud, very drunken mother, completely embarrass you and make sure that you have no chance of pulling anyone in this bar.'

They soon found another table.

On the taxi ride home, I decided that I'd speak to Oliver the following day and make sure he was on board with the abstinence thing. I planned what I'd say, in the least confrontational or demanding way possible. And maybe if I did it in a really sexy dress and flirted a little, I'd get a better idea of just how irresistible he finds me.

Sunday February 12th

Trying to flirt with someone who knows you inside out is mortifying. Standing beside me in the kitchen was the man who witnessed a baby emerging from my foof and now he was about to witness me disappear up my own arsehole, trying to convince him I'm still sexually alluring. Lucy had suggested I try and sell myself more, rather than acting like my usual self-deprecating self – you know, the one who isn't getting laid.

My assault on his senses began in the kitchen where I sauntered in, nonchalantly, watching him pull out the roasting tray from the back of the cupboard.

'Honey?'

'Yeah?'

'I meant to ask: you're OK with all this abstinence stuff, right? You'd tell me if it became too much?'

'What? Oh yeah. Sure. Can you grab the chicken from the fridge, please?' The tray clattered noisily as he pulled it out.

'Did you have a good day?' I continued, brushing my hand across his back as I passed him to get to the fridge. I'd worn the little red slip dress I'd bought in the January sales; a tad overdressed for Sunday night dinner but it made my tits look spectacular.

He nodded. 'Yeah. I was here. With you. All day ... but yeah, I guess it was fine. Is that—'

'Why yes, this is a new dress,' I replied. 'Thanks for noticing.'

He smirked. 'Right ... I was going to say *"Is that chicken OK to reheat?"* but yes, your dress is very nice.'

See? FUCKING MORTIFYING.

I told him that the chicken was fine, touching his back again for reasons unknown, before propping myself up against the kitchen worktop, hoping my tits would be enough to distract him from my faux-pas. I needed to make him think of sex. And me naked. Naked and wet.

'I might have a shower later,' I said, watching him busy himself with dinner. The moment I said it, I regretted it. I'd basically just told him that I was thinking of having a wash. A WASH! How is that sexy?!

But of course, I carried on rambling because it's me and I fucking suck at this.

'I could get soapy . . . you know . . . soap myself up . . .' Oh GOD, now I was simulating 'having a soapy wash' with my hands while he paid little to no attention.

'Get the gravy, will you?'

My hands went back to my sides and I sighed. 'Sure. Will do.'

This was obviously the wrong strategy. Subtle, deranged, mime Phoebe wasn't working. I need to think of something else.

Monday February 13th

'Hi, I'm looking for Jay? I'm Phoebe from *The Post*. He's expecting me.'

The terrifyingly facially-contoured girl behind the bar stopped stacking glasses and sighed, walking off towards the back and through a small black door without saying a word, leaving me alone in the empty bar. Despite Downtime Bar being two streets away from the office, I've never been here. Now that I'm the wrong side of thirty, I tend to frequent bars which don't make me stand beside twenty-year-olds and wish I was younger or dead. It has the feel of a former dive bar, artfully disguised by plush booths, a vegan-friendly menu and an expensive cocktail list on the wall behind the bar.

I reached into my bag and put my phone on silent, preparing myself to meet my final bore of the day. The self-importance that radiates from some managers is—

'Hi. Phoebe?'

I stopped fiddling with my phone and looked up to see a face I'd seen before. Only I couldn't quite place him.

'Jay?' I replied. 'Nice to meet you. Thanks for seeing me . . . sorry, but have we met before? You seem very familiar.'

He smiled. 'No, I don't think so. I must just have one of those faces.'

He motioned me over to sit at a booth while I hoped desperately that I hadn't accidentally shagged him at some point. He's hot, it could have happened. I definitely remember punching above my weight in the past . . . Christ, I ended up with Oliver. He's a nine even when he's hungover.

I tried to scan Jay's face without it seeming too obvious. Black hair, thick-rimmed glasses, tattoo of an owl on the underside of his forearm . . . no, I'd remember that tattoo . . . unless he got it after I shagged him . . . maybe if I saw his cock, I'd be— 'So what have you got for me?' he asked, interrupting my very unprofessional train of thought. 'I should warn you, our advertising budget is pretty minimal.'

'You're familiar with our Entertainments section?'

'Not even a little bit.' As he grinned broadly, his whole face lit up. Damn, he's handsome. I hope I did sleep with him. Just for my ego.

I opened my presentation binder and began casually talking over readership, demographic, ad sizes, sponsorship banners . . . and then it hit me. I remembered. Eleven or so years ago, the Christmas before I met my ex, Alex (throws holy water), I pulled a guy in The Garage nightclub and we ended up shagging at his parents' house while they were away on holiday. He made me toast in the morning and I broke one of his mum's plates, much to his dismay. Jay . . . his name isn't 'Jay'; that's his initial! He's really called Jason and he doesn't have a fucking clue who I am.

'We always recommend doing a run of adverts and obviously you'll get a discount,' I awkwardly continued, thinking, *How the hell can you not remember someone you've slept with?*

'And our production staff can help with any artwork, etc., if you need it.'

(Oh God, I must have been so unmemorable. Back then I was a lot less adventurous – even I wouldn't remember sleeping with me. Maybe I just look different. Of course I do, I'm almost 39 and approaching maximum hag.)

We continued my boring sales pitch and I left him with my business card, which he took in a very uninterested manner, before yelling at the bar girl to 'bloody do something other than your face'.

'Thanks for coming in,' he said, turning back to me and shaking my hand. 'I'll be in touch.'

'Thanks for your time,' I mumbled back, just wanting to leave. Coming face-to-face with the Shag of Christmas Past is bad enough, but I was also faced with the fact that this super-hot man hadn't even saved me in his wank bank. My ego is rescinding its offer to remember.

Tuesday February 14th

Oh fucking hell, I had THE most inappropriate dream last night. I'm still unsettled. I got into a taxi and Lucy's boyfriend Kyle was the driver and we ended up shagging in the car park of the Science Centre. But the worst part is, it was hot as hell. There was hair pulling and hands pressed against steamy windows and WTF IS HAPPENING? I'm dream-cheating on Oliver with my best mate's boyfriend now? Am I so sex starved it's come to this? Oh God, I can never see him again – I think the skin on my face would literally combust with embarrassment. The fact that it's Valentine's Day doesn't make it any easier either. It's making me feel guilty when I haven't even bloody well done anything! I DID NOT HAVE ACTUAL SEXUAL RELATIONS WITH THAT MAN. I did get two Valentine cards though – one from Molly that she'd made in nursery and one from Oliver which had a plain red love heart on the front and a handwritten message inside.

Roses are red
My balls are blue
In one more week
I'll be inside you

Technically not the most romantic thing I've ever read but it did come with the Alexander McQueen perfume I've had my eye on. He's become far less serious these days, I think we might be on the right track here. For his present, I got him a VR headset for his phone and some of those truffle things from Thorntons he likes. Well, I like. He might hate them but that's not important.

Surprisingly, the only person at work to get flowers was Dorothy, who placed them in the middle of the room for us all to enjoy. Within twenty minutes, Kelly was sneezing and demanding they be removed. Brian accused her of being allergic to other people's happiness.

By half eleven, my gnawing guilt had subsided a little but

the memory of how sexy that dream had been was still very much alive. It seemed my shocking dream betrayal had made my libido go from zero to sixty. I had to text Oliver. I knew he'd be working but I didn't care.

> I'm really horny right now. Seriously. I'm so wet, it's distracting . . .

I didn't hear anything back for two hours but then −

> Damn. Do you think me sliding a hand into your knickers is against the rules?

Oh fuck me.

On the way home from work, I bought a giant romantic lasagne from Tesco and we all ate together. Molly told us about a boy in nursery who made Ruby a card and then Ruby's mum made her point him out at home time. 'I heard Ruby's mum say that he didn't look right. That wasn't nice. Jack looks more better than her mum.'

'It's just "better" honey,' I reply. 'But you're right, it wasn't nice. I'm not sure she's a very nice person.'

Molly laughed. 'Ruby says her mum cries in the bathroom like a baby all the time. Can I have some more bread, please?'

As I passed Molly the garlic bread, I felt a pang of sadness. As much as I dislike Lord Wilson, no one deserves to be crying alone in a bathroom . . . and no child should have to hear that. Oh fuck, I'm going to have to be nice to her now, aren't I?

Wednesday February 15th

Last night was intense. After our afternoon text exchange, it was obvious we were both up for it but of course we couldn't physically do anything about it. We lay in bed, side by side, and every time our skin came into brief contact, it was like a jolt of electricity (the sexy kind, though, not the kind where a doctor shouts 'CLEAR!' first).

'When you sent me that text, I fucking throbbed,' he said, staring at the ceiling. 'You haven't texted me filth in a long time. Jesus, I love that.'

It turns out that my sexy dress, kitchen seduction was misjudged. All Oliver needed to wake him up was me being obscene. Part of me wanted to apologise for being lax in my dirty talk duties; admittedly it's not top on my list of priorities after Molly, work, paying bills and perpetually trying to flatten that weird kink in my fringe, but we used to do it frequently and I'd forgotten how much he loves it. But I didn't apologise. Instead I decided to try to make him more aroused than he'd ever been in his life.

'I've been thinking about your text, too,' I mused, staring at the same spot on the ceiling. 'About you sliding one hand into my knickers . . . I imagine you pushing me up against the wall and doing it slowly . . . maybe using your other hand to pull back my hair . . .'

There was movement under the duvet. He squirmed. 'Are you still wet now?'

'There would be an easy way to find out,' I replied, turning towards him. 'But you're not allowed to, are you?'

'You could check . . .'

'Hmm, if you wanted me to . . .'

'I do.'

'But what if I get carried away . . .'

'You won't.'

I started to run my hand down my body. 'Maybe just one finger but—'

'OH FUCKING HELL, JUST DO IT!'

(I win.)

After we'd visually established my level of arousal, Oliver was practically climbing the walls. 'There isn't one part of you that I don't want to fuck, right now. Seriously, your nipples are like bullets and I'm not supposed to touch them! Fuck this shit.'

My plan to turn Oliver on had one glaring flaw. Now I was also gagging for it.

'Oliver, you're so hard, this duvet is practically levitating.'

I threw back the covers and straddled him, pinning his hands back and leaning in close to his face. 'We should wait,' I whispered, gently moving myself against him. 'Think you're hard now? Just imagine how hard you'll be when we—'

'DAD! THERE'S A SPIDER ON MY CEILING!'

We both stayed silent, hoping that she was either sleep talking or that the spider would just eat her.

'DAAAAAaaaaaaAAAAADDDD!'

I sighed. 'Hang on, Mol,' he yelled back, getting one quick kiss in before I was forced to dismount. I loosened my grip on his arms and climbed off. 'Is she ever going to get her own place?' I said, as he tucked his cock into his waistband and threw on a t-shirt. We both knew that once they'd established that there were no spiders, she'd ask for a drink, try and keep him chatting and possibly ask to sleep with us. In other words, our brief, hot moment had passed.

Nonetheless, I plumped up the pillow and turned on to my side, still feeling giddy. 100% the most erotic thing that had happened in ages. Pam Potter – you are a Queen.

Thursday February 16th

At lunch today I told Lucy all about my progress with Oliver; the kitchen, the text exchanges – everything. She listened intently while stuffing her face with a baked potato.

'I cannot believe you didn't fuck him,' she said, quite impressed. 'Or even slip the tip in. Honestly, that takes a certain level of restraint that I just don't have. I've got a tingle just thinking about that.'

I laughed. 'Molly interrupted us anyway. And you're really not supposed to get turned on by me and Oliver. That's weird.'

'Not you. Just him,' she replied, smirking. 'Before you guys got together, I had many an impure thought about that big Irish man.' She started to blush, unusual for Lucy.

'Lucy Jacobs, are you telling me you fancied my boyfriend?'

'Shut up,' she dismissed. 'I was just messing.'

For a split second, I considered telling her about the dream I'd had about Kyle. How he'd kept his glasses on. How he'd licked my neck. But if she went into detail about what she's imagined doing to Oliver, I might think she still harboured secret feelings for him. It's ridiculous but I couldn't guarantee I'd be rational, so why would she be?

'What did you do Valentine's Day?' I asked, trying to steer the conversation back towards her own boyfriend.

'We had dinner at Red Onion,' Lucy replied. 'Amazing risotto.'

I cringed. 'Oh God, I haven't been back there since I had that atrocious date with the guy I met online. The one who was hung up about his weight, remember? Ugh, I'd forgotten about that until now.'

Lucy started sniggering. She was the one who convinced me that internet dating was a great idea when it was possibly the worst idea since Brexit. 'You should go back again and create a happy memory there,' she replied. 'Take Molly. She'll probably be better behaved than he was.'

'Oh, I forgot to tell you!' I exclaimed. 'Remember I had that meeting at Downtime? Turns out the manager is some guy I shagged years ago.'

'Oh shite. Was it awkward? What did he say?'

'It was awful.' I flopped my head on to the table, narrowly missing my soup. 'He didn't remember me. How humiliating.'

Lucy moved my soup bowl and laughed. 'No one can remember *everyone* they've slept with, silly. It's a good thing! You can do business without both of you constantly remembering that he's been up you.'

I nodded, my head hanging off the desk.

'I don't know why you're bothered anyway,' she continued. 'Random shags mean nothing. We've all had unmemorable ones. Go home and be with your stupidly lovely family. At least they're likely to remember who the fuck you are.'

Friday February 17th

Hazel came round at lunchtime with carrot cake and some of Grace's clothes that she'd outgrown, which I gratefully accepted. I always find it bizarre that people buy designer clothes for their kids when they've already grown out of them by the time they leave the shop. Molly is already wearing age 6 clothes on account of her being a giant.

'I think I'm going to get my face resurfaced,' Hazel announced while I made coffee. 'There's a clinic doing a deal at the moment, I went to an open night. £500.'

'Resurfaced? Oh God, you're not going to get one of those laser jobs where you have to hide indoors for a week and your face literally sheds right off the bone? Are you?'

She shook her head. 'No, it's like tiny needles that shoot radio waves or fucking gamma rays into your skin – something like that. I was too busy looking at the before and after photos to listen properly. To be honest, if it makes me look refreshed, they can do what they want.'

Hazel has always had hang ups about ageing. Years of sun worshipping hasn't helped, but she's nowhere near as haggard as she implies. She's a very beautiful, elegant-looking woman. I'm lucky that I haven't begun to wrinkle yet, but I put that down to having oily skin which never gets a chance to dry out.

'So tell me,' she continued, cutting into the cake she brought, 'how is the therapy going? I must say, it's a very different approach to what we were offered. Ours was mostly talking and learning to appreciate each other again. Lots of learning to reconnect as individuals and not just as a couple. All very wanky but it seemed to do the trick.'

'Yeah, Pam is unusual, but that's why I've been going to her for so long. She seems to get me. Oliver says it takes an oddball to understand an oddball. I think he secretly likes her. But the abstinence part is going well – Oliver's a walking hard-on.'

She laughed. 'And you?'

'Don't ask,' I replied. 'I had to go for a walk yesterday to stop me humping the furniture.'

'Jesus. How long to go now?'

'One week,' I replied, blowing on my coffee. 'You're still taking Molly on the Friday night, right? There's no way she can be around when I pounce on him.'

'Yup, I have a movie night planned. And I'll bring her back late afternoon so you can sleep in . . . or have more sex. Whatever.'

I fucking love my friends.

Saturday February 18th

I think we did 'frottage'. I'm not even entirely sure that's a word but we did rubbing. Fully clothed, fully erect, body rubbing. It was completely unexpected. One minute I'm in my jammies, changing the bedcovers and the next, Oliver was on top of me, bare mattress, fully covered arse. He didn't speak, he didn't kiss me, he just buried his face into my neck and breathed me, slowly grinding away as I ran my fingers up and down his back. It was one of the most fucking intense moments ever and now I'm a grinning fool, still sitting on the edge of an unmade bed.

Sunday February 19th

Molly Skyped with my parents and their new dog Daphne this afternoon and was surprisingly into the whole thing, given her recent dog hatred.

'He's so cute, Mum! He looks like he's smiling.'

I placed her lunch in front of her, hoping she wouldn't notice that I'd left the crusts on her sandwich. 'I think Daphne is a girl,' I replied. 'It's a girl's name.'

'Whatever. We should get one.'

Ugh. I fucking *knew* it. I don't want a bloody dog. I have enough to do. 'A dog is a lot of work, Molly, and it's not fair to leave them alone all day. Your Nana and Papa are retired; they can spend lots of time with her. Besides, only Canadian dogs smile. Scottish dogs are very grumpy.'

She bit into her ham sandwich and chewed slowly, considering this. 'DAD? ARE SCOTTISH DOGS GRUMPY?'

I heard Oliver laugh from the kitchen.

'They are, sweetheart. Just like the people,' he called back. 'Look how grumpy your mum is in the morning.'

Molly looked at me and nodded while I was busy being quietly miffed that she didn't instantly believe my bullshit dog lie.

Oliver appeared with an omelette he'd made for me, complete with wholemeal toast and a little salad on the side. I thought he was making me cheese on toast with the heel of the loaf he refused to throw out.

'That looks fancy, Dad,' Molly said, her swinging legs inadvertently booting me in the shin. 'Is that for Mum?'

'Your mum deserves fancy things,' he replied, casually. 'Even if they are made out of eggs.'

'Did I come from an egg?'

Oliver and I looked at each other. Neither of us were close to ready to have THAT talk.

'No,' answered Oliver. 'In fact, you were dropped off on our doorstep by a huge green monster, the scariest monster who ever lived – he said that you were too much trouble, too scary, even for him! But we liked the look of you and decided you could stay.'

Molly giggled with glee and booted me again. I could tell she hoped this was true.

Monday February 20th

Oliver and I took our sexting a step further today when he sent me a photo of his cock – it was starting to look angry. I in turn nipped into the work toilets and sent him a photo of my less irate boobs, asking him if he could think of anything he'd like to do to and/or with them. I had considered taking a vag shot but I had on long boots and tights and, well, logistically it just wasn't happening without getting undressed at work.

When I got home, he had plenty of ideas, cornering me in the bathroom to relay them in great detail.

'I want to oil them up and stick my cock in between them.'

'Oliver, I'm trying to run Molly's bath.'

'Or, I'd just cum on them. Just have you suck me off and then let me—'

'*Keep your voice down!*' I pushed the bathroom door closed. 'I'm glad you like my tits. I mean they're saggy as fuck since breastfeeding but—'

'Enough of that,' he replied, seriously. 'They're fucking massive, Phoebe, and I won't hear a word against them ... and those nipples. Why are they not in my mouth?'

I turned off the water and dried my hands, aware of just how mental this whole abstinence deal was making him. So of course, I made it worse.

'These nipples?' I asked, slipping my boobs out of my bra. They always look better with a bit of wire support still underneath them, otherwise Oliver would be staring at my knees. I propped myself against the sink and let him look at me. 'You're in so much trouble,' he whispered into my ear. 'You have no idea the things I'm going to do to you on Friday.'

'Oh, I think I can guess,' I replied, grabbing his arse with both hands. 'Just as well we have an entire evening in which to do it.'

He moved his mouth millimetres away from mine. 'I really need to kiss you. But if I kissed you right now, I wouldn't be able to control myself. This is torture.'

'Maybe you should have a cold shower after Molly has her bath?' He watched as I returned my boobs to their under-wired home.

He shook his head. 'Fuck no. The moment I undressed, I'd be all over myself. I'll give Molly her bath – you get out of my sight before I have you bent over this sink. Dirty bitch.'

I slipped out of the bathroom and put Molly's pyjamas over the radiator to warm up while Oliver helped her wash her hair. It would have been easy for me to have a little play while they were busy but I'm determined to wait it out, just as Oliver has.

God, Friday night can't come soon enough.

Tuesday February 21st

'You smell like fucking jasmine and vanilla. What the hell are you trying to do to me? I WILL LICK YOU, HENDERSON!'

It's clear that Oliver isn't coping anymore. All I did was use some body spray after my shower this morning and he lost it. He's all testosterone and manly and quite frankly, if we weren't seeing Pam tomorrow, I'd be licking him first. From someone who only had brief moments of being sexual, he's turned into someone who looks at me like he's seeing me for the first time again. My fear is that we have a couple of shags and he's back to looking at me like I'm just his mate.

Wednesday February 22nd

Back at Pam's office today to discuss our near fortnight of not touching. She welcomed us in to the smell of burning incense and faint fart aroma.

'Forgive the smell,' she apologised, gesturing for us to sit down. 'My last client brought her baby son with her, who proceeded to have rampant diarrhoea towards the end of the session.'

I smiled politely, reassuring her it wasn't a problem, but Oliver lost it. What started as a faint shoulder shudder turned into a full blown, crying, can't breathe, fit of the giggles.

Eventually he calmed and it was his turn to apologise. 'It's not even that funny, I think I just have a lot of pent-up feelings.'

'Interesting,' Pam replied. 'Have these last two weeks been difficult?'

Oliver took a tissue and wiped his eyes, still giving the occasional snicker. 'I don't know how we managed,' he confessed. 'It's been tough at times. I think Phoebe's Nine Inch Nails song is particularly accurate right now.' He placed his hand on my knee and gave it a little squeeze.

Pam looked amused. 'And you, Phoebe? How do you feel?'

'It's been quite successful, I think,' I said, trying to be mature about the whole thing and not just launch into how utterly disgusting and distressingly undersexed we both are. I wanted to just agree with Oliver so we could move on to the next stage but I had that question that's been nagging me since Tuesday.

'We're definitely ready to have sex again,' I began, 'but what . . . what if we get all of this sexual tension out of our system and then we're back to where we started?'

'It's a good question,' Pam responded. 'You got to a point in your relationship where things stopped working. Sometimes seeing your partner on a purely sexual level comes way down on the list after being a parent, a household contributor, a friend . . . it's important to focus on the way you both felt about each other when the sexual attraction was . . . intoxicating . . . urgent. From the way you're responding to each other today, perhaps you've already had a glimpse of that urgency.'

We both nodded in unison.

'Good. Then this next part will be far more enjoyable than the last. But it takes a great deal of trust and requires you both to be completely vulnerable with each other. What I want is for you both to focus on the other person. Indulge them. Their wish is your command. Almost like you're having sex for the first time. Remember how much you wanted to please each other back then?'

'So we get to have sex then?' Oliver asked, clearing his throat.

Pam laughed. 'As much and in as many ways as you can think of . . .'

Thursday February 23rd

I could tell by the look on Lucy's face that she was eager to find out how my session with Pam went this week. Rather than yell across the office, I emailed her.

From: Phoebe Henderson
To: Lucy Jacobs
Subject: Next instalment

We've to make a sex jar. We write down our desires on pieces of paper and choose one or two a week. At the moment my greatest desire is to get someone to make my ironing pile disappear. We're not seeing her for a month, so it gives us time to work on our ideas.

From: Lucy Jacobs
To: Phoebe Henderson
Subject: Re: Next instalment

SEX JAR, SEX JAR – YOU'RE A SEX JAR ♫

So what, instead of Oliver telling you directly that he wants you to lick his balls, he just writes it down like it's some big secret? Ooh, I like that actually . . . that's quite hot – see, it's even working on me.

From: Phoebe Henderson

To: Lucy Jacobs

Subject: Re: Next instalment

Oh GOD, he's going to want me to do something vile, isn't he? I don't trust him with this task – if he tries to teabag me, he's losing a testicle.

Friday February 24th

4.40 p.m. I was about to take Molly over to Hazel's house when she suddenly decided that she didn't want to go. I tried to appeal to her better nature by saying that Mum and Dad needed to spend some grown up time together but she didn't care. Instead she's just accepted the £20 note in my purse and a promise of two new outfits for her Build a Bear ponies. This shag is already costing me a fortune.

5.39 p.m. Oliver is stuck with a client. I've threatened to kill both him and his client and make it look like an IT-related accident. Oliver has informed me that I'm being unreasonable and also that I'm sexy when I'm desperate.

7.30 p.m. I am sitting here, shaved, scrubbed and wearing underwear that actually matches for once. I have champagne on ice and enough lube to hold a slip and slide for fifty people. The only thing that appears to be missing is Oliver. ARE YOU FUCKING KIDDING ME?

11.05 p.m. DRUNK! Turns out a whole bottle of champagne to yourself will do that. I hope my heartburn tomorrow won't stop me from kicking Oliver's arse.

Saturday February 25th

So Oliver made it home at midnight, or so he says. I was asleep. Still there's nothing like being woken up at 6 a.m. by your boyfriend going down on you, which in turn started a chain of filth which continued until 1pm . . .

As expected, our first time didn't last that long – Oliver was at the vinegar strokes from the moment he started, pulling my legs over his shoulders and forcefully thrusting as if he was trying to make my IUD shoot out of the top of my head like Inspector Gadget. The second time, however, was far more considered; lots of oral and teasing before I climbed on top and took charge, making sure he felt everything before we both came. The third time was unexpected; he flipped me on to my stomach and pounded me for ages, making me bury my face into the pillow and scream. I don't even think he came a third time but I did. Twice.

By the time Molly got home at 3 p.m., we were both dressed and pawing at each other like teenagers. Goddammit, even now I can still feel him inside me. I'm so excited to be with him again, especially now that I know what Pam's third step has in store. Ugh, please don't let us fuck this up.

Monday February 27th

Yikes. I logged into my computer at work this morning to find an email from Jay waiting for me. He wants me to 'pop in' at some point. He's either going to give me some business or present me an invoice for a broken side plate.

Thinking that the six minutes of sunshine we had this morning was an indicator of the weather for the rest of the day, a raging Kelly arrived into work, umbrella-free and sopping wet.

'Don't say a word,' she threatened, hanging up her dripping jacket. 'I'm frozen to the bone. I'm going to end up with bloody pneumonia.'

Lucy and I both looked at Brian, who was clearly trying to think of something clever and witty and scathing to say. But he's a mouthy little shitbag who works on recruitment and is an all-round sexist pig, so clever and witty he is not. I'm so grateful I never asked him to help me with my sex list all those years ago; I'd never have lived it down.

He screwed up his face. 'Man, you're gonnae be damp all day – like a wet dog. If you start to reek, I'm moving seats.'

Kelly calmly walked over to his desk, leaned forward and wrung out her hair into his freshly-made coffee. 'Makes a change from me spitting in it, eh?'

Now THAT was funny.

Tuesday February 28th

I returned home from work to find that Oliver had cleaned out an old Ragu jar, covered it in a picture of American

Gothic and placed it on top of our dressing table. Laughing, I carried it through to the living room, where he sat tapping away on his laptop.

'So this is our sex jar? Nice picture. Looks like us. Please don't leave this out though; I'm not ready to explain to Molly what Daddy has written, or drawn, about his knob.'

He grinned. 'Yeah, we can't afford therapy for us *and* Molly . . . you got any ideas yet? I'm eager to see what you come up with.'

I smiled coyly and walked back through to the bedroom where my smile changed to a look of panic. We only have to come up with three each but so far I've come up with fuck all. The whole point of this is to get us out of our comfort zone, so writing 'any old sex – I DON'T CARE!' on the back of an old receipt kind of defeats the purpose. Of course I want to have all of the filthy sex, but the truth is I've become lazy and it's depressing. I need to snap out of this. It's not so much that I've lost my sex drive, it's just become fleeting and purposeless, like one of those sneezes that builds up and then changes its mind.

Still, after our session last week, I'm more than motivated to come up with something good. What do I really want to try? The more I think, the more I'm convinced we did everything last Friday . . .

MARCH

Wednesday March 1st

Maggie called last night to say that her son had some sort of weird rash so it was probably a good idea to keep Molly away until it had been checked out by the doctors. Luckily I wasn't working so I did the morning nursery run.

As it was still damp and cold outside, I wrapped Molly up until only her tiny face was showing from beneath her hat and scarf. I love that face. I could kiss it forever. Ruby didn't appear to be there today, which meant I could avoid another interrogation from Sarah Ward-Wilson, no doubt wanting to ask how Oliver is and how much our combined income was. I hadn't forgotten what Molly had told me about her crying in the bathroom at home but I was glad not to have to deal with it this morning.

Returning home, I plonked myself down on the couch with a pen and paper, trying to work out what on earth I could put in the jar. I noticed that Oliver had already written two notes but we agreed not to snoop. I fucking love a snoop. It's killing me.

Forty-five minutes later, I had come up with fuck all, so I grabbed my phone and called Lucy at work.

'Can you speak?' I asked, grateful that she picked up her

extension and I didn't have to make small talk with my colleagues. 'I need some advice . . .'

'On what?' she answered with a slight pause. 'Oh God, you're not pregnant again, are you? Why would you possibly want to have more people in your life?'

'No!' I laughed. 'I need some ideas of stuff to try with Oliver for the sex jar.'

I heard Dorothy call her name in the background. 'I need to go but I'll have a think. But if my ideas are so sexy, you get pregnant again . . .'

'I'M NOT GETTING PREGNANT AG—'

'See you tomorrow.'

She hung up.

Thursday March 2nd

'Right! I have an idea for you,' Lucy said, placing some salt 'n' vinegar crisps inside her ham sandwich. 'You should pretend to be someone else for the night.'

'Someone else?' I questioned, watching her crunch into her sandwich. 'Like who? John Travolta? Joan of Arc?'

She snorted. 'No. I mean, like role play. You create a different persona. And so does he. Meet up in a hotel bar or something.'

I groaned. I remembered the various role plays we'd done years earlier. It had ranged from awkward to downright embarrassing but we'd had a good time. Maybe I was just too old for this kind of thing now? Lucy saw the look of uncertainty on my face. 'It doesn't have to be elaborate. Just give yourself a night off from being you; from being "mum". Be the woman who meets a hot man in a hotel bar and gets a room.'

As she goes back to munching on her sandwich, I begin warming to the idea. Molly could stay with Hazel. I could buy new underwear. I could pretend to have an affair. I could be the filthiest— 'Earth to Phoebe,' Lucy laughed, knowing exactly where my imagination was headed. 'I definitely think you should do it. And then report back.'

'Yeah,' I replied, grinning. 'It has certain merits . . .'

After lunch I went to visit Jay, who fortunately appeared to be a tad less bored to see me this time.

'Oh! You've come. Great. I've convinced my boss to take some advertising,' he informed me. 'We'll do four adverts – quarter pages. We've been open for a year now, so we're having a few promotional nights to celebrate. I'll email all the details over.'

'Wonderful!' I replied. And it was. Not only have I bagged a new client, but it means I have less space to sell to the other poor chumps who don't realise what a fucking money pit advertising is. 'I'll get you a top-right position if it's available.'

He smiled at me, and walked behind the bar. 'Good to know. You want a quick beer while you're here? Soft drink?'

'That's very kind, but I have another meeting soon.'

I collected my things and thanked him, wondering why he didn't just email everything in the first place, and headed back to the office.

Of course the meeting thing was a total lie. I could have had a beer. I could have had a shot of tequila, kicked off my shoes and showed him the new dance routine Molly and I had been working on, but it's hardly professional. Also there's the small matter of HE'S SEEN MY VAGINA to consider (even if he doesn't remember it). It's too weird.

Friday March 3rd

With Molly in bed, we retreated to the bedroom to begin our dalliance with the sex jar. I sat at the head of the bed while Oliver retrieved the jar from the top of the wardrobe. This felt so fucking weird. Like we were being forced to tell each other sex secrets, hoping the other didn't shout, 'THAT'S DISGUSTING! I DON'T EVEN KNOW WHO YOU ARE ANYMORE!' and storm out. I was nervous.

Oliver reached into the jar and grabbed one of my requests between his fingers before lifting it up to his nose.

'This still smells of pasta sauce,' he inhaled near it twice, just to make sure.

'Will you stop sniffing it and just read it!' I insisted, plumping up the pillows behind me, completely aware that I'd now have to sniff it too because I'm easily led.

'Chill out,' he replied. 'I'm going to . . . this isn't going to ask me to piss on you or anything, is it?'

'OLIVER!'

He laughed and unfolded the paper, taking a moment to read to himself before he looked at me and raised one eyebrow. He cleared his throat, reading aloud my first request.

'Control my orgasms. For three days, you have the power to control how and when they happen.'

'Fuck, Phoebe,' he breathed. 'You really want that?'

I nodded. 'Is that weird? It's just when we were abstinent, you worked me up into such a frenzy . . . Oh God, it is weird, look – you don't have to—'

'It's hot as fuck,' he interrupted, reading the request again. 'So you can't cum unless I allow it? Wow . . .'

As he scrunched up the note and put it in his pocket, I realised that I was either going to fucking regret this or be in a constant state of arousal until given further notice. And the fact we were now both sitting in silence thinking about him having control over my next orgasm was already the best thing I'd done this year.

Saturday March 4th

I met Lucy and Hazel for lunch, not only because we all had the afternoon free but also because Oliver had already begun messing with me.

'He's just sent me a lengthy text describing going down on me,' I informed them, stabbing my salad with a fork. 'Oh, and this morning he came into the shower, pressed me up against the tiles and, well, he got me halfway there before he stopped. It's so intense. I'm dying here. Everything he does is carefully planned to make sure I'm thinking about nothing else.'

Lucy picked up her napkin and fanned herself, laughing. 'Oh my. And this was your idea? I'm so fucking impressed. I'm totally doing this with Kyle.'

'Why didn't I go to your therapist?' Hazel moaned, ripping her bread roll in half. 'In fact, I'm tempted to stop sleeping with Kevin, just so we can visit her. We never do any cool shit – well, not to this extent.'

Lucy stole the other half of Hazel's roll, ignoring her request to 'fuck right off'. 'I wonder what Oliver has written down,' she pondered, smothering the bread in butter. 'It'll have something to do with his knob. Men are very basic.'

We all nodded.

'You'd better tell us,' Hazel insisted. 'I know he plays football with Kevin sometimes but I promise I won't say a word. It'll be our little secret.'

'And Kyle's.'

We both turned to look at Lucy, who stopped chewing for a second. 'WHAT?! Oh, come on – this shit is gold. You can't expect me not to share with the man I love . . .'

I poured more vinaigrette dressing over my salad and smiled. 'It's fine!' I reassured her. 'Of course you'll share. Oliver was the first person I told when Kyle went through that phase of preferring you to wank him off using your feet.'

Lucy scanned the room to make sure that no one had overheard, while Hazel just lost it, weeping with laughter.

'Fair enough,' she conceded quietly. 'Let's stop doing that.'

Sunday March 5th

It's the second day of my sex jar request #1 and I'm ready to explode. Everything is turning me on. I was practically drooling over his stomach watching him get dressed this morning (it's frustrating – since I had Molly, my stomach now has two apron-style folds, one on each side, and a variety of stretch marks – which if inspected closely, will result in your murder). And later this evening, he insisted I watch *Secretary* with him, knowing that I find the film disturbingly sexy, especially with him lightly stroking my neck as we watched it.

'What if I just pulled down your jeans right now?' he said quietly. 'Just let my fingers do the work?'

'Oh, thank God!' I exclaimed. 'Yes, let's do that.'

When he leaned in and kissed me hard, my body went up in flames. When he slipped his hand into my knickers, I moaned so hard, I feared I'd wake Molly.

'Is this what you want?' he asked, moving his hand slowly but with enough force to make me gasp. 'You think if I did this hard enough you'd cum on my hand?'

I could barely speak, I just nodded and let him continue, knowing that it wouldn't take long.

'God, you're making me hard,' he confessed, pulling my jeans down a little further. The sound of the film faded in the background against the sounds of our breathing, the sound of clothes being removed and the sound of him pounding me hard with his hand. I reached down to feel him but he stopped me.

'My rules, remember. I might not even let you cum yet.'

'If you want to retain the use of that hand, you'll keep going.'

He grinned. 'This hand? Oh, just wait until the rest of me gets involved.'

What followed was the most extreme, three-fingered, two-lipped, one-tongued orgasm that I've ever experienced in my life! I swear he must have researched this on the sly. God bless the internet.

We went to bed shortly after, me with wobbly legs and a flushed face and Oliver looking very pleased with himself. He kissed me goodnight and just before he turned off the light said, 'We've still got tomorrow. Prepare yourself.'

Monday March 6th

'Mum, I asked for jam, not peanut butter. You know I hate peanuts.'

I turn around to see Molly standing with the plate of crustless peanut butter and toast I'd made her for breakfast.

'Molly, you chose the peanut butter. You've eaten half the jar already. What happened between yesterday and today to make you hate this poor defenceless jar of delicious sludge?'

She shrugged. She didn't need a reason. She's four.

'I'm not wasting food, Molly. If you eat that, I promise you'll never have to eat it again as long as you live.'

She grudgingly took back the plate and walked to the living room where CBeebies was already playing loudly on the television.

After his comment yesterday, I had hoped for some early morning fumbling but Oliver had already left early for a meeting, leaving me to get Molly and myself organised and out of the door for 8.15 a.m.

Jay from Downtime had emailed over his advert copy and dates he wanted it to run, along with an invite to the party itself on Thursday. As awkward as I feel around him, it's a closed venue with a free bar. How the fuck can I not go? I'll take Lucy.

As mind-numbing as my day was, things took an interesting turn around 3 p.m. when Oliver texted me.

Take your phone into the bathroom.

What? Why? I'm working!

Just do it.

Confused, I left my desk (where I was terribly busy looking at cat gifs) and took myself off to the bathroom. Given the nature of what was about to follow, I'm grateful it was empty. I checked my phone again.

Get in a cubicle.

I chose the end cubicle, nearest the hand dryers. I locked the door just as my phone began to ring.

'Hello? Oliver, why are you being weird? If you want to hear me pee, we have a perfectly good bathroom at home. But don't do that.'

'Shut up. Remember that scene in *Secretary* when she's in the bathroom at work? You're going to do that.'

'Oh, am I? And what are you going to do?'

'I'm going to listen.'

'But I'm not even turned on!'

'I am. In fact, I'm hard right now. I came home early. I'm naked and I'm going to get off, listening to you. Now put your fucking hand down your pants.'

Ten minutes later, me and my shaky legs exited the bathroom. Sex jar request #1 completed.

Wednesday March 8th

I texted Lucy this morning to remind her that she was going to this birthday thing at Downtime with me tomorrow and could she give them a quick email on my behalf to say I'd be coming along? She responded almost instantly.

WHAT DID YOUR LAST SLAVE DIE OF? (but free bar, right?)

There's a part of me that thinks I shouldn't go to this party at all. Under normal circumstances, I'd be going along to support a client, but this isn't just a normal client. This is a client that has seen my bare arse – and from what I remember, from several different angles. Thankfully, my arse (and the rest of me) seems to be quite unmemorable, though, so at least I can do business with him without him thinking about it, too. Oliver is slightly miffed that I'm going out as he's champing at the bit to get started on his first sex jar request, but I've promised we'll do it on Friday. God knows what he has in store for me.

Thursday March 9th

Against my better judgement, Lucy and I attended the private birthday party for Downtime, which was heaving with guests who all shared the same love for a free bar on a school night.

Lucy, dressed in skinny jeans and a sleeveless cape, went in first, heading towards the nearest open space at the bar.

'Two tequilas, please,' she requested, smiling at the contoured girl I'd seen here previously. 'And a couple of vodka tonics – no ice in mine.'

'It's roasting in here,' I complained, taking off my coat. My armpits were already beginning to stick to my top. 'I won't be able to stand this for too long.'

'Yeah, yeah,' she replied, rolling her eyes. 'Nothing to do with the fact that you've shagged the amnesiac manager.'

'Shhh!'

We took our shots and downed them, wincing as the alcohol burned in our throats. Lucy sucked on her lime, demanding I point Jay out.

I scanned the room, spotting him in a booth near the back. 'Over there,' I indicated, trying not to look obvious. 'White shirt, brown hair. Beside the woman in the blue dress.'

'Oh my.' She took a sip of her vodka tonic. 'I can see why you're pissed about this. He's hot. I'd want him to remember me.'

'I'm not *that* bothered!' I protested. 'Sure, he's good-looking but—'

'He looks dirty,' she continued, ignoring me. 'He looks like he'd leave a handprint.'

'Stop it.'

'He looks like the kind of guy who would spit on his own cock.'

I started to laugh but subsided when I noticed him waving me over.

'He's waving you over,' Lucy confirmed.

I waved back. 'Right, let's say hello.'

As we walked towards his table, Lucy whispered, 'He looks like the kind of guy who would change the safe word during sex and not tell you what it was.'

'I will kill you . . . Hi, Jay! Great party. Thanks for the invite!' Oh God, did he hear her? Was I blushing? I hoped not. I hoped that Estee Lauder Double Wear covered both imperfections and mortified-as-fuck syndrome.

'Glad you came,' he replied. He smiled at Lucy, who in turn smiled back, though I could tell she was secretly wondering if he had a sex swing in his office.

'Sorry, Jay, this is my friend Lucy. She also works at *The Post*.'

'Admin,' she informed him, shaking his hand. 'I'm not one of the sales wankers.'

He laughed. 'Good to know. Listen, have a drink, and I'll try and catch up with you later, Phoebe.'

I nodded and pulled Lucy away before she had the chance to ask to see his office.

Forty minutes and two tequilas later, I'd relaxed enough to forget about my history with Jay. Unfortunately, Lucy hadn't.

'If you weren't with Oliver, I'd be telling you to fire into him,' she declared, licking the excess salt off the back of her hand.

I sighed. 'Why? Because the first time was so memorable for him? I think not.'

'Hmm – actually, scrap that. If I wasn't with Kyle . . .'

'Behave. I have to work with this man. In fact, now would be a good time to leave. Wait here while I say bye.'

Lucy bolted to the bar to get one last shot in while I made my way over to Jay; he was just heading into his office.

'Sorry, I know you're busy,' I said. 'I just wanted to say bye and thanks again for the invite.'

'Leaving so soon?'

'Work tomorrow,' I lied. 'But I'll be in touch about your ads.'

The sound of a glass breaking, followed by a loud cheer from the bar. I turned to see the culprit, Lucy, clinking shot glasses with a biker twice her size. Jay started to laugh.

'I'll be taking her with me,' I reassured him. 'Sorry.'

He shrugged. 'Don't worry, at least it wasn't *you* breaking my shit again.'

'Pardon?'

'My mum was really pissed about that plate ... anyway, see you soon! Safe home!'

I stood there, stuck to the spot while he entered his office and closed the door. All I could think was: he remembers me? Yay! He remembers me!

OH.

GOD.

HE REMEMBERS ME.

Friday March 10th

11.59 a.m. Lucy has been sending me laughing gifs over WhatsApp all morning because she finds it hilarious that Jay knew who I was all along. I started ignoring her after the twelfth 'owned' gif but she's still going strong.

3.15 p.m. Just back after picking Molly up from nursery. She made me some sort of papier-mâché jam jar creation with a love heart on one side and what looks like a bit of snot on the other. I've been carefully avoiding touching that in case it was sneezed there by accident. Oliver should be back around six – I imagine he's keen for me to choose his first piece of paper from the sex jar from the way he keeps saying, '*I cannot wait to see which one of mine we're doing first*' repeatedly. God help me.

Saturday March 11th

I'm not saying that Oliver's first choice isn't perfectly reasonable in the grand scheme of things, but he's definitely pushing my boundaries in terms of things I said I'd never do.

'Really? You want to unload on my face?'

'Unload? Phoebe, we're not running a haulage company.'

I sighed. 'You know I hate all that. It's degrading.'

Oliver sat down beside me on our bed as I held his little piece of paper in my hand. 'Is it, though?' he enquired. 'You know I love and respect you . . . and look, even if it is – why can't we throw a little bit of degradation in there? I don't feel that comfortable when you ask me to call you a filthy bitch but I still do it.'

'Well, that's completely diff—'

'Actually, fuck it; who am I kidding? I love all that.' He took the note out of my hand and pushed me back on to the bed. 'I want you to be my filthy bitch. I'm not even sorry. I want you to suck my cock and let me finish on your face.' He started undoing my jeans.

I have no idea whether it was the forceful approach Oliver

took or the fact that he'd called me a filthy bitch twice and it turned me on, but moments later I was on my knees in front of him, telling him to avoid my hair.

To be honest, it wasn't as awful as I thought it would be. In fact, when I saw how excited Oliver was by the whole thing, it made me wish I'd tried it sooner.

Monday March 13th

'Well, I have to say I'm impressed,' Lucy remarked as we made coffee before the morning meeting. 'Though, I think you should prepare yourself for most of Oliver's suggestions to be ejaculation-related.'

We hadn't even noticed the cleaner standing behind us, until she coughed like a disapproving parent. We took our cups and walked back through to the office.

'You enjoyed it, though?' I nodded, holding open the corridor door. 'Yeah. I guess it was pretty hot. He looked pretty hot doing it. God, I liked making him feel like that.'

Lucy squeezed past me. 'Well, my dear, you know what that makes you then?'

'Um . . . a good girlfriend?'

'Nope. A great big cum slut! Soon you won't be happy until your face looks like it's being prepared for wallpaper— Morning, everyone!'

Unable to finish this conversation, we both headed through to the meeting room where Dorothy had an announcement to make. 'Well, as much as I've enjoyed working with you all, I've decided it's time for me to move on. It'll be officially announced later this week.'

'Does this mean your position is open?' Kelly asked almost immediately. 'Is it being advertised internally?'

'No one's letting you run the office, Kelly,' Brian responded on behalf of everyone.

Before they had time to argue, Dorothy stepped in. 'As far as I know, the position is being advertised both internally and externally. I'll keep you up to date but I'm due to leave at the end of the month.'

Blimey! I wonder who'll replace her. Fuck, if Kelly did get the job, I think I'd leave. Maybe that's what I need to get me out of here finally! I'll ask her if she wants a reference.

Tuesday March 14th

Oliver is still chipper as fuck about the other day and show-ing his affection in various ways, like holding one of my boobs while we sleep and pulling me in from behind for hugs and neck-nuzzling. We even had a really slow, really deep spoon this morning where he was forced to cover my mouth with his hand to quieten my moans. Next sex jar request is scheduled for Thursday – my turn. Gosh, we only have another two each to do before we see Pam again to dis-cuss our progress.

Wednesday March 15th

Oliver has assured me that eating out-of-date hummus won't kill me. If I do die and the police are reading this, please arrest him.

Thursday March 16th

Sex jar time again! Oliver practically frogmarched me into the bedroom the moment I'd put Molly to bed, unwilling to meet with my 'let me do the dinner dishes first' demands. As he closed the door behind him quietly, I noticed that he'd already placed the jar on the bed.

'Someone's keen,' I teased, hopping on to the bed. 'Have you had a peek already?'

'Nearly,' he confessed, closing the blinds. 'But it's far more fun if I see your face while I read it.'

I watched him pick one of my yellow slips of paper from the jar. He didn't look happy.

'You want to fuck a stranger? What the hell, Phoebe? Why are you smiling?'

I guessed this was not the face, nor the request, he was expecting. 'Relax.' I laughed, placing my hand on his arm. 'I want you to be the stranger – well, you, but not *you* exactly.'

'You're so fucking weird,' he said quietly, reading the note again. 'But OK. I'm listening.'

'I want us both to be other people for the night,' I began, trying to explain more eloquently. 'I'm going to book a room at a hotel. And I want to meet you in the bar. Maybe we're both there on business. Maybe we're just hanging out ... maybe I'm in a mood with my boyfriend who didn't do the dishes while I put our kid to bed—'

'But I was going to aft—'

'Whatever, we can work out the story. But I want you to flirt with me like we just met. I want to get a little tipsy. But most of all, I want the only thing on your mind to be how you're going to get me up to that hotel room with you.'

He was suddenly very interested. 'And when we get there?'

I leaned in. 'Then I want you to do whatever the fuck you want to me.'

He ran his hand through his hair and muttered, 'I'm fucking framing this,' before pulling my face into his and kissing me hard.

I can tell this is going to be a good one.

Friday March 17th

'I have a huge favour to ask.'

Hazel looked at me suspiciously from the other side of a clothes rail. 'What have you done?'

Perhaps the middle of TK Maxx wasn't best time to discuss this, but I carried on regardless. 'Nothing! It's just ... we're seeing Pam next week and we still have a few things to do from the ... jar. Can you watch Molly tomorrow night?'

'Oh, I would, but Kevin and I have plans. Grace is having a sleepover at her friend's house.'

I sighed and put down the hideous blouse I was holding. 'Dammit. We need to stay a night in a hotel.'

'Ask Lucy.'

I grimaced. 'I trust Lucy with *my* life, but Molly's? I dunno ...'

Hazel laughed. 'Nonsense. Lucy's sat for Grace a few times. And Molly loves her. She might dye her hair or pierce something, though – you'd just need to take the risk ...'

'What?!'

'I'm kidding. Text her. She'll say yes.'

8.55 p.m. She said yes, agreeing to stay over at our place so Molly didn't feel uncomfortable in a strange house. Why didn't I think of this before? She also recommended a hotel she'd been to and I've just booked the last room available for tomorrow night. We're all set! Bring it on!

Sunday March 19th

(Sex Jar #3 update from last night. Current state: cannot walk.)

I got to the hotel at 6 p.m. to get ready in the room before Oliver arrived at 8 p.m. But upon seeing it, my heart sank. Sure, the hotel was modern like Lucy said, but in my hurry to book the last room I hadn't noticed that it had NO FUCKING WINDOW. We were essentially going to shag in a cell. Thankfully the shower was hot, but seriously – no direct sunlight? If we'd been role playing a couple of horny vampires, this would have been perfect.

Even though we were playing strangers, we'd decided to keep our names, as I didn't trust him not to come up with something stupid like *Rusty* or *Tarquin* and fully expect me to use it all night with a straight face. However, everything else would be invented, including jobs, home life and whatever else we could throw in to liven things up. I'd decided to keep my job the same (fuck making up too much on the spot) but I'd be unhappily married and childless.

The receptionist looked a little confused to see that I'd

arrived in jeans and high-tops but was now wearing a business suit to relax in the bar on a Saturday night. Regardless, I marched through fifteen minutes early to get a table before Oliver showed up. Why was I nervous? I've known this man since I was sixteen.

The bar area was small but brightly lit, with dark brown, wood panelling, trendy rectangular spotlights all over the ceiling and the odd pink chair scattered around for a burst of colour. I hated it. No windows and pink chairs. Lucy's an idiot. Oh God, I've left my child with an idiot.

Reminding myself that I wasn't there for the décor, I bought a Jack and Diet Coke and picked a table beside the window so I could remember what the outside looked like for the next couple of hours. In front of me sat two women drinking hot chocolate and from what I could hear by unashamedly eavesdropping, Woman 1 had a very nice time at Kelvingrove Art Gallery and Woman 2 had a blister on her effing heel.

'Is this seat taken?'

Fucking hell, I nearly jumped out of my seat. I turned to see Oliver, standing there in a blue suit, his dark, curly, grey-flecked hair dishevelled. He looked like he did when we did a student/teacher role play a few years ago, albeit a little older. Still as sexy as ever. If he'd worn his glasses, I'd have straddled him there and then.

I shook my head and gestured for him to sit down, getting a small frisson of excitement as he placed his drink beside mine.

'Oliver,' he announced, holding out his hand, which I shook in a I-have-never-met-you-before-you-complete-stranger manner, complete with a look of mild disinterest. I didn't want to appear overly keen. Saying that, in real life I'd probably have told him to *sit at one of the other empty tables, fuckface,* so maybe my approach was redundant.

'Phoebe,' I responded. 'Nice to meet you.' He unbuttoned his jacket, aware I was watching him. He fucking wore that suit on purpose to throw me off my game. But he won't win. I've got this.

The next few minutes were awkward. I checked my phone and stared out of the window while Oliver grabbed a newspaper from a nearby table and noisily flicked through the pages.

'Nice evening.'

I nodded as he continued to scrunch the paper.

'There are other tables here if you'd like to read noisily,' I said, keeping my eyes on my phone. 'I came here for a quiet drink.'

He smirked and folded over the paper. 'Phoebe, wasn't it? Yes, there are, but none of them are near you. And I'd really like to buy you another drink.'

'Oh, that's smooth.' I laughed. 'Sure, why not? Jack and Diet Coke.'

'Be right back.'

As he went to the bar, the woman with her back to me at the nearby table turned around.

'Is that man bothering you?'

Yes. God, yes. For over twenty years.

'Oh, no,' I replied. 'It's fine. I'm fine. I think he's just lonely . . . he's probably on day release or something . . .'

She smiled awkwardly, not knowing how to respond and

returned to her friend, no doubt telling her to call the police if I started blinking at her in code. I couldn't help myself. I took an old receipt from my bag and scribbled down 'woman at next table is worried you're a weirdo. Which you are.'

Oliver returned with a bottle of champagne and two glasses. 'You don't mind, do you? I thought we might get a little tipsy.' I slyly handed him the note and watched him grin.

'How forward of you,' I quickly retorted. 'But I need to make sure you're not a dangerous psycho first. Have you ever been arrested?'

The glint in his eye was unmistakable. 'Um ... before I went to prison, yes, I was arrested.'

I tried my best not to laugh. 'Why did you go to jail?'

He poured me a glass of champagne and then himself, purposefully giving himself time to think. 'It wasn't anything brutal. I just happened to borrow some money from my employers without their permission.'

'Borrow? Ha! How much? If that's not too personal a question?'

'Enough,' he replied. 'It was enough. But that's in my past. I'm sure you have things in your past you'd rather not discuss in public?'

I knew that this was Oliver's way of inviting me to invent something just as elaborate.

'Perhaps,' I answered coyly. 'Nothing quite as illegal, however.'

If popcorn had been offered to the women at the next table, they'd have taken it.

Oliver leaned forward and touched my knee under the table. 'But since we're sharing, Phoebe ...'

My plan to become different people for the evening had suddenly become far more interesting than I'd ever expected, but my mind was going blank. What could I have done in my past that I'd rather forget? Punched a dog? Slept with a Sky engineer for extra channels? Fed a burger to a cow?

'I used to do phone sex lines,' I blurted out, instantly regretting it.

Oliver laughed. 'What? Phone them or take the calls?'

'I took the calls.'

He raised an eyebrow. 'You don't look like a sex line operator.'

'Well . . . you don't look like a "borrower".'

'I should hope not – they're tiny.'

That was when I lost it. I started laughing so hard, champagne came out of my nose. It was then that the two women at the table in front took their coats and left. No one in need of help would be laughing this much.

'So tell me more about your sex line work, Phoebe,' Oliver continued, watching the women walk away. 'Although, I should warn you: I'm already incredibly attracted to you.'

'Oh, yes?'

He moved to the seat directly beside me. 'Yes. So don't ruin it.'

I did my best not to smirk but one crept over my face without my permission. 'It's simple, really. Men would call me up and I'd talk dirty to them.'

He downed the remainder of his champagne before pouring us both another glass. 'Really? How dirty?'

It was my turn to lean into him. '*Incredibly* dirty,' I said softly. 'So filthy I'd have to get myself off just talking about it. The things they wanted to do to me . . .'

'Like what?' he asked quietly, before taking a sharp breath as I ran my hand up his thigh towards his crotch.

'Exactly what you're imagining doing to me right now, I'd presume . . .' I slid my hand up a little further. 'Yep. I thought so.'

As Oliver took another long drink, I could feel him get harder under my hand.

'Fuck,' he muttered. 'Are you staying at the hotel, Phoebe?'

'Maybe. Why?'

'You know the answer to that.'

I noticed that the bar had suddenly filled up to capacity. I was so freakin' into this, I hadn't paid attention to anything else. 'Look . . . Oliver, wasn't it? I'm not in the habit of just letting strangers come to my room, let alone ones that—'

Oliver took his glasses out of his inside pocket.

'Ones that what?' he asked, putting them on. 'You were say—?'

'You fucker. Room 203. Meet me there in five minutes.'

I left the table, making my way hurriedly to the lifts and back to the room. I was excited for what was about to happen, but mainly I really needed to pee. I just had time to freshen up before I heard him knock on the door, undoubtedly using his hard-on.

I had barely opened the door before his hands were grabbing at my clothes and his mouth was on mine. I'd seen him eager before but this was on a whole new level. I pulled away for a second as the door shut behind him.

'What? What's wrong?' He wiped my lipstick from his mouth.

'Nothing ... it's just ... you're so intense.'

'And?'

I gasped and narrowed my eyes. 'Prison's changed you.'

He sniggered and pushed me towards the bed, undoing his belt. 'You said if I got you here I could do whatever the fuck I wanted to?'

I nodded.

'Then bend over.'

We fucked over the bed, on the bed, on the floor, against the desk, on the chair and even against the door while we heard people walking past. I don't think there was an inch of that room, or me, that wasn't covered. There was pounding, there was spanking, there was squirting, there were several moments of religious bellowing and by the time Oliver had finished with me, I finally understood Lucy's wallpaper analogy.

We lay panting in bed at 3 a.m., too tired to do anything except sleep, both pushing each other away to get some air. However, the last thing I remember is Oliver gently clutching my hand as I drifted off. It was sticky but perfect.

Monday March 20th

It was Lucy's birthday today. When I saw her at work this morning, she was still laughing at the state she'd seen me come home in on Sunday. She also had on a *birthday babe* badge which was roughly the size of a dinner plate.

From: Lucy Jacobs
To: Phoebe Henderson
Subject: GOOD MORNING

How's it going, John Wayne? Have you recovered?

From: Phoebe Henderson
To: Lucy Jacobs
Subject: Re: GOOD MORNING

HAPPY BIRTHDAY! I feel like I've been battered with a penis. Honestly, maybe it's my age, but fucking hell, I ache in places I don't even have.

BUT TOTALLY WORTH IT. I feel sorry for the hotel staff, having to clean up that room. They may as well just set it on fire.

From: Lucy Jacobs
To: Phoebe Henderson
Subject: Re: GOOD MORNING

You lucky bitch. How many of these things do you have left? You should just keep doing it until one of you dies, to be honest.

Oh and thank you for the birthday wishes! I'm very special and I hope your gift later reflects this.

From: Phoebe Henderson
To: Lucy Jacobs
Subject: Re: GOOD MORNING

My gift later? You asked for vouchers you maniac.

I have one request left and Oliver has two. We're supposed to have them finished by Wednesday but I can't see that happening unless neither of his involve my vagina. Or having to move. I'm too unfit for this shit.

From: Lucy Jacobs
To: Phoebe Henderson
Subject: Re: GOOD MORNING

You'd better be in reasonable shape for my gathering tonight, bitch. It's bad enough that you and Hazel are both bringing your children to my dinner, I don't want your internal injuries getting in the way of my fun. I shan't stand for it.

(Molly is super sweet btw – she put my hair in bunches and didn't scream once when we watched *Nightmare on Elm Street*.)

I glared over at her as she waved at me from her desk. I hope to God she's kidding.

5 p.m. Taxi has been called to take us to Lucy's house. We have roughly three and a half hours before Molly starts getting tired and cranky. That should be enough time to do presents, eat food and have a couple of glasses of wine. I am a considerate and highly efficient mother and friend.

Tuesday March 21st

OMG OMG OMG!!!
Lucy's birthday dinner last night. HOLY BALLS.

So we got there at half five, Molly carrying the extravagantly-wrapped box that contained Lucy's specially-requested vouchers and Oliver carrying the pink champagne I intended to open as soon as possible.

Kyle ushered us in to the living room where Hazel, Kevin and Grace were already seated. Lucy, looking as excited as she had been at work all day, whooped when she saw us.

'Yay! We're all here! Kyle, grab my phone, will you, I need a photo before booze ruins our good looks.'

One Oscar's-style selfie later, we sat down to eat a massive pizza that Kyle had lovingly bought on his way over, complete with garlic bread and wedges. I've never understood the reasoning behind garlic bread with pizza. *I'd like some dough to go along with my other dough, please.* Regardless, the kids soon vanished in front of the telly while we all celebrated Lucy turning thirty-seven.

'Paul sent me a card from New York!' she said, grabbing it off the mantelpiece. 'I miss his big gay face.'

Our mutual friend Paul had come back home to Glasgow briefly a few years ago before deciding it was as shite as he remembered. He then quickly sold his flat and returned to New York with his boyfriend. They got married last year.

'I haven't emailed him in ages,' I confessed. 'I'm a terrible friend.'

Kevin raised his glass to Lucy, to begin our usual round of toasting, which we did to embarrass the shit out of whoever was turning a year older.

'To Lucy!' he said. 'The woman who bought my wife a crotchless cat-suit and to whom I will always be grateful!'

Hazel's face looked exactly like mine when Oliver revealed too much at Pam's office. Men have no filter, it seems.

Next to go was me. Still holding my glass, I smiled sweetly. 'To my wonderful friend. The one who doesn't know where the fuck Nessie lives. The one who hears far more about my sex life than necessary and the one whose lovely face makes going in to work a lot more bearable. You complete me, bitch. Happy Birthday!'

We all began to clink glasses until Kyle stopped us. Kyle with his tattoos and his pierced eyebrow and his disarmingly charming face. Kyle the one who dream-fucked me and now I find it hard to look at him for too long without blushing.

'To my Luce. The one who makes me wish I had more hours in the day to look at her. The one who makes me want to try harder. The one who won't move in with me . . .'

We all 'ooohed' panto-style and she laughed.

'And the one I'm really, really hoping will be my wife.'

We stopped oohing because at that moment every single one of us held our breath. Except Lucy.

'What?! Are you fucking serious?'

He produced a small ring box from under his seat. I felt sick. She won't live with him, why the hell would he think she'd marry him?

As he opened the box, I stood up to get a proper look. We all did.

'Marry me, Luce. I've never been more serious in my life.'

She looked at the ring. And then at me. And then back at Kyle. The silence was killing us all. Until she squealed, 'FUCK YEAH, I'LL MARRY YOU!'

MY BEST MATE IS GETTING MARRIED! But more importantly . . .

I'M GOING TO BE HER BEST WOMAN!!!

That's a thing . . . right?

Wednesday March 22nd

Having only completed three out of our six sex jar tasks, I felt a tad sheepish walking into Pam's office, like I hadn't done all of my homework and would be thrown a disappointed look at any moment. Oliver wasn't concerned in the slightest. He was verging on triumphant.

'Phoebe got to do two and me, only one, but I'm proud of what we've achieved.'

Pam smiled. 'So you feel it's been an effective tool in becoming closer again?' I liked the way her messy bun wobbled every time she spoke. It was comforting.

Oliver coughed. 'Let's just say, there's no humanly way we could have been any closer the other night.'

I whacked him on the side of the thigh. 'I'm sure Pam doesn't need to know that.'

Pam interjected. 'This is a safe space, Phoebe. I'm happy to listen to whatever you'd like to divulge, I'm not here to judge.'

Pausing for a moment, she flicked a page in her notebook, reading something to herself.

'Oliver, you said when we began our sessions that you wanted you and Phoebe, as a couple, to feel like your old selves again. Do you still feel this way?'

He shook his head. 'This is becoming a better version. I'm seeing the side I'd forgotten about.'

'And which side is that?'

He grinned. 'The side that makes me get instantly hard.'

He swiftly moved his leg before I could whack him again.

We have another appointment in two weeks. Plenty of time to finish the sex jar challenges and find out what else she has planned for us.

Saturday March 25th

Lucy texted me a gif of a bride falling down, stating that there were to be *'no fucking stairs'* at her wedding. She's panicking already and they haven't even discussed a date. It's exciting, though. I've never gotten giddy over weddings, or indeed marriage, but it's Lucy. I'm giddy for her. She deserves every little smidgen of happiness that comes her way.

Monday March 27th

Mum's got Facebook. Mum's profile picture is one of Daphne licking her face, with Dad visible in the reflection in her sunglasses. Mum has all of her posts public, including a photo of me holding Molly the moment she was born. Molly looks cute but I look like that kid at the end of the film *Sleepaway Camp*. Mum has friend-requested me. Mum can fuck off.

Lucy is now behaving quite nonchalantly about the fact she's an engaged woman and seems more interested in my sex jar escapades.

'We haven't done any more,' I confessed. 'We've just been busy.'

'Ugh,' she replied. 'Hurry up and stop being so boring. That's what got you into this mess. If you stop having sex again, your hole will close up forever and you'll just pee up inside your own body until you drown.'

'Jeez, FINE. I'll get on it. You're so bossy.'

Tuesday March 28th

So I caved and added Mum on Facebook but I've blocked her from seeing most of my stuff and told her that the moment she tags me in a photo, she's deleted. We've also discussed her publicly sharing pics of Molly. I don't want any old nonce happening upon my child's beautiful face.

Anyway, today was relatively uneventful although Dorothy did have a meeting with a particularly skinny, older gentleman and we all reckon he's the one who'll be replacing her. Kelly isn't happy, of course, not even being considered for the job.

'Utter bullshit,' she moaned. 'I could run this office with my eyes closed. I've been here longer than anyone.'

Brian disagreed. 'Pretty certain Moira the cleaner has been here longer, Kelly.'

'No, stupid, I meant longer than any of you—'

'And by that reasoning, I think Moira should apply,' he continued. 'Makes sense. She's well-liked. Team player . . . hides your mug when you leave it for her to wash . . .'

'Utterly ridiculous,' she protested. 'Moira doesn't know the first thing about . . . she does what?!'

I walked away and left them arguing. I hope when slender man gets the job he fires me immediately. I cannot take any more of this nonsense.

Wednesday March 29th

Molly has a slight cold and fell asleep relatively early, which gave Oliver and I a chance to pick the next request from the jar. I'll miss it when we finish; it's been rather fun.

Oliver's turn this time and I tentatively picked out one of his two remaining pieces of paper, wondering where the fuck he wanted to aim at this time.

I want to watch you masturbate.

'Um . . . why?!' I enquired, a tad perturbed.

He bounced on the bed, trying to find a more comfortable position. 'Are you seriously asking me that?'

'But how is that fun for you?'

'Oh, I'll be playing along. I just want to watch you make yourself cum while I do the same. It's a simple one – probably better after our last jaunt. I'm not sure my cock could take it.'

'Can I use toys? You know how long it takes me using my hand these days. It's a fucking effort.'

He laughed. 'See, I have no idea, it's been so long since I've seen you do it.'

'Likewise,' I replied. 'You sneak off into the shower . . .'

He bounced back up. 'Well, there you go. It's settled. We'll have a couple's wank. You can use whatever you want but I want to see everything.'

Thursday March 30th

'I'm really not sure about this one.'

I scanned the canteen, people-watching, while I patiently waited for Lucy to finish downing an entire can of Irn Bru before answering. 'Sorry. I'm so hungover. I had dinner with Kyle's parents. They're huge whisky drinkers, and when in Rome . . .' She quietly burped, trying not to breathe over me.

'What's the problem with Oliver's request? Me and Kyle do that all the time. Usually he'll pull back the duvet while I'm having a play and join in. It's very rarely scripted.'

'I don't know. I think that it's the fact he'll be looking at everything. Every stretch mark, every wobble. My stupid solo sex face. I don't think I'll be able to concentrate. What if he wants to cum at the same time and I'm still miles away? Fake it?'

'Can I have your water?'

'What? Oh yeah, go for it.'

She mumbled about the evils of whisky and finished off the rest of the bottle. 'Don't fake it. We've had this talk. And don't overthink it, either.'

'You're no help today,' I muttered, 'though I'm not sure what help you can give me, to be fair. Just show me your pretty engagement ring again and we'll say no more.'

She lifted her left hand, displaying the large diamond on a rose gold band.

'It's never not impressive,' I admitted. 'Fuckssake, you get asked for your hand in marriage and I get asked to wank. Where's my fucking ring?'

She laughed into the water bottle, choking herself in the process. 'You get a Molly, I get a ring. Now, fetch me some more water before I dehydrate completely, please.'

APRIL

Sunday April 2nd

We all went to Kelvingrove Park today. Oliver was on a mission to teach Molly how to ride a bike without stabilisers. Being the first Sunday of the nursery break, every bored parent in Glasgow had the same idea, dragging themselves behind their kids who ran screaming towards the swings. I let Oliver and Molly go ahead as I ate some chocolate I'd stashed away in my handbag.

'But what if I don't want to learn how to ride without stabilisers?' I heard Molly enquire, pedalling alongside her dad. 'Why can't I just keep them on?'

Oliver ruffled her hair. 'Because pretty soon you'll be far too big for a kid's bike and they don't make grown up bikes with stabilisers.'

'But mum can't ride a bike.'

'I can!' I insisted, quickening my pace to catch up with them. 'I've just forgotten how to. I haven't done it in a very long time.'

Total lie. I never learned. I wish my parents had pushed me to learn but they parented in the 'let her do what she wants' style, which very rarely came in handy. Bloody hippies. I didn't want Molly to think I was lame. She'll learn that soon enough when she's older.

Oliver smirked at me. He knew I was full of shit but it was easier to lie than to have to explain why I didn't ride but she had to. He stopped Molly and bent down to talk to her.

'I promise that by the end of today, you'll be riding this bike back through the park with no training wheels. Think how cool you'll look when you cycle to nursery.'

She bowed her head and thought for a second. 'Hmm ... Stewart rides his bike to nursery. It's a nice bike, Dad, it has a flame sticker on it.'

'You learn how to ride, I'll get you a flame sticker.'

'Can I get a Yoshi sticker?'

'Deal. Let's get these wheels off.'

I stood back and watched while they interacted. There was something so pure about the whole thing. Molly taking in what Oliver said, Oliver gently pushing, Molly pointing to a squirrel and then falling off – it went on for at least an hour. There were tears, tantrums, Oliver gained another grey hair and I just marvelled. Finally, just as it began to drizzle with rain, Oliver let go without her noticing and off she went, to embarrassingly loud cheers from her parents and an elderly man who'd been watching from a park bench.

My heart nearly burst. Today was perfect. Also, what the fuck is a Yoshi?

Monday April 3rd

'Right, Henderson, we need to get these last sex jar requests done.'

I rolled over in bed and looked at Oliver who was already up and hunting around for a clean shirt. He was back to work today. I was going to remain in my pants until at least lunchtime.

'I know,' I agreed, yawning. 'We will . . . Christ, you look good in those pants. Are those the ones I bought you? Get back in here immediately.'

He glanced over as I threw back the covers. He sighed. 'I wish I could. Early meeting with the boss.' As I pouted, he sidled over and kissed my neck. 'Ugh, you're all soft and warm. Fuckssake. I'm going to be thinking about this all day.'

'You could just put it in . . . just a little . . . just the ti—'

'No!'

I pulled down my underwear a little and he paused.

'What if I just put my hand inside my knickers while you watched? That's what you wanted, right?'

'Oh, you complete shit.'

'And then my other hand began to wander to my nipples? Do you think that would work?'

'Phoebe!'

I laughed. 'OK, I'm sorry. Go to work.'

Finding his shirt, he quickly pulled it on and buttoned it up. 'Promise me you won't touch yourself until tonight. We're so doing this. Shit, I have a semi now. I fucking hate you.'

I rolled back on to my side. 'Hate you, too, honey. Have a great day.'

Yep. Still got it.

Tuesday April 4th

When Oliver got home last night, he was a man on a mission. As requested, I hadn't touched myself for the entire day, but given that Molly was here, it wasn't likely to happen anyway. Perhaps some mothers can have a quick one while their kid is preoccupied elsewhere; I just don't seem to be one of them.

We all ate together, then he played a little *Minecraft* with Molly on the PS4. I didn't think someone with such tiny hands could be so adept at building massive houses. Molly's pretty good at it, too.

If Molly had been younger, I'd have jumped in the bath with her but she's at the age where she just points at my body and either laughs or gives me a disgusted look, so I bathed her first before showering quickly while Oliver read her a story. After popping in to kiss her goodnight (and to make sure Oliver wasn't asleep beside her), I put on some nice underwear, dimmed the lights and sat up in bed, waiting for him to come through. From the point where I heard him say goodnight and close her door, it was like he'd just Quantum Leaped directly into our bedroom.

He sat beside me on the bed for a while, waiting for Molly to fall asleep. He fidgeted, obviously dying to get started.

'It's dark in here, Phoebe.'

'It's called mood lighting. You want me to be in the mood, don't you?'

'Yeah, but what am I? A bat? I need a little more light for this to work . . .'

I compromised by turning the dimmer switch half a

millimetre. Oliver got up and stood at the end of the bed. I suddenly felt very exposed.

'You're just standing there.'

'I know.'

'Can you at least take your shirt off? Women need visuals, too, you know.'

He smiled and started slowly unbuttoning his shirt, while I began running my hands over my chest and stomach. It all felt very unnatural. No one wanks like this. I felt like I was replicating some dodgy porn movie where women suddenly become inexplicably aroused when a man appears to fix their washing machine.

Very astutely, Oliver noticed this and without taking the piss, he quietly said, 'Let me see if I can help things along. Close your eyes.'

I gratefully complied. Hearing my bedside drawer open and close, I began to smile. Oliver was bringing out the big guns.

Placing my vibrator in my hand, he firmly pulled down my underwear and left one side hanging around my ankle. It was clear that Oliver had a very specific visual in mind. I felt him move to the side of the bed and watch me as I used the toy on myself. It was something I'd done many times before, but this time it felt different. This time it wasn't just about me.

Hearing his trousers unzip and his breathing quicken, I slowly opened my eyes and saw him standing over me. Fucking hell, he was hard, he was close and he never took his eyes off me. I reached across and ran my left hand down his thigh and he moaned softly. Hearing him moan made every nerve in my body tingle. I was close too. Part of me wanted to demand he just stop and shag me but this wasn't my game. In my game, wine would have been made available.

'Fuck,' he said, almost in a whisper. 'Tell me when you're going to cum.'

As I did, he came on my tits. And my stomach. And weirdly enough, a little on my elbow. Gross.

I had no choice but to shower again afterwards and he joined me, quietly repeating 'holy fuck' over and over again.

I'm the best girlfriend EVER. Only two more sex jar requests to go and we're done!

Thursday April 6th

Molly and I Skyped Mum this evening as she'd ignored my 'Happy Birthday' messages and Skype attempts over the past two days. I was beginning to worry.

'Happy Belated Birthday! Where have you been?!' I asked, like a total parent.

Mum laughed. 'Dad took me to a fancy hotel. It was marvellous. They had a swing band playing; I think we're going to take lessons. Hello, Molly darling! How are you?'

'I'm good,' she replied. 'I can ride my bike now. With no stabilisers or anything!'

Mum clapped loudly and yelled to tell Dad, who popped his head into view of the camera. 'Aren't you amazing!' he said proudly. 'Maybe you can teach your mum how to ride. She was never really a fan of bikes when she was your age.'

Ah shite. Rumbled. Thanks, Dad.

Molly slowly turned her head towards me like a demonic doll. 'You said you could ride a bike.'

'I know,' I replied guiltily. 'I just didn't want you to think Mummy was a loser.'

Molly giggled. 'Don't be silly. I'll teach you. Then you'll be a winner!'

I cuddled her and whispered, 'I have you. I already am.'

Friday April 7th

I only get twenty days holiday per year and I've had to use five already for Molly's second term break. Now I have fifteen days left and she still has a shitload of time off to come. Not to mention what I'd need for any family holiday that we might decide to take. Oliver will have to eat into his own allowance if I have any hope of making them stretch. I have no doubt that we'll end up paying Maggie to watch Molly during the lengthy summer break, unless she goes away, in which case we're screwed. Happy bloody Friday.

In other news, Lucy texted me to say that she'd overheard Dorothy talking about our new boss and he's due to start on the 24th. They must have hired the skinny man. I hope he's mentally prepared to take on our shit show of an office. I almost feel bad for him. Almost.

Saturday April 8th

Another rainy weekend but I took Molly to see a special showing of Sing-a-long Frozen at the theatre as I'd been given freebies at work. Turns out I knew more songs than I thought, much to Molly's amusement, even dueting with her on 'Love is an Open Door' like a BOSS.

Knowing I had three tickets, Oliver made himself scarce, feeding me some bullshit story about having to work from home. If I checked his browser history right now, it'd tell a different story, I'm certain.

We got pizza for dinner on the way home and I put a very tired but happy girl to bed about an hour ago.

Must remember to dye my roots, I look like a badger.

Monday April 10th

We're opening the sex jar again on Thursday. It's Oliver's turn and then that only leaves mine. To be honest, I'm absolutely in favour of keeping this as a part of our lives forever. It's been very fun. For my last one, I chose 'rough sex' but after our hotel sex, I'm thinking I'll need to change it. That was as intense and rough as it's ever been. What else do I want? I'm guessing 'let me sleep for twelve hours straight' isn't a sex request, no matter how arousing I find it.

Thursday April 13th

I know both Oliver and I are meant to be open, honest and non-judgmental with each other regarding sexual desires, but the moment I read his last request, that all went out the window. As he nearly did.

'WHAT? Nope. Uh-uh – no way. You are not fucking my face. Fuck your own face, fuckface.'

'Are you quite finished?'

'I don't know.'

'It's technically not face—'

'It's deep throat!' I growled, ensuring Molly couldn't hear. 'Do I look like Linda Lovelace?'

'Um . . . it's hard to tell when your face is all contorted like that.'

I put the note back in the jar and closed the lid. 'I give you plenty of head,' I said, grabbing my hand cream off the dressing table. 'Good head, no – INCREDIBLE head. What's the fucking problem?'

He watched me furiously rub cream all over my hands with a mild amusement. 'I'll explain, if you'll listen . . .'

'Hmm.'

'Didn't you give me a hand-job with that—'

'Oliver . . .'

'OK, I'll stop.' He turned me around to face him, making sure I was listening.

'Firstly – your blow jobs are fantastic. I have zero complaints. This isn't about that. Secondly – I do NOT want to face-fuck you. That shit does nothing for me.'

Realising I'd applied far too much cream, I started massaging it into my legs too. 'So what then?'

'It's hard to explain. With someone who can deep throat – it's just a very different sensation. I know not everyone can do it and I've only experienced it a couple of—'

'Who the fuck with?' Oh God, here comes competitive Henderson. I hate her.

'Girl at Uni . . . and Ruth. She could do it.'

Oh, of course she could. Oliver's model ex-girlfriend, with no personality and apparently no gag reflex.

'Look, all I'm asking is that we try it. I'm not going to force you, for God's sake. Just think about it?'

I nodded to say I would but I was busy picturing Ruth swallowing Oliver's entire body like a fucking snake. I needed to speak to Lucy about this.

Friday April 14th

From: Phoebe Henderson
To: Lucy Jacobs
Subject: Help required.

So it seems that Oliver's last sex jar request is for me to deep throat him. Turns out that Ruth (remember her, the one who came to Skye with us) could do it and despite my initial concerns, I'm now solely intent on being better at it than she was.

But I'm not sure I can do it. I gag when I'm brushing my tongue ffs.

From: Lucy Jacobs
To: Phoebe Henderson
Subject: Re: Help required

Jesus, it's only half nine in the morning, dude.

Only kidding – I'll text you a couple of sites where they teach you how to do it. Warning though, I have thrown up a little doing this. Grim. But apart from that, you'll be rewarded in heaven by never having to do it again!

I waited twenty whole minutes before she sent me two links through WhatsApp, both how-to guides on how to take a whole dick into your throat for beginners. There's no way I'm reading these while Molly is around.

Saturday April 15th

Oliver took Molly out on her bike this morning which gave me time to read through the links Lucy sent me.

Practise first! Use something penis-shaped like a banana or a dildo and insert it into your mouth until it hits your gag reflex. Practise doing this for a few minutes at a time until the need to gag has gone. This can take anything from a day to a few weeks.

A fucking banana ... I'm going to have to simulate oral sex on A FUCKING BANANA?! I threw my phone down on the bed.

I have so many questions. Do I keep the skin on? What if I do it unpeeled and it breaks and then I die with an entire banana wedged in my oesophagus? Or what if it gets stuck but I can still breathe through my nose and I have to go to A&E and explain why I don't eat bananas like a fucking human?

Can I use a vibrator instead of a dildo? Do I need to take the batteries out?

Did perfect Ruth have to do this or was she born without a gag reflex as well as body fat?

Fuck, did LUCY DO THIS? I texted her immediately.

Please tell me you didn't go down on a banana to perfect this.

Fuck no. I hate bananas. I bought a new dildo. I wasn't putting any of my old toys in my mouth. You like bananas, though. And it's cheaper . . . Plus if you vomit, you can just chuck it in the compost bin.

Don't speak to me or my bananas ever again.

It took me until Oliver and Molly came home to decide whether sticking something down my throat repeatedly until I stopped gagging was worth it. Was an extra couple of minutes of pleasure for Oliver worth potentially vomiting? Did I really need to outdo Ruth, who'd already been dumped in favour of me? Was I really that immature?

Course I fucking was.

Tuesday April 18th

NURSERY HOLIDAYS ARE OVER! NORMALITY RETURNS!

Oliver dropped Molly off at Maggie's this morning as I skipped into work, happy to be free from my darling family for a whole eight hours. Lucy was equally pleased to see me, presenting me with a croissant and latte as I walked through the door.

'What did I miss then?' I asked, wondering why Lucy and I were the only ones in at 9 a.m. 'Jesus, it's quiet. Where is everyone? Ooh, did the dickhead Rapture finally happen?'

She sat on the edge of my desk. 'Dorothy is in London, Kelly is on holiday and fucking "heid the baw" phoned in sick. It looks like it's just me and you, Peggy Sue. I've left a message with Dorothy to phone me back ASAP but since she's leaving soon, I doubt she'll care.'

'Oh man. Whoever decided we didn't need more staff was an idiot,' I replied, biting into my croissant. 'I guarantee someone will get their arse kicked for this.'

Lucy nodded. 'You know what this means though?'

'We order in a pizza for lunch and charge it to the office because we can't leave the phones unattended?'

'Cooorrrect! I'll get the menu . . .'

I opened my emails and sighed as I was faced with two weeks' worth of spam, complaints and nonsense from Lucy she'd sent me in my absence. Literally the moment I turned off my out-of-office message, one popped up . . . from Jay. Shit. I opened it tentatively.

From: Jason Dainty
To: Phoebe Henderson
Subject: Advertising

Hi Phoebe,

I called last week but they said you weren't back until this morning. Would be good to have a chat about future advertising if you have time to drop in at some point?

Jay

I turned to speak to Lucy but she was on a call, so I just flapped my arms in her direction until she got the hint and hung up.

'Jay just emailed me,' I informed her, pointing at my screen in case she didn't understand where emails came from.

She plodded over, lukewarm pizza in hand. 'Anything interesting? What did he say?'

She glanced over the email and laughed. 'Dainty? His surname is DAINTY? Why didn't you tell me this?'

'Because I don't think he ever told me.'

'Check him being all professional. Mr Dainty totally wants to ride you.'

'How on earth do you get *that* from this email?' I looked again to see if I'd missed anything.

'Two reasons,' she said, examining a mushroom she'd just picked off the slice. 'Number one – his bar is far too trendy for our readership and there's no way he's advertising again. Number two – he wants you to go back and see him. This could easily be done by email or over the phone. He just wants to be in a room with you again.' She threw the mushroom into my bin and went back to answering phones while I sat there disagreeing. As much as I hope she's barking up the wrong tree, if she isn't, I'd have no problem knocking him back if I had to. I of course replied in an equally professional manner, resisting the urge to just write FUCKING DAINTY, THOUGH?!

From: Phoebe Henderson

To: Jason Dainty

Subject: Re: Advertising

Good morning, Jason,

Thanks for your email. I'll be happy to pop in – say, Thursday at 3 p.m.? Let me know if this is suitable.

Kind regards,

Phoebe

As I pressed send, I thought, there isn't a handsome, tattooed man on the planet that could make me cheat on Oliver. Especially not a dainty one.

Wednesday April 19th

Oliver has been decent enough not to pressure me with regards to his sex jar request and has no idea that for the past four days I have secretly been practising with half a cucumber. I feel like a fucking idiot but I've convinced myself it's less humiliating and lethal than a banana.

At first I just retched continuously, wondering why I was putting myself through it, but this morning I found I could withstand the gagging – not entirely, but by Jove, it was progress. I think I'm getting the hang of it.

I came in to work today so I could catch up on more of the work that had accumulated while I was away. Dorothy wasn't pleased that Brian had phoned in sick yesterday and that Kelly had refused to take any work calls on her day off. I don't blame her. I wouldn't have either. She left shortly after the morning meeting on 'business', which we all knew was code for 'doing something personal and completely unrelated to work'.

Brian pestered Lucy on whether she'd received any info or paperwork on the new manager of Scottish classified advertising and her answer was 'Fuck off, Brian, I'm busy'. If she had she would have told me anyway.

Molly and I made dinner tonight, breading fish and making chips in the air fryer. She even did her own fish fingers and was very proud of herself. Oliver praised her cooking skills highly.

'I'm going to be a chef, you know,' she decided. 'With my own café.'

'Excellent,' he replied. 'Your mum and I will get free chips forever.'

'Maybe,' she deliberated. 'It might just be a café for girls. I haven't decided.'

I let her watch some television before bed, while Oliver and I did the dishes together, admiring our own child like a couple of smug pricks. After we'd finished, Oliver grabbed a beer from the fridge. He looked weary.

'Tired?' I asked, drying the last of the cutlery.

He nodded. 'I am, actually.'

'That's a shame,' I replied, beginning to cough weakly. 'Because I have this itch in the back of my throat I was hoping you could help me out with.'

He opened his can and took a swig, oblivious to what I was getting at. 'Sore throat?'

I placed the last of the cutlery in the drawer. 'Not sore, no, but it's about six or seven inches down and I just can't reach it myself . . .'

He paused, mid-swig. 'You mean . . . ?'

'Yep. But if you're too tired, I can—'

'I'm not tired. You must have mistaken me for someone else.'

'I see.'

He made his way back towards the living room with a spring in his step, slapping my arse as he passed me. I heard him tell Molly it was bedtime and that if she hurried, he'd read her the cat book she loved so much. Given that he hates that book, it was clear he wanted her in bed and sleepy as soon as possible.

There wasn't much to do in terms of preparation, apart from dim the bedroom lights and move Oliver's old socks the fuck away from me. Gah. That old saying where you're supposed to love everything about your partner and never want to change them is such bullshit. His *dropping clothes at his arse* habit needs to go before I strangle him with them.

I flicked though Facebook while I waited for Oliver, inwardly scowling at the inspirational memes and laughing at a video Lucy had posted of a man walking into a lamp-post. Finally Oliver came into the room, announcing that Molly had passed out during the third re-read of her book.

'That cat is a dick,' he whispered, locking the door. 'Hang on, why are you still dressed?'

I put my phone on the bedside table. 'You only need from the shoulders up!'

He laughed. 'Fair point. But take your shirt off. Let me see your tits at least.'

So I stripped to the waist, aware that swinging boobs and a roll of fat hanging over my trousers was not my best look, but Oliver didn't care. He'd already started groping me.

'Hang on,' I said quietly. 'We need some rules here.'

'Sure,' he mumbled, attempting to get my entire right boob in his mouth.

'If I slap you on the leg, it means stop.'

'OK.'

'Warn me if you're going to cum.'

'I always do . . . God, you're so soft.'

'And go slowly.'

He pulled away from my boobs and cupped my face in his hands. 'You don't have to do this, you know. If you're unsure . . . I'm just saying . . .'

I paused for a moment, biting my lip. 'I read that me lying face up on the bed with my head hanging over is the best posi—'

'Do it.'

It was awkward at first. As promised he did go slowly, just gently moving in and out of my mouth and running his hands over my body. I felt like an idiot but tried my best to keep my teeth away from his cock and breathe. I hadn't had my mouth stretched this wide since I got my wisdom tooth out in 1998. The first time he went deeper than normal, I was ready. I'd trained for this. I was the Cucumber Queen of Glasgow and I prayed to God no one would ever find out about that. I must admit I was surprised at the sound he made. It was almost animalistic. It turned me on. I relaxed my throat and let him continue. However, the moment he said, 'Oh fuck me, I can see it in your throat,' he thrust with excitement and I gagged, slapping his thigh hard.

'Slowly!' I reminded him. 'Ugh, I have spit on my chin.'

'Sorry,' he replied. 'This is just so hot.'

I took a breath and we continued, making sure I took breaks. I wished I'd taken my mascara off first. That shit will make your eyes water – no one warned me about that. Fuckers. We mixed it in with normal blow job stuff, hands and ball play, and it didn't take too long before Oliver announced he was going to cum and I let him, listening to him as he made that sound again, loudly. I think that sound was the best part of this whole experience.

Afterwards we lay in bed, me removing the mascara that had smudged into my cheeks and him just quietly nuzzling against me.

'So what did you think?' he asked, awkwardly. 'I know this was all about my needs so it's OK to hate it. Did you hate it? You're allowed to hate it.'

'Hate's a bit strong.' I laughed, inspecting the mascara-stained cotton wool. 'It's just a bit overwhelming ... and uncomfortable. I guess after a few times it becomes easier, no?'

'You'd do it again?!' He sounded surprised.

I nodded. 'Probably. If anything, just to hear you make that noise again.'

He blushed. 'I have to do something for you now. Name it.'

I held back the urge to shout *PICK UP YOUR FUCKING CLOTHES*.

'It's late,' I reminded him. 'But we still have my last request to do. I'll make sure it's a fucking good one.'

Thursday April 20th

I called in to see Jay at 3 p.m. as arranged, only to discover that he'd been called away last minute and would give me a call to reschedule. I really hoped he wasn't playing games with me, I'm too old for all that shite. Instead of going back to work, I walked around town for a while until Oliver had finished work and we drove to our session at Pam's office together.

She was pleased to discover that we'd been continuing to work through our sex jar and remarked that we'd been holding hands since we arrived – a far cry from how we'd interacted with each other on previous visits. She found it very encouraging.

'So, what's next?' Oliver asked. 'More sex jar stuff? Cos I think we've nailed that.'

'I think I'd like to keep this as part of our routine anyway,' I admitted, glancing at him. 'It's been a lot of fun.' Oliver agreed, a smile appearing on his face to rival Pam's.

I watched Pam take a sip of her tea, noticing her thumb ring which was in the shape of a fairy. Of course it was.

'Our next step is honesty,' she informed us. 'You appear to be in a place now where you're both ready to hear each other. So for next week, I want you to write down two or three things that you feel you need to get off your chest. It can be something about the other person you're not comfortable with, or something you've done that you're not comfortable with – just whatever you feel has become a burden for you.'

'What if there isn't anything?' Oliver asked.

Pam raised her eyebrows. 'I'd be very surprised. Wouldn't you? How many times have you kept something from Phoebe for fear that she'd judge you or start questioning her reasons for being with you? We all do it but carrying that around can take its toll. Believe me, I've seen it over and over again.'

She saw my face and smiled. 'Don't look so worried. How often do you get a chance to tell Oliver to clean up after himself and actually be heard?'

HOW DID SHE KNOW? WHAT IS THIS WITCHCRAFT?

Friday April 21st

Just after I dropped Molly at nursery this morning, I spotted Sarah Ward-Wilson standing by her car, wearing sunglasses and texting furiously. It wasn't until I saw her wipe a tear from her cheek that I realised she wasn't wearing her shades in the rain to look cool.

I walked over, knowing that she'd probably tell me to fuck off, but the urge to make sure she was alright was strong. I've been 'crying in the street' unhappy before. No one deserves that.

She didn't notice me until I was standing beside her and she recoiled slightly in surprise. 'Oh!' She sniffed and tried to regain her composure. 'Hello, Phoebe, how are you? This weather is awful! I'm due to get my highlights done in an hour and—'

'How are you, Sarah?' I interrupted before her voice got any higher. 'I know it's none of my business, but is everything OK?'

Expecting her to insist she was perfectly fine, I was surprised when she shook her head and began sobbing.

'He's lefty!' she bawled loudly.

It took me a second to realise she was saying, 'He's left me.'

'Oh. I'm so sorry. Do you want to talk ab—'

'Fifteen years!' she exploded. (I guess she did want to talk.) 'I gave that bastard fifteen years, four kids and he thinks he'll just fuck off with the mistress I pretended not to know about!'

As much as I wanted to comfort her, and I did, this was fucking amazing.

'Wait. You knew he was cheating?!'

She laughed maniacally. 'Of course I did. He's not so smart. I used his thumbprint to open his phone while he slept.'

I could see other parents glancing at us as they walked back to their cars. Lord Wilson was impressively losing her shit.

I didn't even have to question her further before we were both sitting in her 4x4 while she smoked a cigarette and told me the whole story. I thought about cadging a fag but I didn't want Lord Wilson's drama to be the reason I started smoking again.

'She's twenty-nine, you know – this Hannah one. Twenty-nine, where her tits still point upwards and she doesn't sneeze and piss at the same time. She sent him a fucking video of herself masturbating and calling out his name! I mean, have you *seen* my husband? He's like a blob of hairy custard and she's wanking over him?! *She's wanking over your bank balance, sweetheart. Get real.*'

I wasn't even sure she was still speaking to me but I listened anyway.

'I'm not a fool, Phoebe. I was biding my time. I had planned to stick it out until Ruby was a little older and then fuck off, but the silly old fool thinks he's in love with his PA. He's fifty-five and she'll eventually leave him, and my children will be left with a poor, pathetic, shell of a father who has nothing left. It's so fucking cliché, I want to throw up.' She took a long drag from her cigarette and threw the rest out of the window. 'He's packing as we speak. *Tell the kids I'm away on business,* he said. He doesn't even have the balls to do it himself. Ugh, they're all the fucking same, Phoebe. Men are scum. All of them. They'd stick their dicks into anything with a pulse.'

'I'm really sorry this happened,' I said, knowing this wasn't any consolation to her but also a tad annoyed she'd implied that every man was as shitty as hers. 'If I can help in any way . . .'

She turned to me and wiped her nose with her hand before quietly asking, 'What am I going to do?'

It was then that I realised that Sarah Ward-Wilson was just as confused and miserable as the rest of us.

Saturday April 22nd

Today was mostly spent contemplating what I'd say at our next meeting with Pam. Of course I'll mention the fact that Oliver can be a slob but I think she's after something a little deeper. I consider myself to be an open person though, especially with Oliver, so I'm not convinced I have anything that I've been purposefully hiding . . . Oh. Wait:

- The Kyle dream.
- Jay.
- That aftershave he loves so much that makes him smell like damp wood.
- That sometimes I wish he'd take Molly to Dublin on his own so I could be rid of them both for a few days and play with my friends – but this makes me feel like a bad person.

Shit. So I guess Pam was right. We all have something.

The evening was spent in front of the television, channel-hopping through a disturbing amount of shit Saturday night programmes and eating junk.

'Oh, I never told you about my little encounter with Lord Wilson,' I said, grabbing a fistful of crisps. 'Turns out her hubby has been having an affair with his assistant. She's fucking livid; well, who wouldn't be?'

'Really?' Oliver replied, taking the snack bowl away from me. 'I suppose these things happen, though.'

'It's the biggest mid-life crisis cliché ever,' I continued. 'Next he'll be showing up to nursery in a penis-mobile.'

'We don't know the full story,' Oliver said, continuing to click the remote control. 'We know she's a nightmare. He might have been really unhappy. We shouldn't judge.'

'They have four kids. Unhappy or not, it's a selfish, dick move. Sarah might be a nightmare but she's still a person. Being cheated on is a horrible betrayal. Remember when my ex Alex cheated on me? It fucked with my head for ages – you know that.'

Flashbacks from that time started to dart in and out of my mind and I physically tried to shake them off, which didn't go unnoticed.

'Let's not dwell on this,' he insisted, knowing where my mind had wandered. 'Movie? We could watch the new Spiderman? I hear it's good.'

'I think I'd rather be cheated on.'

He smiled weakly and proceeded to find the movie channel, while I laughed at my own joke.

Monday April 24th

I snuck into work twenty minutes late this morning, ready to explain to Dorothy that I'd been stuck in traffic, when in reality, Molly had spilled milk all down herself two minutes before we were due to leave for nursery.

I stealthily took my seat and quickly turned my PC on before noticing that there was no one else at their desks either. Not even Lucy. I could hear laughter coming from the meeting room around the corner. Oh fuck, I was going to have to make an entrance. Thankfully they all sounded in an upbeat mood. I grabbed my sales sheets and scurried along to join the meeting, wondering why the fuck everyone was so happy on a Monday morning.

'Sorry I'm late,' I apologised, rushing in. 'Traffic was—'

'Good morning, Phoebe. Long time, no see.'

My eyes nearly fell out of my head and all I could think was –

No.

NO.

NO.

'Frank?!'

I couldn't fucking believe it. My old boss. The one who drove me nuts. The one I'd often despised with a passion. The one I'd shagged in almost every part of this office. And his car. And his flat.

And he was here.

He was back.

'Are you alright, Phoebe?' Dorothy looked at me with a confused expression, while I did my best not to fucking faint on the spot.

I quickly sat down in my chair. 'Yes. Sorry, I just rushed to get in. I'm a little lightheaded.'

Why was he here? He'd left for London the year I found out I was pregnant. The year he'd manipulated me into helping him 'woo' Vanessa, the woman he left with! He was a mistake that I didn't ever want to revisit, yet HERE WE FUCKING ARE.

Dorothy passed me some Buck's Fizz. Oh God, they were celebrating his return. I felt sick. I couldn't even look at him.

'So now we're all here,' Dorothy continued, 'I'd like to formally welcome Frank back after six years away. As it's my last day, I'll be spending it getting Frank up to speed, but I'm sure you're all delighted to have him back.'

As everyone clinked glasses, Frank's gaze met mine and I could tell that he remembered Every. Single. Detail. Oh, just fucking shoot me.

I didn't see much of Frank for the rest of the day and invented a 4 p.m. appointment so I could leave the office earlier that night. Lucy found the whole thing hysterical. Of course she had no idea what went on between us. The only people who knew were Oliver and Pam.

'I'm surprised at how well he looks,' Lucy said over lunch. 'I wonder if he's still the wanksock he always was. Maybe life with his girlfriend has mellowed him – oh God, what was her name?'

'No idea,' I lied. It was Vanessa. I knew everything about her because he was an oversharing asshole. 'But I can't imagine him changing for anyone.'

'Let's hope he's lightened up on you a bit,' she replied,

shaking a little sugar sachet for her coffee. 'Remember how he used to haul you into his office and yell at you? We were all surprised you didn't report him.'

I did remember. He did that as an excuse to get me alone. It was such an odd time in my life. I was getting over Alex, I was getting under Oliver, and Frank and I, well, we used each other. We left things on relatively good terms; not best mates, by any stretch of the imagination, but we had a certain respect for each other in small, nay, *miniscule* doses.

I wasn't sure how Oliver would react to him being back in my life. This all happened before Oliver and I were a thing but I distinctly remember Oliver calling him an uptight knob. I might leave it a couple of days.

Tuesday April 25th

Arriving on time this morning, I slipped into the kitchen to make coffee before Frank spotted me. I knew I couldn't avoid him forever but I could have a damn good crack at it. Why the fuck are these men reappearing in my life all of a sudden? How is this good for my mental health?

Lucy had beaten me to it; she was already in the kitchen making coffee for everyone, except Kelly who wanted some of the stinky herbal tea she pretended to like.

She admired her engagement ring as we stood and chatted for a minute. 'I still can't quite believe we're doing this,' she confessed. 'I always thought you and I would end up together like Bert and Ernie.'

'Don't give up on us yet,' I laughed, pouring more milk into my coffee. 'There's still time.'

'Time for what? For me to fuck it up?'

'No, for me to have Kyle killed. I know people.'

She snorted and grabbed the tray of drinks. 'If that's true, maybe you can sort Frank out. He's already put some weird artwork on his office wall this morning. It's like he never went away.'

My plan to avoid him was ruined when one by one, he called each of us into his office to catch up, predictably leaving me till last.

'Phoebe, do you have a minute?'

Here we go. I swivelled around in my chair, swiping my notepad and sales folder from the desk. My heart was racing but I managed to keep calm, casually walking into his office like nothing had ever happened.

He closed the door and cleared his throat. It seems he was as nervous as I was. I waited for him to sit back behind his desk.

'Still a fan of the artwork, I see.' I gestured towards the painting on the wall. 'It's nice that you've done that – most parents just hang it on the fridge.'

'Still a smart-arse then?' he replied, smiling. 'It's good to see you.'

'Um, yes – you too . . .'

'I see you had a baby.'

I blinked at him with a blank expression on my face as he became flustered.

'I don't mean from the way you look – you actually look thinner than I remember – I just meant from your file here. It mentions your maternity leave.'

I put my head in my hands. 'This is *weird*, Frank, I'm not going to pretend otherwise.'

He adjusted the photo of Vanessa on his desk. 'Oh, calm down, woman. What happened ... well, it was years ago. I'm not giving it a second thought and neither should you. God, you're just as infuriating as ever.'

'Infuriating? I've hardly spoken a word!'

'You don't have to. You just ... exist.'

'Yeah? Yeah ... well, you got old as fuck.'

There was a moment's silence before we both started to laugh. The tension was officially broken and Lucy was right. It was like he'd never been away.

Wednesday April 26th

I took Molly to the park after nursery this afternoon and tried to clear my head a little while she played with a couple of her friends. I feel quite unsettled now that Frank has returned, and not because I've been pining for him or that I want to sleep with him again, more because it brings back memories of a time when I was still fucked up over Alex. When my future was bleaker than it is now, but also when I was free to do whatever I wanted. No one relied on me. No one expected anything from me. I don't feel comfortable living in the past but seeing Frank again has dragged me back there.

Thursday April 27th

Oliver was chirpy enough as we walked into Pam's office, making me think that his 'confessions' weren't going to be half as bad as mine. This time, I took the tea she always offered and sat down in my usual spot.

'So, Oliver, why don't you begin?' she requested, handing me a cup with a badly-drawn pineapple on it. 'My niece.' Pam winked. 'She made it at nursery. It's utter crap but I still adore it.'

Oliver uncrossed his legs and sat forward.

'OK ... sometimes I wish Phoebe would take Molly away for a few days, just to give me some space.' He rubbed his forehead and turned to face me. 'I know it makes me sound like a shit and I love you both but ... why are you smiling?'

'Because I was going to say the same thing! I totally get it!'

The relief on his face was priceless. Maybe this wasn't going to be so awful after all.

As usual, Pam sat facing us, smiling. 'Well, that one was easy. Phoebe, would you like to go next?'

I took a deep breath. 'I have a new client at work. And it turns out that I slept with him years ago and I didn't know whether to tell you or not.'

Oliver laughed. 'Really? Who?!'

'Do you remember the guy who lived with his parents and I smashed one of their plates and he lost the plot?'

'Yes! Oh that's fuck—sorry – *fecking* brilliant. Does he remember you?'

'Unfortunately, yes.'

Oliver continued to giggle at my misfortune. I'd forgotten that he knew all about this. I'm so stupid. He found it funny at the time, makes sense that he would now. Pam, however, didn't look so convinced. She narrowed her eyes.

'So you have no problem with Phoebe working with some-one she's been intimate with?'

Oliver shook his head. 'No. I mean, this happened years ago. It would be different if it was someone she had to see every day, or work closely with.'

My heart fell into my stomach.

'Like Frank?' I enquired.

'Exactly,' Oliver continued. 'He was the type of guy you had to watch. Manipulative wanker. Not some idiot who still lived with his parents. Did Phoebe mention Frank?'

'I'm aware of the association,' Pam replied with a slight smirk. 'I think we agreed it wasn't the healthiest relationship to—'

'He started back in the office on Monday.'

Both Pam and Oliver stopped smiling at the same time. 'Frank is back?' Pam asked. Oliver just stared.

'I had no idea he was coming back!' I protested. 'I mean, I knew we were getting a new manager but I had no idea it was him.'

Oliver sat back on the couch. 'So why didn't you tell me on Monday?'

'Because of this!' I gestured at both him and Pam. 'Look at your faces! Seriously, you cannot be jealous of him. He's like fifty now. I never felt anything for him, you know that.'

'I was jealous of him then, why would you think I wouldn't be jealous now?'

'Why were you jealous, Oliver?' Pam enquired.

'Because she sometimes chose to spend time with him over me. It was when I was beginning to develop feelings for Phoebe and she was being intimate with some handsome, rich prick who didn't deserve her. There's history there now. How can I possibly be OK with this?'

Oh God, this was going horribly wrong. Pam decided to step in. 'Oliver, do you trust Phoebe?'

'Of course I do, it's just . . . I know how these things can escalate. How you don't plan on them happening but . . .' His words tailed off.

'What do you mean?' she asked.

'He's referring to a mutual friend of ours who discovered her husband has been having an affair with someone he works with,' I interjected. 'Which is completely different from me working with Frank.'

'Is that correct, Oliver?' Pam was looking at his face intently.

'No,' he admitted. 'This has nothing to do with Sarah or her husband.'

'Then what do you . . .'

The look on his face answered my question. My heart gave one heavy, painful beat and then went numb. Completely numb.

'Who?' I asked calmly. 'Who was it?'

It took Pam a second to understand, too. She then closed her notebook.

'Look, nothing happened, really. It's not as bad as—'

'WHO WAS IT?'

'A temp. Bethany. She worked with us about a year ago. I didn't sleep with her, you need to know that.'

'Did you kiss her?'

'Yes. Once.'

I felt like I was going to throw up. 'I think you should leave.'

'I'm not going to do that. We need to talk.'

'I agree you both should keep talking, but perhaps give Phoebe a few minutes,' Pam suggested. 'If you wait outside, I'll call you back in shortly.'

This he agreed to, leaving quietly.

'God, I'm such an idiot!' I proclaimed, throwing my hands in the air. 'I should have seen this coming. Why the hell did I think that Oliver would be any different to any other man? Why did I believe that he was the exception?'

'Do you believe it was just a kiss?' she asked.

'Does it really matter?' I replied. 'What do you think?'

'It's really not my place to say,' she said, rubbing her hands together, 'however, I don't see any reason *not* to believe him.'

'What about the fact he's kept it hidden for a year?'

'True. But you've also kept secrets. Tell me, if you had kissed Frank or the other man you mentioned, would you have told Oliver? Before you answer, think about it. Would you have told him, inevitably hurting him to clear your conscience? Not many people would say yes. I'm not excusing his actions, I'm simply presenting a reason why he may have chosen not to tell you. I see this a lot.'

I wanted to get out of there but I knew if I left while I was this angry, one of us might not make it home. 'Whatever,' I replied. 'Just let him back in.'

Oliver, along with his now white-as-a-sheet face, returned to the couch.

'I'm really hurt,' I said, tucking my hair behind my ears. 'And angry. If I were you, I'd start explaining myself, pronto.'

He recounted how Bethany had been recruited to cover maternity leave for Sara and how they'd worked really well together. I listened as he described how she'd made the long hours he had to work bearable and how she made him feel important at a time when he felt inadequate and useless as a father and a partner. How they'd opened a bottle of wine at work and how she'd kissed him and he'd kissed her back. And I watched as he cried when he told me how sorry he was.

I didn't know what to say. I looked at Pam, who for once wasn't smiling. 'There are obviously trust issues here now,' she stated. 'But issues that can be overcome if you're willing to put the work in. You may need some time to think things—'

'We'll see you next week,' I replied, my tone cold, almost robotic. I was still numb. Oliver just nodded.

The car journey home was expectedly silent. Oliver understood that saying anything, or pushing his luck in any way, might result in me losing my shit. I just stared straight ahead, the reality hitting me slowly the closer we got to home. By the time he parked, I'd be unsuccessful in holding back my tears. The hurt and disappointment was palpable. All I could think was: *why the fuck couldn't he have been the exception?*

Saturday April 29th

Oliver took Molly out today so I could have Lucy and Hazel over for lunch. He's been quiet since our last meeting with Pam but then again, so have I.

They arrived with the salad and wine I'd asked them to bring, while I'd thrown a pizza in the oven; it was ready by the time they turned up.

As we sat around the table, I began to tell them the events of the last week, doing my best not to cry into the lovely Caesar salad Hazel had prepared. She was the first to react.

'He did what?! When?'

'About a year ago.'

'Was it an actual affair? I don't understand.'

I picked out the croutons with my fingers. 'No. He said it was just a kiss. She kissed him but he kissed her back. I'm pretty fucking gutted.'

'You must be.' Hazel took my hand and gave it a squeeze. 'I'm surprised, to be honest. I never thought Oliver would be so . . .'

'Predictable? Disappointing? Stupid? Arseholey?'

She nodded. 'All of those. I'd cut Kevin's balls off if he did that. I can't believe he kept it hidden for so long.'

'Oh, I can,' Lucy interjected. 'Sometimes you're just not ready to deal with someone's reaction to a certain situation, so you keep it hidden. Sometimes for years. Isn't that right, Phoebe?'

'What? How would I know?'

She grinned broadly. 'We all make mistakes. Sometimes these mistakes even involve people we work with . . . right?'

Oh God. She knows about Frank.

I sighed. 'Who told you?'

She laughed. 'No one told me. I knew while it was going on! Sometimes you smelled of his aftershave. And the way I caught him looking at you . . .'

Hazel motioned for us to stop. 'What the fuck am I missing here?'

'Phoebe was shagging our boss Frank for ages. She kept it

hidden from people who love her more than Oliver and we're not holding it against her.'

Hazel screeched with laughter. 'It's completely different!' I protested. 'Stop laughing!'

'I know it is,' Lucy replied. 'All I'm saying is that I understand why he wasn't ready to share. Yes, he did a cunty thing but we all do. He didn't stick his dick in anyone. He didn't fall in love with anyone. He allowed some woman to massage his ego for a while. You need to let him make it up to you.'

Hazel nodded. 'Oh, and *then* cut his dick off.'

I pulled them both in for a hug. I have no idea why I pay Pam Potter when I have these wise women for free.

MAY

Tuesday May 2nd

I woke at 6 a.m. and watched Oliver sleeping for a while, thinking, 'This is the man I love. This is the man I want to grow old with. This man needs to wake the fuck up and answer some questions.' I shook him awake, telling him I needed to talk and surprisingly he didn't protest too much.

'I need you to answer some questions. And I need you to be honest.'

He perched himself up in bed, rubbing his eyes. 'OK ... shoot.'

'What made you stop at kissing?'

'Guilt,' he answered. 'I felt like a massive prick, the second it happened.'

'Did you ever plan to tell me?'

He shrugged. 'I honestly don't know. The thought that my stupid actions could ruin all of this ... it makes me feel sick.'

'How can I be sure this won't happen again? What if you meet someone that—'

'You don't think I'm scared that you will?! Especially after this. I'm terrified that you'll meet someone who doesn't come with all my bullshit and decide it's a better deal for you and Molly.'

'You're Molly's dad,' I replied. 'And you're my heart. How could there possibly be a better deal?'

'I'm so sorry, Phoebe. You have no fucking idea, just how much.'

We held each other for what seemed like ages. 'I'll make this up to you,' he said, kissing my head. 'I promise.'

'Damn right, you will. I want the grandest of gestures, fuckface.'

We cuddled until the alarm went off at 7 a.m. and Molly bounded into the room. Maybe some women would have dealt with this differently, but I dealt with it in the only way I knew how; forgive with my head and hope my heart follows.

Thursday May 4th

I looked out for Lord Wilson this morning but there was no sign of her. Ruby was dropped off by an elderly woman I can only assume was Granny. I hope she's not slumped in her kitchen underneath a pile of Bordeaux bottles.

Frank was settling back into his role with ease, pacing around the office like a prison guard while we tried our best to ignore him.

'Phoebe, that bar advert you ran last month – are they doing anything else with us? They paid a decent rate.'

I placed my hand over the mouthpiece on my phone, asking Helen from the council to hang on a second.

What I really wanted to say was: *He's messing with me, Frank, because I made the mistake of sleeping with him years ago. Now I'm stuck having to deal with yet another prick who's decided to reappear in my life. Like you.*

'I'm due to see him,' I replied, wondering why the fuck he couldn't wait until I'd finished my call. 'He cancelled on me last time – I'll chase him up.'

Frank continued pacing while I scowled behind his back and got back to my conversation. I glanced over at Lucy, who was smirking. She's never going to let me forget that she knows.

Oliver had already picked Molly up from Maggie's, who apparently laughed too hard at one of his jokes and embarrassed them both. He's not advertising the fact that he's trying to make things up to me but I can tell; little things like flowers randomly appearing in the living room, my favourite overpriced biscuits showing up in the cupboard, or his dirty clothes making their way to the washing machine . . . maybe not the grand gesture I demanded, but it's a good start.

Friday May 5th

Oliver took the afternoon off today but we kept Molly's afternoon session with Maggie so we could go and see Pam. I swear, this woman must be making a fortune from idiots like us.

Dressed in a tartan skirt and pink heels, she welcomed us into a room that today smelled like coconuts. I wondered whether she's started early on the Malibu.

We both refused tea, but Oliver accepted water, nervously sipping as we began.

'How are you feeling, Phoebe?' she asked, settling into her chair.

'Well ...' I said, 'the last week has been tough but we've talked and I don't see why we can't move past this.'

She nodded as I heard Oliver give a quick sigh of relief. 'Fine,' she continued. 'And Oliver? How have you been?'

'Ashamed,' he replied, rubbing his forehead. 'And sorry. Just really, really sorry.'

She didn't allow him to dwell on it too much, but explained our next steps.

'The best way forward is for you to acknowledge what's happened and for Phoebe to know that you are still very much focused on the relationship. And in turn, Phoebe, it's important that Oliver recognises and understands that he hurt you but also that he knows you're not going to let this define the rest of your relationship.'

Bloody hell, she might have been on the Malibu, but Pam was in sensible mode here. Nothing quirky, nothing odd. She might have well been wearing a suit and renting a proper office.

'I know we've already covered music in our sessions, so I won't ask you to compile another list, but each of you take a moment, right now, and choose a song; let's call it a goal song. The song that defines how you feel about love. A song you'd play your partner to show each other you're deeply committed. Besotted, even. Close your eyes and take a deep breath.'

Oh. There she is. HI, PAM.

Oliver couldn't help but glance in my direction, no doubt trying not to pick something stupid that would make his disdain for this process obvious. I just closed my eyes, hoping my brain would not instantly be filled with inappropriate songs. It was. First up was 'The Sound of Silence', followed by

'Down Under', 'Killing in the Name' and then 'Don't Fear the Reaper'. My eyes shot open and rolled at myself before I took a deep breath and tried again. Jesus, the pressure. People put less thought into their funeral music.

Finally Pam gave a little cough to bring us both back to reality.

'Ready?'

Opening one eye, I peered at Oliver. 'Yeah. I think so,' he answered meekly.

'Phoebe?'

'"Sweet Disposition",' I blurted out. 'I choose "Sweet Disposition".'

A smile crept over Oliver's face. I sing this song loudly in the car . . . and in the shower and well, basically at every opportunity. Last week he joked that The Temper Trap wouldn't have written it if they'd known the damage I'd do to it with my voice.

'And why is this?' Pam questioned.

'Because it has an urgency to it,' I gushed. 'It's about someone else making you feel completely alive. To me, that's romantic as hell.'

Pam nodded and wrote something on her little pad. 'Oliver, what did you choose?'

'"Danger! High Voltage",' he replied promptly.

My head spun around to look at him. Was he serious?

'Why?' Pam and I said in unison.

'I dunno, it's the little things,' he replied. 'It's hard to explain. It could be a look, or the way she puts on her lipstick or when she makes me laugh – like really hard. I just lose it. She gets me so fired up, it's unreal.'

His song started playing in my head, suddenly taking on a whole new meaning, so I kissed him. I kissed him like Pam wasn't watching.

Did Bethany kiss him like this? Did she get him fired up? Did he get hard? I stopped and pulled away, cursing the omnipresent voice of fucking doom in my head. 'Are you alright?' he asked.

I shook my head. 'I want to be, Oliver! I really do! I want to kiss you, but when I do ... see, not only did you bring her into our relationship, you brought her into my head. That is so unfair.'

'Good, Phoebe.' Pam smiled while her head bobbed in approval. 'This is a process. Unfortunately you won't know where the stumbling blocks are until you trip over them. Oliver, do you want to respond to Phoebe?'

'It was unfair of me,' he agreed, 'but I don't know what else to say. Couples move on from this, right? We can move past this.'

Pam didn't respond and for once we were both left with the realisation that if we can't move past this, we're in deep shit.

Saturday May 6th

Lucy and Kyle have set the date and she's now panicking in advance. Most couples have at least a year to plan, she now has six months. I had to calm her down over coffee. Hazel, an actual real life married person, also attended.

'The venue I liked had a cancellation. November the 11th. Do people actually have weddings in November?'

'Of course!' Hazel proclaimed. 'You'll be an autumn bride.'

'Oh, God, there's a name for it. Should I be reading up on this? Are there seasonal rules I have to adhere to?'

I slid half of my cheesecake across the table towards Lucy, who looked like she needed it more than me.

'You can have whatever kind of wedding you want,' I insisted, before Hazel could start frantically Googling 'Autumn Brides' – 'as long as you don't make me wear yellow. I'm too pale. I'll look like a corpse.'

'Never mind *your* dress,' she moaned. 'What am *I* going to wear? I really don't think I'm a traditional dress kind of girl ... though I do look good in white. Kyle is hopeless at this stuff – he actually told me to wear "whatever". Who the fuck wears "whatever" to their wedding? Ugh, if only I knew someone who was good at all of this ...'

Hazel was practically foaming at the mouth.

'Oh, just ask her, Lucy,' I insisted, laughing. 'We both know I'm useless at all of this.'

A smile slowly appeared on Lucy's face like a crack in ice. 'Hazel, will you help me plan my—'

'I WOULD LOVE TO.' Hazel reached into her bag and produced six wedding magazines and a notepad. It seems we all knew this was coming and I have no doubt that Hazel will do an amazing job.

Sunday May 7th

At our last visit, Pam suggested that we take a couple of weeks to talk things through and bring any issues we still have to the next session. She's also suggested that we go easy on any intimacy until trust has been re-established on my side. I'm OK with this. I mean, the sex jar hasn't been brought out for a while now anyway, mainly because I haven't felt particularly amorous since Oliver's reveal and he's not pushing things while I'm dealing with it. My final piece of paper in the jar asks for rough sex but I'm not sure I want to go with it. Angry sex would probably be more appropriate but not when I'm still sore at him.

In other news, someone in this block of flats owns a recorder and I'm even more convinced that living in a cave is the way forward.

Monday May 8th

Not only was it pissing down all day, but I had to go and visit Jay first thing. At least he was actually there this time.

'Coffee?' he asked as I placed my umbrella beside the front door. 'I'm just making one.'

Yes, please. How about a cup of what the fuck do you want this time, to take away? Two sugars.

I accepted, smiling graciously. Coffee is important to me, regardless of who's making it.

I sat at one of the tables in the middle of the room and took off my rain-soaked coat, hanging it over the seat. Water began to pool on the floor underneath.

'Oh God, I'm making a mess here, sorry,' I apologised. 'I'm dripping all over the place.'

'That's what she said,' he replied, sniggering as he brought some coffee over.

Oh dear God. He's one of *them*. I bet he knows Brian.

I didn't bother laughing. I'm fed up humouring men who aren't funny. Instead I opened my folder and clicked my pen.

'So,' I began, 'you had a decent response—'

'Sugar?'

'One, please.'

'—from the adverts we ran?'

'I have no idea,' he replied. 'Yes, we were busy, but we always are. It's hard to gauge response.'

My coffee was far too hot but I sipped regardless. 'There are promotions you could run which might help with that. Say, offers on our ads for discounted drinks, etc. That's a good way—'

'Are you single?'

'I . . . excuse me?'

'Did I stutter? Are you single?'

'I don't see how that's relevant, but no. Can we get back to this?'

'Married then?'

I closed my folder. 'Why are you asking me this?'

'Because I'd like to take you out.' He dragged his chair a little closer and I felt his foot rub against mine.

Lucy was right. Of course she was, she's Lucy.

'You would?!' I exclaimed. 'How lovely. Well, in that case, no, I'm not married.'

He grinned. 'Great, well, we could—'

'But I do have a daughter. A big one. You don't have a problem with kids, right?'

His grin began to fade.

'I know that some men are all *I'm not taking on someone else's child,*' I continued, 'but I don't get that vibe from you, Jay. How much do you make here?'

'What? Um . . . I . . .'

'Oh, I'm sure it's enough for us. And Molly loves all the bars I take her to. She'll have fun here.'

He squirmed uncomfortably, looking towards the door as if he was expecting help to appear at any minute.

'Now, I should warn you. Once I tell her dad – we're seeing each other – he won't be happy. He rarely is. I blame it on all the bare-knuckle fighting he did as a kid in Ireland but just stand your ground. Actually, maybe just run – he's tall but he's not fast.'

'Jesus, Phoebe, I get it! Enough.'

I started to laugh. 'Jay, I'm not interested in dating you and if that's the only reason you brought me back today, I'm afraid you've wasted your time.'

He looked a little defeated but smiled. 'You can't blame a guy for trying.'

'Under normal circumstances, no,' I said, 'but in a work situation . . . given our very brief history, it's entirely inappropriate. Wouldn't you agree?'

He shrugged like a two-year-old.

'I'm sure your boss will be able to help you understand when I tell him. Pete Kirby is the owner, right? I mean, I'm not certain that this is tantamount to sexual harassment but—'

'Six full pages,' he interrupted. 'Six full page adverts and we forget this.'

'Eight.'

'Fine.'

I opened my folder again and clicked my pen, triumph-antly. *Clickety-click, you little prick.*

Tuesday May 9th

Having secured enough business to get Frank off my back for the next few weeks, today was a breeze. I'm still stunned at the sheer cheek of Jay bloody Dainty but when I remember back to the first time we met, I was drawn to his arrogance. He pretty much told me I was going home with him that evening, like I had no choice in the matter. I liked that self-assured cockiness in my twenties. Now I just find it irritating.

Kelly decided to reorganise her already perfectly organised desk in an attempt to, as Brian put it, *Feng-Shui it to fuck.*

'Clear desk, clear mind, Brian,' she insisted, her eyes scanning his desk with contempt. 'There's nothing wrong with making sure things run as efficiently as possible.'

'Is that what you tell your fiancé in bed?' he sniggered.

She sighed. 'No, Brian, it's what I tell your dad.'

From across the office, Lucy could be heard picking up the phone and saying, 'Hello? Is that the police? Yes, I'd like to report a brutal owning please.'

Sometimes I wish everyone would just get along but this is far more entertaining.

Wednesday May 10th

Even though I don't get periods anymore (God bless this coil), I still find myself getting a tad emotional around the time they're due. Today was no different. I had a little weep over both Oliver's indiscretion with Bethany and the spot on my chin before my mood abruptly swung me the other way and I screamed along to Hole on my iPod while I tidied Molly's room. I feel much better now. Thank God I wasn't in work or Frank would have been missing a limb.

Thursday May 11th

Work was especially dull today as Lucy had the day off and I was left alone with Kelly, Brian and Frank for company. I helped Kelly out on a deadline with the health and beauty section before Frank called me into his office. As usual, he made me sit for a couple of minutes while he finished off emails before swivelling around to face me.

'Thanks for waiting. I wanted to let you know that there's a managerial meeting in London in August, which I'll be attending, and I thought it might be a good idea if you came along too.'

'Me? Why?' I asked, watching him fiddle with an elastic band.

'We need a deputy here and I think you'd be the most suitable. It's only an overnight trip but it'll give you a chance to meet the MD.'

I stared blankly at him. 'Frank, why on earth would you think I'd be interested in being the deputy? I'm fairly certain you're aware that this job isn't my goal career.'

He gave a throaty snigger. 'Phoebe, you're not twenty anymore. You're a woman of a certain age with a family. This might not be your goal career, but you've certainly been here long enough. What else are you qualified to do?'

His words felt like a punch in the stomach. Never mind that he was speaking out of turn or that he was a condescending bastard, he had a point.

'Just because I haven't figured out that part yet, doesn't mean—'

'You'd need to come back full-time, of course, but it's an additional eight grand on top of your salary, plus petrol allowance and expenses.'

I shook my head. 'Why not ask Kelly? She's dying to get into a managerial role. She likes it here.'

Frank rolled his eyes. 'Kelly would be efficient, yes, but she has zero respect in this office. I need someone who can keep a level head and not cause conflict. You'd all threaten to leave within a week if Kelly was in charge.'

'Fair point.'

'Look, go home and discuss it with your husband. The role isn't being created until after this London meeting, anyway. But please keep this to yourself until then.'

'I'm not married and I'm not inter—'

'Close the door behind you, please.'

There was no point in arguing. I could have hired a plane to skywrite I AM NOT FUCKING INTERESTED, FRANK, and he'd still be convinced he knew best.

But it played on my mind for the rest of the day. Of course the money would be great and I'm sure I could do the job, but it would mean admitting defeat. It would mean that this is all I am destined to do and that's fucking depressing.

Friday May 12th

After a quick jaunt to the supermarket to save me going over the weekend, I saw something which made me grin for the rest of the evening. Nothing makes me happier than witnessing the joy that is *teenage goth being forced to walk the family dog*. His sulk was unmistakable, as was the injustice which radiated from every cell in his lanky body.

I spoke to Oliver about the job offer and the London trip in August. He's not thrilled at the prospect of me doing an overnight with Frank but of course it was my decision. He just wants me to be happy. That makes two of us.

Saturday May 13th

Lucy came over to watch Molly tonight, letting Oliver and I spend some quality time together watching a special screening of *Jaws* at the Film Theatre, followed by a quick drink at Nice N Sleazy after. It was great, like a proper date – I wore fancy heels and Oliver opened doors for me, bought me sweets and laughed when I moaned about people clapping at the end of the film.

'I hate that. Like a room of appreciative seals. It's not a live performance. Stop that, no one cares.'

'I fucking love how much you hate people.'

We got back around 1 a.m. to the sight of Lucy, cross-legged on the floor, flipping through wedding magazines.

'Molly alright?' I enquired, gratefully kicking my heels off.

'Yep! She loves her stories, that kid. We read a book about an asshole cat three times. How was the film?'

'Same as it was the last forty times I've seen it,' Oliver replied. 'Brilliant.'

'I see you've had a productive night?' I said, gesturing towards the magazines. 'Hazel's been busy.'

Lucy got to her feet, brushing down her trousers. 'She's like a well-oiled machine when it comes to this stuff. Did you know that I'm supposed to give a shit about whether flowers match my dress?'

She didn't wait for a reply, grabbing her car keys off the table. 'Be thankful you don't have any of this nonsense to deal with.'

After I'd seen her to the door, I joined Oliver in the bedroom. 'She's stressing over this, eh?' he commented, taking off his t-shirt. 'I couldn't be arsed with it all. I'd just fuck off and get married somewhere. Have a party when we got back.'

We? This was the first time Oliver had even mentioned marriage, never mind including me in it. I'd never considered marriage to be an option. We're not 'that' kind of couple.

'It just all seems a bit pointless,' I replied. 'Archaic . . . of course, you can buy me a big fuck off ring regardless. I won't complain.'

He smiled but stayed quiet. Oh God, he's going to think I'm hinting for an engagement ring now. I stayed quiet too. I'm not digging myself in any deeper, we have enough to deal with.

Sunday May 14th

Took Molly to the park today where we saw Ruby and Sarah Ward-Wilson hanging out by the boating pond. It's the first time I've seen her away from nursery. It felt weird. Like when you were a kid at school and you spotted your teacher out in the wild.

Molly began sprinting towards Ruby, yelling her name so loudly, it startled the swans. The way children run always fascinates me. Adults run with their legs but children run with their feet. They make that completely identifiable, slapping sound you never hear from a jogger. Sarah waved me over and I took a deep breath. If she hurls herself into the pond, I'm not going in after her.

'What a surprise!' she exclaimed. 'How are you? Keeping well?'

She was definitely far more chipper than the last time we spoke. 'I'm good, thanks,' I replied. 'And you? How is everything?'

'Wonderful,' she said, the smile on her face never wavering. She looked over at Ruby to make sure she wasn't in earshot of our conversation. 'He's back in the house. He says he realises that our kids need him around but I think he realised that living in her shitty flat in Govan wasn't all he hoped for.'

'So you're trying again?'

She laughed. It was creepy. 'Of course not. Separate bedrooms. I've told the children their father snores too loudly. He can continue seeing his homewrecker and I will take a lover.'

There were a million questions swarming around in my mind. Firstly, they have four kids. That's four bedrooms plus her own and apparently a spare room, too. How fucking big was their house? Secondly, was she really OK living like this? Also, SHE SAID TAKE A LOVER AND NOW I CAN'T GET 'GLORIA' FROM FLASHDANCE OUT OF MY HEAD.

Supressing the urge to mention any of this, I smiled and told her I was glad she was doing well.

'I'm pleased you're doing better. After last time, I—'

There goes the smile. Her face became cold and motionless. 'What about last time? What do you mean?'

'Nothing! Just in your car . . . at nursery . . . you seemed quite, well . . . distraught.'

She threw her Prada handbag over her shoulder and replastered the smile back on her face. 'I'm sure I have no idea what you mean . . . *Ruby! Time to go, sweetheart.*'

I didn't push it any further. If she wanted to pretend it didn't happen, who was I to insist it did? What good would it do?

Tuesday May 16th

Oliver and I had a massive talk tonight. We discussed how we felt things were going after his confession in Pam's office, the state of our relationship – basically everything that's been on our minds for the last week or so. It was tough at times but I'm glad we did. His main issue was me working with Frank again. It was difficult trying to convince him that not only did I *never* have feelings for Frank but that he didn't have any for me either. I wasn't harbouring any then and I'm certainly not now. From what I can gather, Oliver is more concerned about Frank trying it on, than me.

'He's a fucking toad. There's no way he's not remembering what it was like to sleep with you. And if you go on that London trip . . .'

'I have no control over that,' I replied, exasperated. 'Just as I have no control over who you've slept with previously, and whether they remember it. Just trust me when I say that it's in the past and it's staying there.'

I think I finally got through to him but it's still a real sore point. Can I blame him? I don't know how understanding I'd be if Oliver was still working alongside Bethany. Ugh, even writing her name makes me want to scream. I can't help but wonder how she feels about what happened between them. She knew he had a partner. A family. Does she feel guilty? Embarrassed? Does she pity me? Think she'll be the one to save him from his miserable hum-drum life with the wrong woman?

But most of all, I can't help but wonder if Oliver had feelings for her that went beyond lust. I think that would crush me more than any sexual infidelity.

Wednesday May 17th

I think Pam's session was productive today, with both of us eventually accepting responsibility for the way our relationship had struggled over the past couple of years. I'd love to blame it all on Oliver and get my *'nothing to do with me, I'm perfect'* badge on my way out but I know that's not true.

When you become a parent, naturally everything becomes about your kid. I threw myself into that role head-first, so much so that even I stopped seeing me as me – just as 'Mum'. I organised everyone, not just Molly, and thrived on routine, forgetting that life isn't as linear as I tried to make it. Of course Oliver wouldn't come crying to me because he wanted more attention – I already had one demanding child. I was doing what I was supposed to do – how could he selfishly ask me for more? But it turns out there was someone else willing to do it. I'm just glad he realised that it wasn't only recognition he craved; it was me. Yes, he also behaved like a complete dick but we need to move on.

I questioned him about his feelings for Bethany and he assured me they were non- existent. I can either accept this as true or continue to doubt him until it eats away at me. I'm choosing the former. Even when we got home, the conversation continued into the small hours and for the first time I really believe that we can get through this.

Thursday May 18th

I woke up this morning to the sound of Oliver singing along to 'Love Plus One' in the shower and it made me smile. Actually, it made me melt; that rush I get when he does something cute came flooding back. Then I watched him dress, while Molly barged in and out of our room, bare-arsed, looking for pants.

'Morning, sleepy,' he said, kissing me on the cheek. 'I need to shoot off; can you help the streaker here find some knickers?'

'On it,' I replied, giving myself a shake while he fastened his watch and straightened his tie. 'You look good,' I informed him, unashamedly eyeing him up. 'Really good.'

He paused to look at me, which given my bed-head must have been horrifying.

'Miss Henderson, are you flirting with me?'

I brushed the hair off my face with my hand. 'Maybe . . . yes. Why am I so turned on by the fact you just fastened your watch?'

'Well, my wrists are very manly.'

'And my pussy is very— Hang on, Molly!!'

I dragged my aching vagina out of bed and brushed past Oliver, who told me to hold that thought until tonight.

'We're having sex later,' I informed him, quietly. 'All of it. I'd kiss you now but I have morning breath. Just go before I lock this door and climb you like a gym rope.'

He left the room, casually adjusting himself while I went on an underwear hunt with Molly, finding eleven pairs in the drawer where her pants live. I didn't mind. I was ready to shag my boyfriend again. Today was a good day.

Saturday May 20th

Hazel was stuck for a babysitter this weekend, so we took Grace overnight to let her and Kevin celebrate their anniversary in style. She's agreed to take Molly next Saturday as I have plans for Oliver's birthday.

'We're staying at One Devonshire in the Vettriano Suite, in case anything comes up,' Hazel said. 'Thank God we don't have to take Grace along; there's no way I'm not being naked 100% of the time.' Grace likes staying with us. She gets to impress us all with her *Minecraft* skills and sleep on the bouncy air mattress we keep for guests. Molly was of course delighted that her 'sister' was staying, begging us to let her come on holiday with us this year.

'I'm sure she'll be going away with her own parents, sweetheart. Maybe when you're both older, we can arrange something.' Jesus, being responsible for my own kid abroad is stressful enough, never mind someone else's. We should plan where we're going this year, actually. Last year's holiday in Egypt was fun but being constantly hassled by the spa staff who wanted to thread my entire face wasn't a highlight.

Monday May 22nd

Mum and Dad are thinking of coming over in October for a few days. Their old friend Mitchell is having a huge 70th birthday celebration in Arran so they're hoping to combine the two.

'I hear his new wife is quite a bit younger,' she informed me. 'If she hasn't shagged the old boy to death by New Year, I'll be surprised.'

'Ever the romantic, eh, Mum?' I replied. 'Hang on, what the hell is that noise? It's like panting. Is that Dad?'

'It's Daphne. She gets very excited when I'm on the phone. Do you want to say hello?'

'To the dog? I think I'll pass. Who'll watch her when you're over here?'

I heard her lower the phone and tell Daphne to fetch. 'Our neighbour Bill. He has three dogs anyway, he's happy to look after her. She has a ball over there. He lets them use the outdoor pool . . . oh shit, she's in the rose bushes. I have to go, will email you the dates. Love to Molly!'

She hung up the phone and left me to break the news to

Oliver. As much as he likes my parents, he finds them a little too full on, though everyone is full on compared to his own parents.

Tuesday May 23rd

A very meek-sounding Jay called to make changes to his copy this morning, apologising for his unprofessional behaviour.

'It's absolutely fine,' I assured him. 'Please, let's just forget about it.'

'Great,' he replied. 'I'll email the new photos over shortly.'

I have to admit, I felt a little bad for the guy. Not only had he been shot down, he was also paying over the odds for advertising in a shitty, right-leaning newspaper.

Frank's partner came to pick him up for lunch. She looked completely different. So different, in fact, that I had to question whether this was the same woman Frank had on the photo on his desk. A look from Lucy confirmed that she thought the same.

As soon as they stepped out of the office, Lucy and I rushed into his office to grab a look at the photo. But it was gone. There was nothing left to do but SPECULATE AND GOSSIP.

'They've split up.'

'Who dumped who? I bet she dumped Frank. But why?'

'Maybe she died?'

'Maybe he died?'

'Maybe he had an affair. Ooh, I bet that's it. And he's parading his mistress around town like some Lothario.'

'You have to find out, Phoebe. He'll tell you.'

'Why will he tell me?'

'He's been up you. He'll tell you anything.'

He arrived back after a two-hour lunch, looking flustered. They totally did it. Beasts. I'm going to quiz him next week.

Wednesday May 24th

It's Oliver's birthday so I baked a cake with Molly after she got out of school. I haven't baked since 2001 when some mates and I thought it would be hysterical to make hash brownies without researching how to do it first. We failed miserably.

I let Molly do as much as her little arms would allow, taking over the mixing when she got tired. We decided on chocolate with buttercream icing and some little fondant animals Molly insisted on buying at Tesco.

'This one is a bit wonky, Mum,' Molly commented as we let the layers cool on the rack. 'The animals might fall off.'

I stood back and looked. She was right. One was perfectly level and the other looked drunk. 'We'll just cut a bit to make it more . . . even,' I reassured her. 'Once everything is on, Dad won't know.'

Oliver got home at six and was greeted by Molly holding a lopsided, farmyard-themed birthday cake, sporting huge 3- and 9-shaped candles.

'Happy Birthday, Dad!'

'Oh WOW!' he exclaimed, doing his best not to laugh. 'I think that's the best cake I've seen IN MY LIFE. You must have worked so hard on this.'

Molly nodded. 'I did most of it. Mum says I can light the candles after dinner so we have to have dinner now, 'kay?'

She handed over the cake and skipped off to her bedroom. Her work here was done.

'I thought we'd just get a takeaway?' I suggested, taking the cake so he could get his coat off. 'Chinese?'

'Hell yes. I'm exhausted. Looks like you are too.'

'I have no fucking idea how Mary Berry does this crap on a daily basis. She must have biceps of steel.'

He wandered off to the bedroom to change.

'Would you like a beer, darling?' I asked in my best housewife voice. 'I got some of those craft ones you like.'

'That'd be lovely,' he called back, knowing I'd just implied he was a wanker. 'I'll be on the couch waiting for my presents. I hope your arms still have enough strength to carry them through.'

'First one's in the jar,' I replied.

'What ja— Oh! Really?'

I heard the noise of the jar scraping off the top of the wardrobe. Inside was my last request. It didn't take long until his face popped around the side of the kitchen door.

'When?'

'Saturday. Hazel's taking Molly at 3 p.m.'

He grinned. 'A whole twenty-four hours in bed? That's ambitious.'

'Not really. I thought we'd organise a bed picnic, maybe order a pizza, hook the PlayStation up, watch a movie, laugh at some porn and, you know, fuck my brains out in between?'

As his head disappeared back round the door, I heard him proclaim: 'Best. Birthday. Ever.'

Sunday May 28th

Oh, yesterday was fun. I think this was the best sex jar request yet.

We dropped Molly with Hazel at 3 p.m. before racing home to begin twenty-four hours in bed. It began as I thought it would: frantic, noisy, no-children-around sex which lasted about twenty minutes, before we grabbed food from the fridge and planned our activities. Highlights included:

1. Playing *Friday the 13th* multiplayer on PS4. I was the worst killer ever, everyone lived and some American teen-agers made fun of me.
2. Watching *La La Land*. (I loved. Oliver hated because apparently jazz is for wankers.)
3. Watching *Mad Max Fury Road*.
4. Having very intense sex.
5. Passing out for two hours.
6. Having more sex in the shower.
7. Ordering pizza, hot wings and Irn Bru. Eating like pigs.
8. Feeling sick.
9. Cuddling. Too sore for more sex.
10. Oliver making me laugh so much I almost peed myself.
11. Sleeping until 1 p.m.

It reminded me of when we first got together; all sex and laughing and just messing around. As a couple, we needed this, but as friends we needed it more.

Wednesday May 31st

Molly went back to nursery today (I am so done with these holidays), so I met Lucy for a quick coffee during her lunch hour. I was only in town to return some jeans which claimed to be my size yet were clearly made for someone with bare bones for legs.

'Please let me talk about something other than weddings,' she pleaded, biting into a cookie. 'Honestly, I never thought I'd become this person. I'm sorry we didn't just decide to elope.'

'You still could,' I informed her, blowing on my Americano. 'Oliver said that's what he'd do. Just fuck off and do it.'

Lucy shook her head. 'We've paid deposits now – we're too far gone. Also, WHAT? Oliver talked about marriage?!'

'Calm down,' I replied. 'It was just in passing. Neither of us have any plans. I made a joke about him buying me a fancy ring and I don't think I've ever seen him shut his face so quickly.'

'Shame,' she replied, continuing with her cookie. 'We could have done a double wedding. That would have been fun.'

I laughed. 'Can you imagine? We'd never take it seriously. I'd want to walk down the aisle to Madonna and have my first dance with you.'

Lucy's face broke into a massive grin. 'We could prepare one of those really intricate, surprise dance routines and put it on YouTube.'

'We should do that regardless.'

'He's moving in, you know. In June,' she said. 'We decided we might as well get it over with. Be one less thing to do after the wedd—oh God, STOP ME TALKING ABOUT WEDDINGS.'

An hour later I was back on the underground and on my way home, wondering which Madonna song I'd rock down the aisle to. Would have to be 'Ray of Light'. No, 'Vogue'. Definitely 'Vogue'.

JUNE

Thursday June 1st

I made an excuse to see Frank in his office, asking him about the deputy role he'd offered me. I didn't give a shit about that, I just wanted to start a conversation so I could enquire about his personal life.

'Ah. You're considering it. Wonderful. Well, the role would involve—'

'Where's your photo gone?' Yeah, not very subtle but he was boring me already.

'Photo?'

Oh don't play dumb, Frankie boy. Where's the photo and who's the new woman? What the fuck are you up to?

'Yes,' I replied, trying not to look like I was drilling him for information. 'The one of Vanessa . . . it used to sit right there.'

He sighed. 'I see. This is because Kathryn took me to lunch last week.' Frank might be a dick but he's not stupid. 'You're prying.'

'Of course I am. Spill.'

'Phoebe, I am your boss and this is not an—'

He stopped talking when I gave him a look that said *Really? You want to go down this road?*

'Fine. Kathryn is my divorce lawyer. Vanessa and I are no longer together.'

'I knew—What? Hang on! You're married?'

'Was married.' He started pressing random buttons on his keyboard, nervously. This was obviously uncomfortable for him. 'Three years.'

'Well. I'm sorry. I . . . don't really know what to say.'

'Well there's a fucking first,' he mumbled under his breath.

'I am sorry, though. I feel bad now. We thought you were having an affair.'

He stopped tapping. 'WE? Who's *we*?'

'Oh relax, just me and Lucy. We had nothing better to talk about. I promise this won't go any further.'

He nodded and I quickly left. What I *meant* was *this won't go any further than me . . . and Lucy . . . oh, and definitely Hazel*, but again, he's a smart man. He knows me.

Saturday June 3rd

Oliver's mum and dad have invited us to Dublin during the school holidays but he's less than keen to go.

'I'm not using my holiday allowance to be fucking miserable. I want to be miserable somewhere warm, where my mum won't nag me about getting a haircut. I'll make up an excuse.'

In other news, HOW THE HELL IS IT JUNE ALREADY? I haven't done anything. Is it too late to take back my plan to not make any New Year's resolutions because I feel like I should have had some goals in place. Even Molly has fulfilled her 'pick names for all the cats I see' resolution, though I'm not sure 'big pussy face' was entirely appropriate for the cat who sits on our bins.

Monday June 5th

Frank kept away from me today, probably scared I'd quiz him about his recent divorce, which of course I would have given half a chance. I told Lucy all about it as we walked to the station after work.

'I wonder what he did?' she mused, pushing the button at the traffic lights. 'I'm convinced it must have been his fault.'

'Why?' I asked, stepping back from the kerb. Jesus, the traffic was heavy today.

She glanced at me. 'Hmm. I have to say that him being a massive arsehole was a factor in reaching this conclusion.'

We started to cross the road. 'So,' she continued, 'you never said – does he have a big dick or what?'

Oh God. I felt my face begin to burn. I knew she'd ask about this eventually.

'Because if he has a tiny penis, that could also contribute.'

'He isn't tiny!' I insisted, almost defending him. 'He's normal-sized.'

'I mean, Kyle isn't big—'

My head snapped round to look at her. 'He isn't?'

'Nope,' she grinned, 'but *damn* he knows how to work what he has and I'm never sore afterwards.'

In my dream, Kyle was huge. I'm going to have to adjust this mental image now. We reached the other side of the road and I hoped the end of this conversation, but Lucy was still intent on getting me to talk about Frank's sexual prowess.

'So, was he good in bed? Did you kiss him? Oh Jesus, you kissed him, didn't you? Fuck, I don't know if I actually want to know any of this.'

'I WASN'T VOLUNTEERING THE INFORMATION!' I exclaimed. 'Stop digging.'

She pulled me into Starbucks to grab a coffee. 'But was he? *Tall, skinny vanilla latte, please.* Where did you do it? Did you go to his place? Oh God, I have so many questions.'

I promised to fill her in properly over lunch tomorrow and left her in Starbucks; I had to get back for Molly. I'm not sure if I want to rehash the past, to be honest, but she's never going to let this go.

Tuesday June 6th

Frank is one of those fragile men who need to feel important. It's his oxygen; without it, he'd quickly die and then we'd be obliged to attend his damn important funeral, so we all play along to avoid having to do this. He's so transparent though – he'll make you wait while he finishes a non-existent email or he'll mention how much his suit cost or he'll just randomly shout COME ON, PEOPLE, TIME IS MONEY while clapping his hands. He's a fucking joke and every time I look at him, I'm reminded that I let that clapping buffoon into my knickers.

Wednesday June 7th

I had a dream last night where Kerry Washington invited me to stay at her house but I refused because fuck being in the same space with someone that perfect. Watching back-to-back *Scandal* at bedtime may have been to blame. Oliver always rolls his eyes when I turn it on but he loves it more than I do.

We have therapy tomorrow. I feel things are going pretty well at the moment, both with our sex life and our relationship. Oliver doesn't think we need to go anymore but I'm not so sure. It's been more than useful so far and it's certainly made Oliver far more communicative than he was. I don't think about him kissing the mysterious Bethany as much as I used to but that doesn't mean I don't think about it at all. It's still there. Quietly present. Maybe we can cut back to once a month and see how it goes?

Thursday June 8th

Highlights from our session with Pam today included:

- We're definitely keeping the sex jar. Pam has encouraged us to use it as often as we feel we need to.
- Agreed to cut back our sessions to once a month, unless we feel we need more.
- Most importantly: keep talking and don't go to bed on an argument.

I could see Oliver's mind at work for new sex jar suggestions as we drove home. He appears to be motivated as fuck.

Friday June 9th

Things I know about our noisy upstairs neighbours: the woman's name is Nicole and Nicole never listens. The reason I know this is because the man says it loudly every time they argue. Nicole also exercises after work every day at the same time and it sounds like the fucking Dawn Patrol from the *Jungle Book* on the ceiling above. Him? I have no idea about him, other than he appears to love the sound of his own voice, even though it breaks like a fourteen-year-old during their arguments. Oliver has gone up a couple of times to ask them to keep it down but it falls on deaf ears. We end up just banging the ceiling with a broom until they take the hint or start banging back defiantly. Fucking morons. I make a point of shouting HI, NEIGHBOUR when I see them to wind them up. It's childish but I never claimed not to be.

Sunday June 11th

Hazel was forty-five today and just like every other birthday I've shared with her, she wasn't happy. Kevin had arranged a meal for everyone at COSMO because now we have children, we don't get to eat anywhere remotely high-brow.

'I'M OLD!' she yelled, as we made the mistake of wishing her a happy birthday. 'Next year I'll be middle-aged. This is not a time for celebration; this is a time for panicking and denial.'

Lucy hugged her to calm her down, whispering something in her ear which seemed to work, while we all took our seats. Lucy is the Hazel Whisperer.

We did presents while we waited for our drinks, handing Molly and Grace colouring books to keep them entertained for as long as possible. The place was packed, the lure of a buffet too great for many Glaswegians to resist.

Molly was starving, dragging Oliver and Grace up to the buffet in search of noodles, pizza and whatever else she could balance on her plate before she began destroying the dessert section.

Hazel flashed her new bracelet from Kevin, a white gold affair which dangled delicately from her wrist, while she opened the gift Lucy and I had clubbed in to buy her.

'I love it!' she declared, showing Kevin the spa package we'd got for the three of us. An overnight at Cameron House, with dinner, full use of the spa facilities, facials and massage. It cost a bloody fortune, but what the fuck do you buy someone who doesn't need anything, except mud therapy with her mates?

As Oliver and the kids came back with their plates piled high, the rest of us followed suit, planning to eat at least six plates' worth but struggling to finish a second. Despite Hazel's initial freak out, we all had a fun evening.

Monday June 12th

At lunchtime, Lucy and I went to look at wedding dresses. I was happy to go with her, as it'll undoubtedly be the only time I'll set foot in a wedding dress shop, unless Molly also goes down this route when she falls madly in love with someone I deem unworthy.

We made it all the way to the front door of the shop before

she suddenly froze, about-turned and started hurriedly walking the other way.

'I'm not going in there,' she stated, her pace reaching Usain Bolt level. 'Nope. Uh-uh. It's terrifying. I am not one of those women. Women change once they get that dress on. I've seen it on the telly. They become possessed. They start craving the perfect wedding – like ice sculptures and coordinating heel heights and fucking individually-wrapped kittens as wedding favours.'

I thankfully managed to slow her and calm her down. She plonked herself on the kerbside and put her head on her knees. She was freaking out.

'Are you having second thoughts about this?' I asked cagily, sitting down beside her. 'I hear it's normal ... I mean, if you are.' I rooted around in my handbag looking for anything that might be useful: a brown paper bag to breathe into ... a sedative ... some wiser words than the ones I was currently using – anything.

I found a Milkybar. Luckily, Lucy snatched it from my hand and began tearing it open without questioning.

'I'm not having seconds thoughts,' she insisted, biting into the chocolate, 'I just don't want a fucking dog and pony show. Kyle's parents are trying to make us invite all three million of his extended family, his sister Gayle is insisting she'll take over the seating arrangements in case Charles is sat next to Angus or within breathing distance of Marjory, and I don't even know who the fuck anyone is. Kyle is keeping out of it and quite frankly I'll be murdering him first if he doesn't tell them to back off. I never realised he was such a fucking mummy's boy.'

She finished the Milkybar in two bites (must buy another for Molly) before resting her head on my shoulder. 'I want to run away,' she said quietly.

'So do it.'

She looked up at me, her blue eyes blinking away the little pools of stress tears that had started to form.

'Go away and get married,' I continued. 'Go and do your own thing. Fuck what anyone else wants.'

'But we've paid the deposit on the venue—'

'And you can still use it for a party when you get back. Go to Gretna, just the two of you. Wear a bright green dress. Get married barefoot, whatever.'

'And miss out on walking down the aisle looking fabulous in front of everyone?' She gave me a nudge and grinned. 'No way.'

I laughed. Lucy will never surrender. 'I just want you to be happy, mate. I'll help in any way I can.'

She wiped her eyes with the sleeve of her jacket and began to stand up. 'Fuck it. I'm just going to marry you instead. Forget this place. I'll look at vintage dresses online. It'll give me something to do at work.'

I don't envy Lucy. I can't imagine Oliver's family demanding a religious ceremony and his mum taking over everything. My parents would show up with some hash and a bottle of organic wine.

Tuesday June 13th

Last night I dreamt that Oliver told me he'd kissed that woman again and he was leaving Molly and me to be with her. I woke up with wet eyes and a knot in my stomach the size of a fist. Even though it was just a stupid dream and intellectually I know that this won't happen, my heart hurts. And it *was* stupid; he was wearing a cowboy hat, for fuckssake. I think I'm going to sit with this feeling for a while and if it doesn't dissipate, I'll bring it up at therapy.

Wednesday June 14th

Check-up at the dentist this morning which ended up costing me 120 quid for two fillings, an x-ray and a clean. I think I'd rather have kept the tooth decay. I then had to terrify my own kid with my slurring face and drink my tea through a straw afterwards.

I dropped Molly at nursery, doing my best to not lop-sidedly smile at anyone, but of course Lord Wilson cornered me in the cloakroom and I had to communicate using only half of my face.

'Oh, you poor thing,' she said robotically. 'I'd empathise but my dentist says I have the healthiest teeth he's ever seen ... my sugar intake is almost non-existent, you see; Stevia all the way!'

My urge to just stand there and drool on her Nikes was strong. Lately she's always dressed like she's either been or is heading to the gym, with a water bottle in her hand and a visible camel toe in her yoga pants. I may be podgy and eat a lot of sugar but at least my fanny doesn't eat my clothing.

'Nice seeing you,' I mumbled insincerely, before ushering Molly into her classroom. I hoped that she'd pay attention to someone else but she fucking followed me, chattering about

Wholefoods and her new personal trainer, Marc with a C. Before she could tell me her body fat ratio, I caught the attention of Molly's teacher and pretended to have a pressing nursery-related question until Lord Wilson left. The fact that she refuses to mention or even acknowledge the whole husband affair fiasco is a little disturbing and now it just feels awkward when we meet. I understand that she's probably embarrassed but I can't help feeling like I've been used in some way. Like I was useful at the time but now my services are no longer required.

Thursday June 15th

Frank told Lucy off for looking through bridal websites at work today.

'This is not an appropriate use of either work time or resources. I'm sure you can look at wedding dresses on your own time,' he stated firmly but loudly enough for the whole office to hear from behind his closed door. See? Self-important prick. Thankfully, Lucy was on form as usual.

'I think you're being unreasonable.'

'Well, you're entitled to your opinion. However, I am the—'

'Surely my excellent work ethic is valued enough that you'd trust my judgement to ensure my standards won't slip,' she continued defiantly. 'Have a little faith in me.'

'This isn't up for discussion, Lucy. I've said what—'

'Frank, did you know that planning a wedding is one of the most stressful times in a woman's life?'

'What? Yes, I'm sure it is.'

'And that stress is one of the biggest factors in long-term

sick leave? I mean, what would happen if I became so stressed that I had to be signed off for months? MONTHS, Frank. In fact, even being dragged in here in full view of everyone is making my blood pressure rocket. I may have to lie down.'

'Lucy, I know what you're trying to do here and—'

'Sure, I was looking at dresses on work time. I mean, it's not like we haven't all done something that perhaps HR wouldn't approve of. Wouldn't you agree?'

I could almost hear his jaw fall open. Oh, she went there. Both my ears and my face were burning.

'I liked the cream dress better,' he said meekly. 'The white was too frilly.'

Friday June 16th

I awoke to see the old couple from the sex jar staring at me this morning from my bedside table. Oliver had already gone to work but had slipped a request in there before he left.

Buy lube, Henderson. I want a big, dirty hand job.

I snort-laughed loudly, just as Molly burst into the bedroom. 'Why are you laughing?' I quickly scrunched his piece of paper up and stuck it under my pillow.

'Oh nothing. I just remembered something silly Dad said earlier,' I covered. 'Do you want some cereal, honey?'

She nodded. 'Yes, please. Dad is always saying silly things, isn't he? He's funny.'

'He is,' I agreed. 'He's been making me laugh since we were in high school.'

Molly scrunched up her face. 'Even in the olden days? That's a lot of jokes.'

I suddenly felt very lucky. Not many people get to have laughed as hard and for as long as I have.

Saturday June 17th

Had yet another dream about Kyle last night! However, this time he had really large balls – like two dangling melons. I remember staring at them in horror, a bit like when Mia Farrow stares into the crib in *Rosemary's Baby*. I think I've now quashed any subconscious desires for Kyle. I don't want to see that again. I'm done.

Sunday June 18th

Someone on Facebook used 'lol' today and it put me in a bad mood. In fact, Facebook in general puts me in a bad mood. If it's not endless streams of motivational memes, it's someone posting the same filtered selfie, at the same angle, for the 654th time. You have a face, it has a good side – WE GET IT. Still, at least I'm not on Instagram or Snapchat, that shit is worse. Maybe it's my age, but I really have no interest in what your dinner looks like or that you've added a dog nose and ears to your face – it's hilarious but you're also forty.

Monday June 19th

As I took my make-up off tonight, it suddenly hit me that I'm starting to look old. Not Titanic-survivor-old but certainly not as youthful as I think I am when not confronted by my own face in the mirror. I swore I'd never be one of those overly neurotic women who gets hung up on her age-ing appearance but now that it's happening, I can't help it. I accepted reality when my tits started heading south because my bra dealt with that but now that everything has started heading south, I'm wondering why there isn't a hoist to help. My jaw isn't as defined as it once was and the laughter lines around my mouth aren't going anywhere when I stop laughing. I feel like Pennywise the clown. Not only am I drooping, I'm also producing grey hair at a rapid rate. Per-haps my first belated New Year's resolution should be buying a hair dye to deal with the silver roots landing strip which has appeared on top of my gradually sagging head.

Tuesday June 20th

Popped to Boots after work to buy some dye. Why do I feel like the moment I hover near the hair colourants, people immediately start judging me and my hair? I should have dealt with this a long time ago and now I've reached a level of self-neglect that only L'Oréal, some rubber gloves and a triple sandwich meal deal can help with. I also picked up some new foundation, nail varnish, oh, and some lube for Oliver's forthcoming sex jar request. I'll look groomed as fuck while I'm wanking off my boyfriend.

Thursday June 22nd

Last night I made the very important decision never to buy, smell or be in the same room as strawberry lube, ever again. Oliver's hand job request began with him sitting on the edge of the bed and me kneeling between his legs. Instead of the old reach-across in bed, he wanted to 'look at me doing it, preferably with my tits out' but that was my call.

Having touched Oliver's dick hundreds – nay, millions – of times, I knew what he liked – the pressure, the ball cupping, the double-handed moves that made him thrust towards me without warning – so this should have been a no-brainer. As I pulled the top off the lube and squirted some into my hand, the overpowering smell of overly sweet fake strawberry made me want to gag. And if that wasn't bad enough, the texture of the lube was all wrong. It didn't glide; it was sticky. It was sticky and it stank. Oliver appeared oblivious, eagerly waiting for me to begin while I casually tried to prize my now-gummy hands apart. Telling myself that what this situation needed was simply more lube, I squirted half the tube over my hands, his knob and the bed-covers, wishing to fuck I'd just bought baby oil.

At first it worked. My hands moved over his cock easily as he watched, occasionally reaching down to make sure my boobs were still bouncy for reasons known only to him. But the lube dried quickly, the smell was becoming overwhelming and the more I applied, the more ridiculous the whole situation became. I was up to my elbows in strawberry glue while dodging the intermittent squirming of a man who was definitely getting the worst hand job of his life. Eventually he moved back on the bed and away from my grasp.

'OK, enough!' he exclaimed, picking up the sticky bottle of lube. 'What in the hell is this shit?! It smells like a mixture of Starburst and spermicide . . . and it's not even lubey!'

I could feel it crusting in between my fingers. 'I know,'

I replied, shaking my head. 'It was on offer. It was an impulse buy.'

'It felt like you were pulling my foreskin off at one point.' He looked so deflated.

I placed my hands on his thighs to push myself up from the floor, pressing into a blob that had escaped and gone rogue. That was the final straw. 'Right, fuck this. We both need to shower and I especially need to set fire to these sheets.'

He didn't even argue, he just threw on some underwear and headed for the bathroom while I pulled the duvet cover off the bed.

We showered together, scrubbing each other to remove every trace of that lube, like we were cleaning up a crime scene and vowing never to speak of it again.

'Can you hand me that shower gel one more time?' I asked before he turned off the water. 'I think I missed a bit.'

Admittedly Oliver didn't get the hand job I'd planned but it turns out zingy lime and lemon shower gel could save the day.

Monday June 26th

So, today was bizarre. Running late for work, I dropped Molly at nursery only to discover that I'd driven there with a flat tyre and no spare in the boot. Of course Sarah Ward-Wilson was the one to inform me because that woman misses NOTHING.

'Oh, silly you. Just call the RAC. You do have roadside recovery, don't you?'

Silly me? Oh, do shut the fuck up, you annoying woman.

'I do,' I replied, putting up my umbrella. The rain began bouncing off the streets in huge, heavy drops. 'But I don't have time to hang around. I'll just call a cab into work and deal with it later.'

'A taxi at morning rush hour? In the rain?' she scoffed. 'You'll be waiting just as long as it would take to get your car fixed. Where do you work? I'll drop you.'

Her random offer of generosity startled me. 'What? No. No, that's very kind but—'

'Get in,' she insisted. 'We can chat on the way.'

I found myself agreeing and getting out of the rain and into her car, unsure whether she'd drive away with me and never come back.

Thankfully, I arrived at work, dry and grateful to Sarah for driving me. We talked about my job, and how she regretted not returning to her career in hotel management after she got married. Maybe she does have a good heart, she just keeps it hidden behind that snobbish façade.

Fifteen minutes late, I made my apologies and told Frank about my car troubles, but either he didn't care or he knew that it was pointless reprimanding me. I settled down at my desk, ready to enjoy another uneventful day at the office.

'Can I help you?'

I glanced over to where Lucy sat in reception and saw Lord Wilson looking around the room, completely ignoring her question. 'Phoebe! You left your umbrella in the car.'

Before I had the chance to open my mouth, she was marching through the office like she owned the place, casually glancing at the rest of the staff who stared in disbelief.

'Thought you might need it,' she stated as she advanced upon my desk. 'Nice office. Smaller than I imagined.'

Imagined? She'd literally only found out where I worked ten minutes ago.

'Can I help you?'

The second person to ask this was Frank. Frank who'd bounded to my desk the moment he'd seen the blonde woman with the big fake tits approach it.

'Sorry, Sarah was just returning my umbrella,' I informed him, watching his face light up as she smiled at him.

'Sarah, this is my boss Frank. Frank, this is—'

'Sarah Ward-Wilson,' she interrupted, sticking out her hand. 'Sorry to interrupt, I just hated the thought of my good friend Phoebe being caught in the rain without her umbrella. Her car had a flat this morning, so I gave her a lift.'

Good friend? I don't even know her phone number.

Frank laughed. 'I thought she'd made that whole car story up. Well, that was kind of you. Phoebe's very lucky to have you.'

He's talking about me like I'm a five-year-old. There was a pause while they both just smiled at each other; Frank adjusting his tie and blingy watch, while Sarah groomed her hair into place. Oh dear God, they were flirting and it was weird.

I glanced at Lucy who'd noticed this too and was now pulling a *wtf* face from behind her desk. I coughed loudly, snapping them both out of their disgusting display of mutual attraction. I couldn't cope with this shit at 9.30 a.m.

'So . . . thanks, Sarah,' I said, standing up between them.

'I'd better get on with some work now. I'm sure you have a busy day ahead, too.'

'Not really.'

'OK, good. Bye now and thanks again.'

Frank sidestepped me and cleared his throat. 'Let me show you to the lift, Sarah. It's just this way . . .'

I watched dumbstruck as Frank led Sarah out of the office while Lucy rang my desk.

'How do you know a Real Housewife?'

'She's that woman from the nursery I've told you about. Husband had the affair.'

'Oh shit, that's her?! Bloody hell, I thought Frank was going to faint. I don't think I've ever seen two people flirt so openly in my life. Shit, he's coming back. Speak later.'

For the rest of the day, I tried to ignore what I'd just witnessed but it was impossible. Somehow, the two most frustrating people that I've ever known have unexpectedly met. And I have the feeling it won't be the last time.

Thursday June 29th

Today was my little Molly's last day at nursery. Ever. They gathered all the kids in the brightly-decorated classroom and the parents watched as they were presented with A4-sized graduation certificates and their very first school tie. Oliver grinned so much I thought his face might split in two but me, I cried. Not an embarrassing wail, just a small blub, interspersed with sniffing and assuring Oliver I was fine. I could tell that Sarah Ward-Wilson wasn't handling it very well either. This was the last of her brood now headed for

Primary School and her mascara was making its way towards her chin in protest.

I agreed to go into work tomorrow instead of using another holiday to witness this strangely traumatic event. Afterwards we took Molly for lunch to celebrate her successfully playing with other kids for two years.

However, this now means that Molly is free to roam in the wild for six bloody weeks before school starts all over again. SIX WEEKS! We're all doomed.

JULY

Saturday July 1st

SPA TRIP!

Having agreed to drive, I picked up Lucy and Hazel at half past ten this morning, giddy with excitement. Even though it would take less than an hour to get there, I'd loaded my iPod with tunes and provided granola breakfast bars for everyone.

Lucy looked like she was going on holiday; hair swept back in a bandana, massive sunglasses and a small glittery overnight case. Hazel wore her gym gear, putting my flabby ass to shame.

'I think you are my body goal,' I admitted as she bounced into the back seat. 'Jesus, do you have any extra body fat, woman? I have some to spare if you need it.'

She laughed. 'Stop it. Though, if you want to lend me your tits for an evening, I'm pretty sure Kevin would thank you.'

The weather was beautiful, which of course meant everyone within a twenty-mile radius had decided to leave the house and drive slowly in front of us. Still, we had a playlist full of Garbage, Basement Jaxx, Bowie and Fun Lovin' Criminals to pass the time.

An hour and ten minutes later, we pulled into Cameron

House, which sat on the banks of Loch Lomond. We couldn't have chosen a more beautiful day to sit inside and sweat profusely in a sauna.

'Look, Lucy!' I exclaimed. 'There's another Loch for you to misidentify.'

Hazel sniggered while Lucy muttered for me to shut my wee face before exiting the car. As our rooms wouldn't be ready until later, we left our small amount of luggage and caught the shuttle service to the spa.

It was a riot. Our first treatment required us to cover each other in mud before sitting in a steam room laughing at how fucking ridiculous we looked. This was then followed by showering, more showering and cries of 'get this fucking stuff off me' until we were clean. I fell asleep during my massage and Hazel got uncontrollable giggles during her facial, so much so that the therapist had to leave the room and come back when she'd calmed down.

We got back to the hotel around 3 p.m., where we'd booked a room for Hazel on her own while Lucy and I shared. We could have gone for a stroll, or to the boathouse, but instead we chose to pass out face first until dinner.

We ate in the Grill restaurant, which was a tad old-fashioned for Lucy, but we dressed up, drank champagne and put the world to rights over stuffed Dover Sole and flambéed prawns.

Lucy was the first to show signs of alcohol mismanagement. 'Do you realise that by Christmas I'll be a married woman?! I'm the last one to finally reach maturity.'

I poured myself more wine. 'Nonsense. I spend many days in bed pretending to be Jason Voorhees on the PlayStation.

I hope I never mature. Hazel is the only proper grown up here.'

'It's true,' she agreed. 'Husband, kid, mortgage, self-assessment . . . God, I'm dull. Did I ever tell you that I spent the night in the cells when I was twenty?'

Lucy's glass hit the table with a loud thunk. 'Shut. Up. You did not!'

She nodded proudly. 'Yep. I fell asleep on a bus, gave the driver grief, passed out again and he called the police. I was far too drunk to remember where I lived so they banged me up for the night. I USED TO BE WILD AND IRRESPONSIBLE.'

A couple in their sixties glared at us as they exited the dining room. It seems Hazel was just as tipsy as Lucy and also a hooligan in a previous life. It seems we're all struggling with the realisation that being an adult is shite.

Sunday July 2nd

Devoured a massive, sausage-heavy breakfast at the hotel this morning so felt pretty sluggish most of the day. Lucy and Hazel recovered from their hangovers impressively quickly and were both delightfully chipper on the drive home – well, until a wasp flew near Lucy's open window and she had a small heart attack.

When I arrived back at the flat, Oliver and Molly were having a jammies day and sat cuddled up on the sofa watching some old episodes of He-Man that Oliver had found online.

'Enjoying yourselves?' I enquired, chucking my overnight bag into the bedroom. 'I haven't seen this show in years!'

Molly was too engrossed to welcome me home, simply nodding in response.

'I'd forgotten how brilliant it is ... well, was,' Oliver replied, motioning for me to come and join them, which I did, pulling the blanket from the back of the couch over me.

'You smell like a Yankee candle,' Oliver noted, sniffing my hair. 'It's nice.'

'I'm freakin' exhausted,' I replied. 'De-stressing has destroyed me.'

'You're such a lightweight.'

'That's blatantly untrue.'

Twenty minutes later I was asleep on Oliver's lap with the sound of Skeletor laughing in the background.

Monday July 3rd

I've checked the holiday board at work and I can take ten days from the 19th July so Oliver and I will need to plan our holiday around that. Guaranteed it's going to cost a bajillion pounds because it's the school holidays, so we'll have to choose wisely. I've explained to Molly that we can't afford to hold a big party for her birthday *and* go on holiday but she's fine with that. Apparently nothing will top her bouncy castle party last year anyway. Thank God she's not a difficult child.

Frank was hovering around my desk at work today, asking questions about Sarah Ward-Wilson. How long have I known her, was she married, how many children does she have ... it couldn't have been more obvious that he was fishing for her number, which thankfully, I don't have.

'Jesus, Frank, just Google her like a normal stalker! Pretty certain she'll have a Facebook or a Twitter account or something.'

'I looked,' he said sheepishly. 'Couldn't find anything useful.'

'Oh well . . .'

'But you could give her *my* number . . .'

Oh God, no. I was not getting involved in this. He seems to have forgotten that I helped him snag his last wife Vanessa – this is not part of my job description. Besides, it means I would have to go out of my way to talk to Lord Wilson and I'd like to not do that.

'Sorry, Frank. School holidays. I won't see her until the new term starts in August,' I replied. 'You'll just have to figure this one out on your own.'

He sloped away back to his office, tail between his legs. If there's one thing I know about Frank, however, it's that he's determined. If he wants to get in touch with her, he'll make it happen.

Tuesday July 4th

'Egypt is pretty cheap.'

I looked over at Oliver who was scrolling away on his phone. 'There's loads of kid-friendly hotels,' he continued. 'We could do the pyramids and stuff, too.'

'They're cheap because no one wants to get terrorised by terrorists,' I replied. 'I'm not even sure the tour operators fly there at the moment. Same with Tunisia.'

'Phoebe, I don't think anywhere hasn't been targeted by nut jobs.' He continued scrolling. 'This place in Turkey looks pretty decent. Four-star, all inclusive. Big waterpark.'

'But wasn't Turkey—'

'Subjected to terror attacks at some point?' he interjected. 'Yep. As was London and Paris and America and Germany and . . . you see where I'm going with this?'

'I know, I'd just like to be as far from the action as possible, thanks very much.'

'Phoebe, some idiot tried to drive his car bomb into Glasgow Airport, remember? No one is ever going to be that far away from it.'

I started to laugh. 'I do remember. The baggage handler jumped in and booted one of the terrorists in the balls. Fucking love Scotland. OK, fine, I take your point. Email me over the link to have a look at.'

Two hours later, we were booked up for ten days in Turkey. Sun, sea and as much food as I can eat without an intervention being staged. Bring it on.

Thursday July 6th

From: Phoebe Henderson
To: Lucy Jacobs
Subject: Holiday

I need holiday clothes and a swimming costume. A big one. Would it be inappropriate to wear a burka as I really don't want my flab on display?

From: Lucy Jacobs
To: Phoebe Henderson
Subject: Re: Holiday

Who the fuck is going to be looking at you? There will be twenty-somethings with flat stomachs and perky tits to bear the brunt of the male gaze and the female scorn. We've paid our dues – just wear something that keeps those giant boobs strapped down, Dolly Parton.

She makes a sad, yet valid point. I'll nip to the shops at the weekend. I saw some really nice swimming kaftans in Dorothy Perkins that I could cover up with. They had pockets. Pockets are everything.

Saturday July 8th

While trying on swimming costumes this afternoon, I came to the realisation that as much as I try to embrace my body, the truth is, I'm just not there yet. Maybe I'll never be. It's not going to stop me wearing a swimsuit, but it doesn't mean I'm not going to feel self-conscious as fuck. Lucy was right, no one will be looking at me, but that's not the point because no one will ever be harder on me, than me. I really have to make sure none of this bullshit rubs off on Molly. I wonder if Bethany has a beach-ready body? I bet she does. I bet she's throwing herself around the gym when she's not throwing herself at my damn boyfriend.

Anyway, I bought a navy blue one piece with a red bow, a couple of kaftans, some three-quarter-length trousers, a couple of maxi dresses, a swishy skirt for swishy times and a whole trolley full of sunblock so we don't all suddenly explode like the Terminator 2 dream sequence.

Monday July 10th

Sarah Ward-Wilson has emailed Frank. Well, she emailed Lucy's admin address looking for Frank's direct email and of course Lucy informed me of this new development the moment she hit reply.

'I'm pretty sure she still lives with her husband,' I said. 'They have a weird separate bedrooms arrangement. He's doing some younger woman he works with—'

'—and soon she'll be doing Frank. Poor cow. I think they'd make a good couple, though,' Lucy insisted, chewing on her pen. 'They both look like vacant arseholes – like attracts like and all that. He can buy her a designer vagina. Just be grateful he doesn't want to buy you one.'

She's right, of course, but the whole thing just leaves me feeling uneasy. What if he lets it slip that we were briefly intimate? What if she gets all weird about it and stabs me in my sleep? If things progress between them, I might have to have a word. I'll be seeing this woman five days a week when school begins, the last thing I need is her giving me evils for having seen Frank's knob first.

Tuesday July 11th

I got an email from Downtime today, only it wasn't from Jay. It was from some woman called Denise, a new manager, who politely declined any future advertising. Methinks that Jay got the sack and the new woman is wondering why on earth he'd spent so much on promos in a newspaper whose biggest advertiser is orthopaedic beds and Saga holidays. Damn, I'll have to find another sucker to take my space now. Some sales people thrive on this shit. To me, it's nothing but a massive ball-ache.

Wednesday July 12th

Oliver and I have been so busy recently that neither of us have looked at the suggestions that remain untouched in the sex jar. In fact, apart from a half-arsed morning attempt last week, we've barely touched each other. I texted Oliver to remedy this as soon as possible.

> I am hereby scheduling a shag. Meet me by the jar tonight after Molly goes to sleep. Message ends.

He responded:

> New phone. Who dis?

> Idiot.

I already had my hand in the jar when Oliver came into the room, closing the door quietly behind him.

'Isn't it my turn to pick?' he asked, watching me lift out a piece of paper. 'Although, the hand job one was a bit of a write-off . . .'

I shrugged. 'I don't care whose turn it is as long as I get laid.'

'You're so romantic.'

I unfolded the paper and smiled at the handwriting, handing it to Oliver who read it aloud.

'Missionary – slow, hard and deep . . . Phoebe, this is verging on *normal* sex. I'm disgusted.'

'But you have to follow my instructions,' I explained. 'You go at my pace, none of this thrusting willy-nilly.'

He nodded. 'My willy shall remain nilly-less. Now take your fucking clothes off.'

Thursday July 13th

FFS Henderson! Last night – I swear when you made me go balls-deep and just hold it there, I thought my entire body would explode. That was hot as fuck. You win this round. See you later x

I put my phone back in my pocket and smiled to myself, hoping the other people on the train wouldn't notice the last night's sex glow which radiated from every pore in my body.

Friday July 14th

Oliver and I watched *It Follows* in bed tonight which was clearly a mistake as now I can't sleep and I'm sitting bolt upright in bed while he's snoring away like nothing happened. Did he not see the same thing I did? I AM SCARED. I keep expecting to see a shadow under the door or someone walk past the window, despite the fact that we're on the first floor. Evil doesn't follow the rules of gravity, it doesn't need to; it just needs to MURDER MY FACE. Why do I do this to myself?

Saturday July 15th

I SURVIVED THE NIGHT!

I also only got four hours' sleep and had to be alert and coherent for Lucy and Hazel who arrived at lunchtime to discuss wedding plans. As usual, Lucy was panicking.

'He wants "Africa" by Toto for the first dance!' she exclaimed. 'Can you believe it? How the hell am I supposed to dance to that without looking like I was born in the seventies? No offence.'

'None taken,' I replied. 'Though, like you, that song came out in the eighties, so you're just as screwed as the rest of us.'

'It's a great song, though an odd choice for a first dance,' Hazel agreed, diplomatically. 'What did you have in mind?'

Lucy grinned. ' "Kiss" by Prince. Who wouldn't want to kick off their married life dancing to Prince? Kyle says it's not *unique* enough. Fucking hipster. What was your first dance, Hazel?'

'At which wedding?' she smirked. 'Let's see – for my first we danced to "Your Song" by Elton John. With Kevin, we chose "Real Love" by John Lennon.'

'I always forget you're a divorced woman,' Lucy remarked. 'I hope I'm as splendid as you are when I get divorced, which will be the day after the wedding if Kyle plays bloody "Africa". What would you have, Phoebe?'

Both sets of eyes fell on me.

'"Rasputin" by Boney M.'

I really didn't want to think about this because I wasn't getting married. I was dating a man who'd kissed someone else.

They continued to stare.

'Fine. Well, we had to think about songs recently for therapy and how they reflected our relationship . . . or something like that, I can't remember the logic. Anyway, I'd choose "Sweet Disposition" by The Temper Trap. There would be no discussion. It's perfect.'

I saw Lucy's eyes light up. 'OMG. I'd forgotten about that song. I'm going to suggest it to Kyle.'

'You should!' I replied, slightly miffed that she'd stolen the song I wanted to use when I never got married. 'As long as you get everyone up for the chorus. Or just me. Whatevs.'

I made some tea while we looked at dresses that Lucy had seen online, instantly dismissing anything bright pink and eventually agreeing to wear flower garlands in our hair to keep Kyle happy. Why does Kyle want us all to look like fairies? Doesn't matter, I'll rock that shit, regardless.

It looks like everything is coming together nicely. Hazel should do this full-time.

Tuesday July 18th

8 p.m. We're all organised for tomorrow with only one small *where the fuck are the passports?* incident late afternoon which was simply resolved by finding them. Surprisingly, Molly went to sleep quickly and Oliver is grabbing a shower now as

I write this. Taxi is booked, suitcases are by the door and I've set four alarms to make sure we don't all sleep in and miss the flight. Maybe I should set six alarms? Just in case . . .

Wednesday July 19th

3 a.m. We groggily got up and ready before making our way to Glasgow Airport for our 6 a.m. flight. Unsurprisingly, Molly was in good spirits because she's four and won't let something like lack of sleep interfere with her bouncing around plans. Check-in was painless enough with the majority of the queue behind us (all looking like cast members of *The Walking Dead* who'd had emergency spray tans the previous day), which left us to make our way through security before finding coffee and sugar to keep us upright.

'I am going to go on the biggest waterslide ever,' Molly announced, sipping her apple juice. 'I'm so *excciiitteeeddd*.'

'Your dad will have to go on the big slides with you, sweetie,' I reminded her, wishing she had a volume switch. 'And you'll be a bit wee for some of the massive ones.'

'Aren't you coming on, too, Mum?' she asked, ignoring my voice of reason. 'We could have a race.'

I used to love waterslides as a kid but as an adult they scare the shit out of me. I think it's a height thing. I don't want to plummet to my death from anything, let alone attached to an inflatable doughnut, thanks very much.

'Maybe the small ones,' I replied, hoping she'd change the subject soon. 'We'll see.' I felt like such a killjoy. I got up to collect some sweetener from a nearby table, noticing a woman in her twenties with a kid around the same age as

Molly. She had the determined yet fucking demented look of a single parent and I felt nothing but admiration. She wouldn't get a relaxing holiday – she'd get a week of being on constant stranger danger patrol, sunblock duty and being confined to her hotel room when her daughter decided to fall asleep. At least Oliver and I can take turns escaping for a bit of peace and quiet.

4 p.m. After a five-hour flight to Antalya, followed by a ninety-minute coach ride to the hotel and sixteen thousand 'we'll be there soon' reassurances for Molly, we made it. Hotel is gorgeous, right on the beach, and we can see the waterpark, outdoor stage and main pool from our balcony, which thankfully has an extra-high balcony guard to appease my already-ridiculous fear of falling to death. There's free water and snacks in the fridge, a wet room shower, a huge king-size bed and bunk beds that Molly has already claimed as her own. I think we chose well.

6 p.m. Back from the beach. It's so fucking hot. I didn't expect it to be this hot. Even my sweat is sweating. I helped Molly wash the sand out of every orifice before jumping into the shower after her and doing the same. This is why people sit on blankets on the beach.

7 p.m. All-inclusive buffet restaurants will be the reason I'm forced to buy two seats on the plane home. Food is amazing. Baklava is my spirit cake. The other guests seem to be mainly German, British and Russian, friendly enough but we're only on day one.

10 p.m. Molly and Oliver crashed out on the main bed leaving me to sip a really bad white wine on the balcony before bottom-bunking it with a stuffed cat toy named Pablo and a piece of baklava I didn't finish at dinner. I'm having a blast.

Thursday July 20th

8 a.m. We ate breakfast in the main restaurant, a large dining area with white table covers, really cool staff and food stations making omelettes and pancakes as well as a huge array of bread, cheese, olives, meats and the best honey I've had in my life. Man with Yorkshire accent at the next table complained repeatedly that his orange juice had bits in while his wife refused to touch 'that turkey bacon muck.' Molly had pancakes. All of them, I think.

9 a.m. Waterpark for three hours before lunch. Decided that I'd brave some slides with Molly and be a fucking adult about it. Realised I'd made a terrible mistake as I hurtled down a giant snake slide at warp speed, screaming uncontrollably. Luckily Oliver caught the whole thing on video, including my clumsy departure from the inflatable ring. Prick. I wasn't alone, though; it's heartening to hear so many different nationalities and languages all uniting in the same high-pitched terror shriek.

8 p.m. Kids' mini disco was fun. Molly participated enthusiastically, wiggling along to unknown classics such as 'Chocolate Choco Choco', 'A Ram Sam Sam', 'Veo Veo' and others I'm sure I'll be having night terrors about before the week is over. Oliver and I sat like proud parents who loved their child and were also off the hook for thirty minutes to drink beer and swear. We were only on our second day but already I was starting to burn while Oliver was getting a healthy glow.

'I swear my shoulders are melting,' I complained, pulling my shawl over them. 'Can you rub some of that aloe vera stuff on me when we get back to the room?'

'I'll rub anything you want when we get back to the room,' he said, glancing at my cleavage. 'That dress looks good on you. Really good.'

'Oliver Webb, are you trying to seduce me?'

Nodding, he took a swig of his beer. 'Like you wouldn't believe. I think it's the sun. The sun makes me want to fuck the shit out of you.'

'We're moving country.'

He moved in closer, pushing my hair behind my ear and whispering, 'Seriously. All I can think about right now is cumming deep in your—'

'Sorry to interrupt!'

We turned to see a woman standing in a pretty white summer dress with a flower in her hair. I felt my face turn as red as my shoulders. It was the single mum I'd seen with her kid in the airport.

'I hate to ask,' she continued, 'but my daughter Jodi is up dancing beside your little girl and I *really* have to use the bathroom . . .'

'Go for it,' I replied, watching her shuffle from foot to foot uncomfortably. 'If they finish before you're back, she can sit with us.'

'Oh God, thank you. I'll be two minutes, tops!'

We watched her bolt towards the main building, trying to stay out of view of her daughter who might panic if she happened to see her leave. These are things they don't warn you about before you have kids. That you might be forced to ask strangers for help in a foreign country or risk pissing yourself in public. Luckily Jodi was far too distracted by the other twenty kids with zero rhythm to notice that her mum had vanished from view.

A few moments later she returned, looking far less stressed, entirely grateful and carrying two of the beers we'd been drinking. 'You saved my life,' she gushed, placing the beers on the table. 'That was a close call.' She turned to go back to her table but Oliver insisted she sit with us, because fuck letting anyone spend their entire holiday alone.

It turned out that Lydia lived in Dennistoun, worked shifts in a nursing home and had been saving for a year to take Jodi on her first holiday. 'Her dad had leukaemia,' she informed us, waving at her daughter on the stage. 'He passed when she was five months.'

As I listened to her story, I gave Oliver's knee a little squeeze under the table. I wouldn't want to be doing any of this alone. Lydia couldn't have been any older than twenty-five. What a brave woman.

Molly and Jodi bounced back over to the table once the disco finished, grabbing bottles of water like two tiny ravers.

'Can I go to the kids' club tomorrow, Mum?' Molly asked. 'My best friend Jodi says you get to colour and there's ice cream for free. FOR FREE!'

I wish I could announce that someone was my best friend immediately upon meeting. 'Of course,' I agreed. 'I'll take you after breakfast.'

'I'll be taking Jodi anyway,' Lydia said. 'It's supervised but I like to sit nearby ... you know, just in case. Why don't I take them both and give you guys a couple of hours off? Least I could do.'

Before I had the chance to open my mouth, Oliver had accepted her kind invitation and arranged to meet them for breakfast. It didn't take a genius to work out why.

Friday July 21st

9 a.m. Had breakfast with Lydia and Jodi. Molly went to the kids' club.

10 a.m. Half a shag accomplished before housekeeping turned up to give us towels and water. Oliver nicked some cans of Coke when she wasn't looking. Rebel.

11 a.m. Rest of shag complete. Oliver grabbed my sunburned shoulders while he fucked me from behind and I threatened to cut his fingers off.

11.30 a.m. More aloe vera applied lightly to shoulders and Oliver kissed them to say sorry. Kissing led to second shag with no shoulder contact.

12 p.m. Had to stop sex to collect Molly from the kids' club. Arrange with Lydia to do this on alternate mornings so we all get a break. We get to shag, Lydia gets spa time. Now I also want spa time. Stolen cans of Coke useful for rolling on sunburn.

Sunday July 23rd

Today's highlights included:

- Random kid told Molly her sunglasses were stupid. Molly told kid her face was stupid.
- Saw a man touch and sniff some baklava before putting it back on the serving plate. I'm now done with baklava.
- I have three mosquito bites in various locations and I want to claw my own skin off.

We didn't see much of Lydia and Jodi after this morning's kids' club. I guess they wanted some alone time which is understandable. I don't know if I'd want to be hanging around with a couple who are nearly twice my age for the entire holiday.

Monday July 24th

Woke up in the middle of the night, convinced I'd left my straighteners on at home and that the flat would be burnt to the ground by the time we got back. The fucking things are in Turkey with me but there's still a little voice in my head that's unconvinced. I'm sure all women must be plagued by this.

Tuesday July 25th

As it's Jodi and Lydia's last full day, we all went to the spa together, taking advantage of the kid's package which included a chocolate facial and gentle body scrub. It wasn't cheap but as the hotel is in the middle of fucking nowhere we had little else to spend our Lira on.

Oliver went for a Turkish shave which I later learned involved hot towels, an extremely sharp straight-edge razor, hair singeing and threading. Afterwards he was completely smooth and completely traumatised.

'How the fuck do women do that threading thing on a regular basis? And he fucking burned my ear hair off with fire! I can still smell it. Never again.'

Wednesday July 26th

Oliver is getting ratty now.

'If I have to sit beside one more moron who's getting hammered on shitty beer in the morning in front of his kids, I'll fucking lose it. Seriously – go and play with your kid; build a fucking sandcastle. You're not on a stag weekend in Ibiza.'

Molly begged me to go on another slide which had a plug hole you disappeared into before whooshing out into the pool below, upside down. Initially I refused until I saw a woman in her eighties do it and felt like a prick for not being braver. I have to admit – it was fun. I went on it three times and redeemed myself for acting like such a fragile wreck on the snake slide.

Friday July 28th

We leave at some ungodly hour tomorrow morning so we spent the last day in the waterpark, making sure Molly got to ride as many slides as possible. She's pretty devastated to be leaving whereas I cannot wait to get the fuck home because:

1. I am sick of smelling like sun cream.
2. I am sick of everyone else smelling like sun cream.
3. Other people are annoying.
4. Being constantly harassed by staff to go to the spa when we have been to the spa is getting on my tits.

It's been a pretty successful holiday though, apart from my inevitable sunburn. Even Lucy tans better than me and she's a redhead. Still, I conquered my fear of falling off waterslides, had sex four times, let my skin go make-up free, watched my kid dance her little ass off, discovered baklava and saved a very nice woman from wetting herself on holiday. I'm a damn champion.

Sunday July 30th

I'm still finding sand in everything, despite having washed our holiday clothes twice. Fuck nature, it's ruining my washing machine.

It's a tad deflating to arrive home to grey skies and showers but my skin is grateful. Lucy popped over with some healing cream she swears by.

'I think it's used for burn victims or something. Burn victims and redheads. So how was the holiday?'

'Exhausting!' I admitted. 'I'm glad to be home. There are only so many kids' discos you can sit through before you lose your mind. It was nice to get away from everything, though. You know, I didn't think about Oliver or his stupid kissing colleague once while I was away. Maybe this is exactly what we needed. How are you anyway? I take it work still hasn't burned to the ground?'

'Sadly no,' she replied. 'Though that Sarah woman was back in seeing Frank for lunch. She sat in your chair, waiting for him. She's bold as brass, that one. I had to politely remind her that she didn't work here so would she please not do that.'

'I don't want her sweaty gym arse on my seat! I'm going to have to bleach it now,' I responded. 'Who the fuck does that? She's very strange.'

Monday July 31st

My baby is five today. FIVE! I've had the pleasure of gazing adoringly at that wee face for 1825 days but it's flown by and I'm feeling many feelings about this, goddammit. As much as I'm excited to see how she's blossoming, I'm also a bit sad that very soon she'll no longer be my baby and will leave home and then I'll be stuck looking at Oliver's big face until one of us dies.

However, I kept this to myself and rearranged my work schedule so I could have today free and work Wednesday, instead. Oliver also took it off – we wanted to make sure

Molly had a lovely day. It involved presents, a trip to the cinema to see *The Boss Baby*, dinner at Frankie and Benny's and finally a Just Dance tournament when we got home. Mum and Dad Skyped her this morning and transferred some money for her into my bank while Oliver's parents rang her from their landline because other forms of technology scare them.

When we finally got to bed, Oliver was pretty overwhelmed by the whole day.

'How the hell is she starting school next month? She was only born the other week.'

I laughed and pulled the covers over me. 'I know. I've been wondering the same all day. I think she had a good birthday, though. She loved the Pokémon stuff Megan sent her.'

Everything was silent for a moment until Oliver said softly, 'We made a good one. She's amazing.'

I nodded sleepily and turned off the light.

AUGUST

Thursday August 3rd

'So have you thought any more about coming to London at the end of the month?'

I'm really not sure which one of the NO responses I've given Frank so far is confusing him. I sat across the desk from him and sighed. 'I have no interest, Frank. Truly. Why are you persisting with this?'

Now he was sighing. 'Look, any of you could do the job, it's not remotely taxing. I'd just be happier bringing you to London. You're far more . . . well, fun.'

It didn't make sense. I do nothing but argue with the man. Kelly or Brian would be far more respectful and grateful for the opportunity. I suddenly had a creeping suspicion that Frank's idea of fun involved both of us being drunk in his hotel room. I bet that fucker hasn't been laid since his divorce; well, not unless Lord Wilson has dropped her drawbridge for him.

'I have no interest in being *fun* anymore, Frank,' I said coolly. 'I hope that clears the matter up. Please ask someone else.'

Damn . . . the look on his face. He looked almost hurt.

Sunday August 6th

The stage show Wicked is touring so I've told Molly I'll take her to see it, despite her protests that she doesn't even like the Wizard of Oz and witches are annoying. How is that possible? I'm starting to think she's adopted.

Mum has emailed dates she'll be here in October – three days here with us and then they're off to Arran for the rest of the week. I think the only reason I look forward to seeing my parents is because it doesn't happen very often. I feel terrible saying that but it's true. They've always preferred to live independently from me and the feeling is mutual.

I've also been thinking about Frank's reaction to me refusing the London trip. I think he's lonely and I'm sure that Lord Wilson is in the same position. Perhaps those two getting together would result in them getting the hell away from me . . .

Monday August 7th

'Did you hear, Phoebe?' Kelly shouted across the office as I walked in. 'Frank's asked me to go to London to discuss being assistant manager.'

The look on her face was a mixture of smugness, pride and bloodthirst. It was quite startling. Brian was just quietly shaking his head in disbelief.

'I hadn't heard,' I replied. 'Good for you! You must be very happy!'

She nodded. 'The substantial increase in salary will come

in very handy and yes, it'll be nice to finally get some respect around here.'

'Does that mean I'll have to talk shit about you behind your back, instead of to your face?' Brian asked. 'Cos that'll be a bummer to be honest. I'd prefer if my dislike for you wasn't hidden away.'

'When I'm assistant manager, I will rise above your pettiness,' she replied haughtily, peering into the small mirror on her desk. 'But until then, EFF OFF, you little rat-faced nuisance.'

He clutched his heart like she'd wounded him and I laughed. I don't particularly want their dynamic to change. I'll be sad when she reports him to HR and they are finally forced do something about it.

Monday August 14th

Molly is beyond excited about starting school on Wednesday. She's already had a little taster session with her old nursery – they all went for a morning, met her teacher, sampled the school dinners and generally got a feel for the place to make it less daunting on their first day. She's got a new everything – pencil case, crayons, lunchbox, water bottle, gym shoes and hair bobbles with cats on – but she isn't too impressed with the uniform. I made her try everything on earlier, to ensure it fitted properly.

'This shirt and tie is stupid,' she said, pulling at the collar with her finger. 'Why do they want to put everything tight around my neck? This is not comfy at all.'

It's a valid point. I'll teach her how to undo the top button and hide it with her tie later. She only has to deal with it for the next twelve years.

Despite having my mind on Molly all day, I still managed to find time to occasionally think about Oliver kissing Bethany. This is ridiculous. I can go for weeks and then BAM! the scenario starts to play out in my head – the look they shared before they kissed. The point where they both knew it was going to happen. Ugh, why am I torturing myself? It was a kiss – he didn't run off into the sunset with her.

Wednesday August 16th

9.35 a.m. I've just dropped Molly off for her first day at school and I'm a bit shell-shocked, to say the least. Oliver and I took her into her class, along with all the other parents who looked as nervous as we were, except for Sarah Ward-Wilson who almost mowed down the lollipop man in her 4x4 then parked in the disabled bay. *'Mornings are frantic, thank God for Pilates!'* I heard her say to a mum in a duffle coat. Duffle coat woman gave her a 'what a fucking bellend' look behind her back and carried on helping her kid settle in. Molly was a little champ, finding her seat quickly, utterly delighted that she was sitting beside Ruby. We all said our goodbyes and shuffled out of the classroom, leaving our little people behind to start their adventure. I need a cry. Or a gin. Fuck me, this is weird.

10.50 a.m. I've calmed down a little. Oliver called when he got into work and I had a bit of a blub, insisting that she's growing up too quickly and there must be something we can do to stop this. He doesn't have as much faith in time reversal as I do but he listened anyway.

'What if she misses me? What if she's horribly unhappy and the other kids are mean to her? What if—'

'She'll be fine, Phoebe. She's more prepared than you think. She's going to kick ass, trust me.'

I know I'm being overly anxious. Fucking hell, she's gone to school, not war. I need to get a grip.

3 p.m. I picked Molly up at the school gates and she zoomed down the playground eager to tell me about her first day, which involved singing, colouring, writing her name on her new books and how her new teacher Mrs Ali can play the piano 'super good'. I was utterly relieved that it went well and utterly exhausted by the whole event. Maybe when you have more children, this stuff becomes second nature? You just launch them into the playground, leave and trust that the teachers know what they're doing? I bet Sarah Ward-Wilson didn't spend the entire day being a fretful prick. I'm the worst. How do I learn to enjoy these milestones in her life? It's bullshit.

Thursday August 17th

I totally forgot Oliver is off to his Chicago office next week. Of course I'll miss him but it'll give me a chance to do my own thing for seven whole days! I'm sure he's looking forward to the break too – I'm aware that I'm not a fucking delight 100% of the time. I think I'll have Lucy and Hazel over for dinner one evening. I need my girlie fix.

Monday August 21st

Oliver left at 5 a.m. for his flight to Chicago and I couldn't get back to sleep so I watched *Broad City* in bed until it was time for Molly to get up for school. He doesn't travel for work as much as he used to but it still feels weird when he goes. Mainly because he's in charge of spiders. Exhausted, I still had to go into work and was forced to listen to Kelly go on about her forthcoming trip to London with Frank – the trip I'd turned down because being a manager here would be like admitting my life went very wrong somewhere. Maybe they'll offer her a better job down there . . .

Tuesday August 22nd

I didn't sleep well *again* last night. That's two nights in a row. For some reason my brain won't shut the fuck up. It's all 'HEY! REMEMBER THAT STUPID THING YOU DID WHEN YOU WERE FOURTEEN? LET'S REVISIT THAT' and 'HEY! WHAT IF BETHANY WORKS IN THE CHICAGO OFFICE NOW? WOULDN'T THAT BE A HOOT?!'

I just have too much in my head right now between Oliver's bullshit creeping back in, Molly starting school, Frank coming back. I need some quiet. Perhaps cutting back our sessions with Pam to once a month wasn't the best idea.

I'm going to download some sleep hypnosis mp3s and see if they help. Perhaps listening to someone else's voice will help drown out mine.

Wednesday August 23rd

I picked Molly up from school and she happily informed me that her new best friend is a boy called Adam because Adam enjoys playing with Monster High dolls as much as Molly does. I like the sound of Adam already. For dinner I made tuna pasta with sweetcorn and forced her to eat five pieces of broccoli at gunpoint. We read a book about a badger with a job and she fell asleep halfway through.

As I lay in my own bed, I realised that Oliver and I hadn't had sex since our holiday. Perhaps I'm sexually frustrated. I realise he's not physically here to do anything about it but we always have webcam.

Thursday August 24th

As Chicago is six hours behind the UK, I finally managed to get Oliver on video chat in his hotel at 2 a.m. so we could be long-distance perverts.

Having caught myself off-guard with my front-facing camera, I vowed to *never* hold the camera at that angle, ever again. I then propped it up on the table beside me in a far more flattering perspective, where I could also watch Oliver at the same time.

'I haven't slept properly for ages,' I moaned, watching him open a can of Sprite with one hand. 'I think I have your jet lag.'

'I've slept like a baby,' he replied. 'Truth is, I'm not even here for work, I just needed to be three thousand miles away from your snoring.'

'I'm too tired to reply to that.'

I made him give me a quick sweep of his hotel room, show-ing me the amazing view he had of an alleyway and the really creepy painting of an old house that hung above the bed. It looked like Amityville.

'If I never hear from you again, I'm going to make sure they check the windows in that painting. I guarantee they'll see your face staring back.'

'You're such a ghoul,' he replied, bouncing back on to the bed. 'Also, please take that fucking old t-shirt off. I thought this was supposed to be a dirty call. I need flesh, dammit!'

Ten seconds later my t-shirt was on the floor and I was lying back in bed, admiring the deceptively flattering angle I'd chosen. He started to unbutton his shirt, telling me where to start touching myself.

Oliver had no reason to keep noise down, grunting and moaning as loudly as he liked, while I, on the other hand, was one loud moan away from waking up Molly and ruin-ing the whole thing.

'I can't hear you,' he breathed. 'Fuck the video, I need to hear you moan, even if it's low. Put the phone to your ear.'

We finished that way, him getting off on my quiet gasps while I did the same as he told me all the things he wanted to do to me. It felt like we were doing something we shouldn't be – something illicit – and it was hot as hell. This is defin-itely one for future sex jar suggestions.

Friday August 25th

I was totally convinced someone had broken into the flat last night and with Oliver being away I decided to heroically confront the intruder, grabbing the first thing I could find, which was a hairbrush. I mean, really, what the fuck was I going to do with that?

'*Reports indicate that the intruder was found with a side parting.*'

Of course, there was no one there. I think my sleep deprivation is making me go a little bit nutty. I power-napped on the couch while Molly was at school, so now I've not only fucked my sleep pattern, I've knocked it up and will no doubt be forced to marry it.

I found some videos on YouTube designed to help with sleep but I could hear the guy smacking his lips as he talked and I'd rather never sleep again than have to endure that.

Saturday August 26th

Lucy, Hazel and Grace came over for dinner tonight, which meant I was in charge of cooking for five people. After much deliberation, I called Domino's and ordered pizza, because fuck spending my entire Saturday cooking for five people.

They arrived at half six; Lucy brought two bottles of fancy wine and Hazel brought some profiterole tower thing from Waitrose which had been badly knocked around in her car and now resembled a chocolate tumour.

After devouring dinner, the kids went to play in Molly's room, leaving the grown-ups to sip wine and discuss wedding dresses, something that Lucy was already fed up with (and to be honest, so were we).

'So we don't have a *theme* as such but I'll be going more Bohemian than Princess,' she stated, scrolling to a picture on her phone. 'I'm thinking something like this.'

Hazel and I looked at the photo and grinned. An ivory-coloured lacy wrap-around dress with long, flowing bell sleeves. It was perfect.

'You're going to look amazing,' Hazel said dreamily. 'A little garland in your hair, some simple make-up . . . you'll be stunning.'

I nodded in agreement. Lucy was going to wear the shit out of this dress. 'I envy you,' I said. 'I will never have a reason to wear something this beautiful. Have you thought about our dresses yet? Can we all wear these, like a girl group?'

She laughed. 'I'm thinking either lilac or mint green. Maybe long, side-split dresses . . . off the shoulder. Chiffon, maybe.'

Hazel was Googling as Lucy spoke, saving photos as she went, while I had the important job of opening another bottle of wine. We had this wedding shit nailed.

Later in the evening, I voiced my concerns that I was still a little hung-up on Oliver's kiss, even after our zillion therapy sessions and heart-to-heart talks.

'Is this it for the rest of my damn life?' I asked. 'Forgiving him but never being able to forget?'

'Have you really forgiven him?' Hazel asked, filling up my wine glass. 'Because it doesn't sound like you have. It sounds like you've just accepted it.'

'What's the difference? It happened. I'm powerless to change it and life goes on.'

'You're still angry,' Lucy interjected. 'Sure you've accepted it, but as you said, you're powerless. I think when you forgive someone, you take back some of the power. You haven't done that.'

'It's this bloody mystery woman,' I replied, throwing back my wine. 'Who the fuck is she? I don't know what she looks like, how old she is – nothing.'

'You want to know what was so special about her that made Oliver risk losing you?'

I nodded.

'Thing is, Phoebe, you'll never forgive him until you realise that this isn't about you. This was Oliver's misguided way of dealing with his own shit. You're both equally responsible for the relationship but only *he* is responsible for his actions.'

'Damn,' Lucy said, opening a can of Coke. 'That's some insightful shit right there.'

Hazel laughed. 'I had a good therapist. He made sense.'

'I'm going to call you Dr Phil.'

'Lucy, you're ruining the moment.'

'Good,' she replied. 'I'm sick of talking about men and relationships and problems and weddings. It's exhausting. We should just dance.'

'Dance?'

'Yes, Phoebe, dance. I'm sure therapy is very worthwhile but nothing is better for clearing the mind and soul than dancing.'

Without saying another word, she put YouTube on the television and found a 90s playlist. It didn't take long for the kids to come through and join us. I hope that when Molly grows up, she finds friends just like mine.

Sunday August 27th

I finally slept like a baby last night. Perhaps it was the wine or the pizza or just the good company that relaxed me enough. Maybe my brain just ran out of things to try and shame and torture me with.

Oliver is back tomorrow which is cool as Molly has missed him. I have too but not as much as she has. Apparently he does funny voices better when he reads to her. Mine all sound the same. This is clearly untrue. My Billy the Badger voice is a triumph.

Monday August 28th

With Frank and Kelly in London, the office was super quiet today. Brian hammered through his work in the morning which left time for him to arse around all afternoon. My day wasn't particularly productive but that's normal.

When I arrived home at six, Oliver had already picked Molly up from the childminder and they were playing Connect Four at the dining table. While Molly was obviously thrilled to see her dad, I can't say that I was quite so enthused. His presence can be confusing – as much as I despise what he did, I still fancy the arse off him. I'm confused by my ability to feel sad, annoyed and aroused by him at the same time. It's very frustrating. The sadness concerns me, though: what if it never goes away? Can I stay in a relationship that constantly weighs heavy on my heart? It's doubtful, and that grieves me most of all.

Tuesday August 29th

I saw Lord Wilson at the gates this morning, chatting loudly on her phone. I kept my head down, hoping she wouldn't spot me, but she did, yelling my name in the middle of the parents' car park.

'I was just talking about you,' she informed me, popping her phone into her handbag. 'Your boss says hello.' She giggled like a possessed doll.

'Frank? You were talking to Frank?'

'Oh yes!' she beamed. 'We've been chatting occasionally. He'll be asking me out to dinner any day now, I just know it.'

'Well, I'm glad that's working out for you,' I replied, doing my best to sound sincere. 'I'm sure you two will get along famously.'

'If you have any pointers you can give me, I'd appreciate it. He seems like quite a complex man.'

'Complex? Really?' I could feel my head tilt in confusion. Complex isn't the first C-word that springs to mind when describing Frank. 'I'm afraid I don't know Frank well enough to help you in that department,' I lied. The truth is I know him better than I'd like to; from his terrible taste in furniture to the splodgy-looking birthmark on his inner thigh.

She looked peeved that I wasn't being more useful. 'You look tired this morning,' she said, scrutinising my face. I frowned. Everyone knows that *you look tired* is actually code for *you look like dog shit*.

'You not getting the full eight hours?' she continued without any encouragement from me. 'I read somewhere that the less you sleep, the shorter your life will be. It's all about being the best version of yourself, Phoebe! Anyhoo, must dash. Spin class in fifteen.'

I watched as she strode back to her car, wondering why the real life harbinger of doom goes to the gym in a full face of make-up. The best version of myself? But what if the best version of myself is me doing lines of coke off 1980s James Spader's ass while driving my car the wrong way through traffic? She didn't think that through.

Wednesday August 30th

I called Pam to discuss whether it would be appropriate for me to see her individually while she was also seeing us as a couple for therapy. She said probably not and recommended I see a different therapist while Oliver and I are working together with her. I don't want to see a different therapist. I love her! I'd rather get a different boyfriend. I've arranged for us to go in and see her next month. I think we've made great progress since we first shuffled into her office but I'm still quite raw about what's come to light since we did. I know I have to discuss this with Oliver but sometimes I want to just rant alone without risking any hurt feelings.

Thursday August 31st

At work today, inappropriate conversations were rife. Brian was telling us in graphic detail about a woman he's dating who has one defunct nipple.

'I swear you could take a blow-torch to that thing and it won't respond. I've tried everything to make it hard.'

Kelly is looking for a new bikini waxer after the lady she uses 'literally ripped the skin off my labia'. She showed Lucy the photos – I refused to look.

And finally, to put the cherry on the top of this disturbing office sundae, Frank called me in to his office just before five o'clock to tell me that he'd finally asked out Sarah Ward-Wilson. WHY AM I BEING DRAGGED INTO THIS SHIT?

'You do realise that this is none of my business,' I told him. 'Sarah and I aren't close. Or even friends really.'

He smiled. 'Yes, you seem like an unlikely friend for her. Regardless, I just thought, since you introduced us, you might like to know our situation.'

An unlikely friend. How does he manage to make every word that comes out of his mouth seem insulting?

'I didn't introduce you! Well, not on purpose. Really, I honestly have no use for any of this information. Date whoever you want! I must be getting home.'

Ugh, he's so infuriating. I'm convinced there's a tiny part of him that thinks I might be jealous or something.

SEPTEMBER

Saturday September 2nd

Molly had her little friend Adam over to play this afternoon. I don't remember ever having boys over to play when I was her age, mainly because they were disgusting. They still kind of are. I was ironing in the kitchen when Oliver came in looking slightly concerned.

'Do you know where the screwdrivers are?'

'Hall cupboard, I think. Why?'

'I had a listen at Molly's door a second ago and I'm pretty sure I heard Molly say "Adam, just put your hand around it" so I'm going to take the door off the hinges.'

I laughed a little louder than I meant to. 'You're going to be a fucking nightmare when she starts dating.'

'Damn right, I am,' he agreed. 'If we had a porch, I'd be permanently posted there with my shotgun.'

Since Oliver got back from his trip, things have been relatively normal. We even slept together last night. But I still can't help wondering what exactly went on with him and Bethany. The less he tells me, the more I imagine, and it's not a healthy place to be. Sometimes I feel like he believes if he just soldiers on as normal, then I'll forget what happened. But it's having the opposite effect.

Monday September 4th

We have a session booked with Pam on Wednesday. From the way Oliver's behaving, I think he feels that everything is fine now – and it is to a certain extent – but the hurt still takes me by surprise every now and then. I want to be able to say, 'That happened. It felt shitty but life goes on,' but there's still a part of me that wonders what the fuck she had that was special enough to turn his head, even just for a moment. I'm aware that the answer might be as simple as 'a great body' or 'big stupid doe eyes' but what if it was more? What if she made him wonder why the hell he was with me?

Tuesday September 5th

'He's taking me for dinner tonight!' I heard a disembodied voice yell as I waved goodbye to Molly at the school gates. I spun around to see Sarah Ward-Wilson hanging out the driver's side of her car, which was spread over two parking spaces in case someone accidentally breathed near her beloved 4x4.

'That's nice,' I called back, walking slowly back towards my own car. 'Hope it goes well!'

'We're going to that new place on Royal Exchange Square,' she continued. 'At those prices, I expect it to be fabulous!'

I sniggered internally. Frank knows the owner. There's no way he's paying for anything other than the tip. Frank rarely pays for anything if he can throw a free advert their way.

I didn't want to keep this conversation going. I was late

for work but more importantly, I didn't care. I gave her a thumbs up and disappeared into the front seat of my car, just as she began arguing with a guy who noticed her shitty parking. God speed, foolish man.

Wednesday September 6th

'Honestly? Yes, I've had fleeting thoughts about Oliver's kiss ... and a dream ... and it throws me. Not because I'm scared he'll be tempted to do it again, but because the kick in the chest I feel when it hits me hasn't seemed to lessen any.'

Oliver began to rub his forehead as Pam listened. A lot was coming out in our session today, the first one we'd had since before our holiday.

'And did you talk to Oliver about this?' she asked.

'No, she didn't,' he responded on my behalf. I couldn't tell if he looked pissed off or hurt.

'I didn't see the point,' I replied. 'It was a dream. How can I ask Oliver to defend a dream?! That's not fair.'

'How did it make you feel?' she asked.

'Sore,' I replied. 'My heart felt sore.'

Oliver sighed. 'I will never not feel shitty about this. I don't know what else to say. But you should have talked to me. I need to know when you're not OK.'

'He's right,' Pam agreed. 'You're not trying to punish him. You're trying to process what happened, both individually and as a couple. Including him in the process can stop any resentment before it begins.'

Oliver turned to face me. 'You know it'll never happen again, right? You must believe that.'

'I do. I don't even think the dream was about that. It was about me. It made me feel unimportant . . . second best. It's a horrible place to be.'

He bowed his head a little.

'I'm not trying to shame you; I'm just telling you how I felt. Perhaps I don't feel as secure as I used to.'

I left Pam's office feeling both relieved and guilty. I don't want to keep rehashing this because I have no doubt that Oliver feels like a giant arsehole already – I want to move past this. But being able to get it off my chest helped tremendously.

Thursday September 7th

I'm feeling less negative today. I hate that I do this to myself. After my shitty, disastrous relationship with my ex Alex, you'd think I'd have learned not to be so hard on myself. Why do I expect the perfect happy ending? We're all just idiots, frantically rubbing our bits against other idiots in the hope that we'll spark enough to start a fire. But I never feel like that's enough. I find myself yearning for the big grand gesture to show me that out of all women, I am the best one. It's fucking ridiculous. We should all just be grateful that another human being finds us tolerable enough to not kill us on sight.

Friday September 8th

The soles of Molly's school shoes have already started talking so I took her into town to act outraged in the shoe shop until they issued replacements. On the way back I noticed the new Mexican restaurant Lucy had been talking about at work.

'Shall we go and meet your dad after work and take him for fajitas?' I asked Molly, who quickly agreed as long as she didn't have to eat the spicy ones. 'It's a lovely night, we could sit outside.'

We strolled towards his office, stopping to look in book-shops and to watch some terrible dancing buskers in silver trousers, who looked like they were doing it for a bet. When we reached Oliver's work, I stopped at the main door to call him and let him know we were downstairs intending to surprise him, but forgot that security wouldn't let us in because we didn't work there.

As I held the phone to my ear, I ushered Molly away from the smokers who had grouped together outside. 'Hey, handsome. There are two women out front who want to take you for dinner. Yes, you are incredibly lucky. OK, see you in five.'

I put the phone back in my bag and sat on a nearby wall with Molly, who was getting hungrier by the second.

As I casually looked around, I noticed a younger woman on my right, mid-twenties with fabulous hair, smoking and texting with her thumbs. I still can't fucking do that. I need to tap away with my middle finger because I'm old as fuck.

Soon Oliver appeared from the side door. I watched him walk towards us from the left, smiling and waving at Molly. And then he caught sight of something behind me that made his smile fade and his pace quicken. I turned to see the thumb-texter staring at Oliver and then at me, before quickly stubbing out her cigarette.

I didn't register what was going on until a random stranger stuck his head round the main door and put everything into place.

'Bethany, I know you're on your break but you're needed in the conference room.'

Bethany . . . BETHANY? Oh, you have got to be shitting me.

Sunday September 10th

It's fair to say things have been a little strained over the past couple of days.

After finding out that Oliver had lied about his little kissing partner not working there anymore, I lost the plot. Not in front of Molly, of course, we still went and ate Mexican food like a normal, happy family – just one where Mummy sent texts to Daddy throughout dinner telling him she was going to punch his fucking face off.

When we got home and Molly went to bed, we had the whisper fight to end all whisper fights.

'You had the cheek to have a go at me for still working with Frank when she was still working with you!'

'Because I knew you'd fucking overreact. Like you're doing now!'

'The look on her face! She knew who we were. I felt so fucking stupid. Standing there, waiting patiently for the man who probably finger-banged her in the office.'

'What? I didn't finger anything, it was—'

'Of course you did, I'm not stupid. You'd have been grabbing her tits and up her skirt like a shot. You think I don't know how you operate? It's your trademark move.'

'Like I don't fucking cringe knowing that you've had your boss's cock in your mouth? I'm fully aware of your moves, too. It makes me want to vomit.'

'Oh, fuck off.'

'You fuck off.'

That was at 10 p.m. on Saturday night. Neither of us has spoken a word to each other since unless Molly's been there.

Fuck.

Monday September 11th

'You guys really need to shag this out,' Lucy advised over lunch.

I put down my water and glared at her. 'Did you hear anything I just said? She still works there.'

'Oh, I heard and if you'll stop giving me evil looks, I'll explain what I mean.'

I retracted my eyeballs.

'Look, I understand why he didn't tell you she still worked there. I would have done the same thing. Knowing that wouldn't have made a bad situation any easier. And the fact that this seems to all be coming down to sex makes me think that you need to be having some of the angry kind.'

My retracted eyeballs started to roll.

'He's already mentioned he thinks about you fucking Frank, you obviously think that he's been finger-banging the twenty-something, and it's like you both have something to prove. I say punish the fuck out of each other and let me eat my tuna baguette in peace.'

Tuesday September 12th

By 8 p.m. tonight, I'd had enough. I waited until he'd read Molly a story and pulled him by the shirt into the bedroom.

'I'm so fucking angry with you. You haven't spoken to me in days, like this shit is my fault.'

He removed my hand from his shirt. 'Because you're being irrational. I want to talk about this, you want to accuse me of doing shit I didn't do. You fucked the man you work with and I'm supposed to be OK with that?'

'You're fucking jealous of a fling I had before we even got together! Are you that fucking insecure?' I was grabbing his shirt again. I didn't even realise it until he firmly removed my hand once more.

'You're the insecure one,' he replied. 'And stop fucking grabbing me! You're nuts.'

'I'm nuts? I'm not the one running around kissing women who – who … text with their THUMBS!'

'What?'

We stood there, inches apart, seething, neither of us backing down. Until I grabbed his shirt again, pulling it out of his trousers and moving quickly on to his belt. He pushed my hands away and hesitated for a moment before whispering, 'Fuck you'. He spun me around to face the wall, his hands frantically lifting up my skirt before tugging my underwear down so forcefully I felt it graze my skin. With his hand over my mouth, we had sex over my dressing table, hoping that Molly wouldn't wake up and force us to snap out of this, whatever this was. I watched him behind me in the mirror, almost hunched over me, every thrust deep and deliberate; he didn't take his eyes off me the entire time.

When we got to bed, I didn't kiss him goodnight or even cuddle him. I may have worked out some frustration but my anger was still raw. Still, there's no way he'll forget this. No office twit will ever shag him the way I can.

Thursday September 14th

'This can't be normal,' I said, panting as I lay on the floor. 'We've angry-fucked four times this week already. I have carpet burns.'

Oliver stood up and stretched. 'I feel like I've gone fifteen rounds with Conor McGregor. Even my arse cheeks hurt. You're going to put me in the hospital.'

'Here's hoping.'

'As much as I'm on board with this conflict resolution, are you really still that pissed with me?!'

I sat up and wiped my brow on the t-shirt he'd ripped off me earlier. 'Yes! You lied to me! She still fucking works there and—'

'I'm not going over this again,' he said, getting up. 'I feel like I'm banging my head off a brick wall. If we need to go back to therapy, fine, but for now, I'm done talking about it.'

'Good, because I'm fucking fed up hearing your lame excuses for being a lying prick.'

I pulled on my dressing gown and walked to the kitchen, cursing him under my breath.

When I returned to the bedroom, he'd left to sleep on the couch.

Friday September 15th

Today I had to stealthily avoid being stalked and confronted by serial bore Sarah Ward-Wilson in the car park. You can totally tell that there will come a point in her life where she'll round up her offspring and utter the words 'Kill for mommy'.

I also stepped on my iPod and now it's broken. I'm raging. I hate using my phone for music; it drains the battery too much. Goddammit. I'll just drop hints until someone buys me a new one.

Saturday September 16th

'We're going out tonight.'

'Lucy, it's half past eight in the morning. I'm still in bed. This is why we have text messaging.'

'You'd take too long to reply and then come up with an excuse to stay home and be dull.'

It's a valid point. 'And where exactly are we going?'

'I have no idea but I know that it will involve dancing. We're going dancing.'

I switched the phone to my other hand and sat up in bed. 'Lucy, I'm nearly forty. I am not going dancing!'

'Well, THAT'S the worst excuse I've ever heard.'

'But . . . that *thing* happens when you have kids,' I insisted. 'That mum dance disease. It happened to Hazel – she used to be down the Arches every weekend and now she dances side to side, clapping out of time.'

I could hear her laughing. 'We'll go somewhere age-appropriate – I have no desire to inadvertently get into a dance-off with a twenty-year-old. But I need this. YOU need this.'

I started to flashback to the many, many nights of clubbing Lucy and I had been involved in. The sheer fucking joy of it all – well, minus the idiot men we'd inevitably pull. But we had fun. So. much. fun.

'I do need this,' I conceded. 'Oliver and I are still fighting. I need a break. Fine – find somewhere that won't require arse implants for entry.'

'I fancy that new eighties bar. I'll meet you in town at eight tonight.'

'Make it nine,' I replied. 'I'm going to need time to iron my face.'

Sunday September 17th

When I was in my twenties, seeing anyone over my age in a club was pitiful. These oldies, clinging to their youth, unable to grow old gracefully – it was sad to watch. But last night, I was that older person and I finally got to tell that twenty-something in me to fuck right off. When you're twenty you don't realise that you will feel exactly the same about fun when you're forty. Or sixty, I'd imagine. Sure, different responsibilities mean you may have less time for it, but the need to go out with your mates and get lost in a song never leaves you.

By the time we got to the eighties bar, the crowd was a

mixture of ages, ranging from all the single ladies to all the Tena ladies and the men hoping to pull them. It wasn't perhaps as hip as we'd like but regardless we drank, we danced, and I still remembered all the words to 'Whip It' by Devo. Oh, and it turns out I still dance like a fucking legend. Result.

Wednesday September 20th

This morning, I took Molly to school and then went to see a morning showing of IT at the cinema. It was just me alone in the cinema with a cup of shitty coffee and the occasional jump scare for company. I loved it, even though I spent the whole time thinking that if Bill Skarsgård was inviting me down into the sewer, I wouldn't need much convincing. I'd be halfway into the drain before he could change his mind. I'm such a weirdo.

It felt weird not having Oliver with me. We'd both been excited about the film coming out but we're not even on speaking terms at the moment, except around Molly. God, I feel so sad even writing that.

Thursday September 21st

It's the autumn school holiday, which means no class for Molly until Tuesday and no work for me until next Thursday. I'm glad my birthday falls on a Sunday this year; it's bad enough that I have to age, without doing it in front of my work colleagues. Oliver reminded me that we'd booked an overnight in Aviemore tomorrow, some voucher deal he'd found online ages ago. Rather than cancel and Molly miss out, we've decided to go. They have an outdoor adventure playground, a pool, a spa and a room that I won't be in charge of tidying. Who knows, maybe a weekend away will ease some of the tension.

Saturday September 23rd

We arrived back from Aviemore about an hour ago and it went reasonably well – lots of outdoor walks and we took turns taking Molly swimming so the other could have some time to use the rest of the facilities. I got three new spots on my face from the sauna and Oliver pulled his hamstring on the treadmill because he hasn't been on a treadmill ever. We've gone from not speaking to being civilised, which is a relief but it's still strained.

Predictably, we got stuck in traffic on the way back. Had three polo mint races with Molly, played two games of I spy and sang the entire soundtrack from *The Little Mermaid*. Oliver does an excellent Ursula. He's such a dark horse.

It was good being away from the flat. Though we simply ignored our problems for two days rather than addressing them, at least we're talking again. My rage has diminished but now I just feel sad. I don't even feel like celebrating my birthday tomorrow.

Sunday September 24th

7.30 a.m. 'I cannot believe I'm thirty-nine. This is the last year of my thirties! I feel like I should do something big to commemorate this. Like skydive. Or get something pierced. Or murder.'

I pulled the covers up to my chin and lay there watching Oliver get dressed and listening to the rain battering off the window pane. He leaned over and kissed me on the forehead.

'Happy birthday! Even though you just articulated the need to murder.'

I smirked. 'A kiss on the head better not be my gift. Give me presents and I'll let you live. Big, expensive ones.'

'Tonight,' he promised, stepping into his work trousers; he'd been called in unexpectedly to deal with an emergency. 'All will be revealed tonight.'

I reluctantly got out of bed and went through to the kitchen to make Molly's breakfast. Thirty-fucking-nine. How did this happen?

When I got to the kitchen, sitting on the worktop was an unopened box of pastries, some orange juice, a single pink rose in a small glass vase and a handmade card from Molly propped up against it. She'd made me breakfast!

'MUM, DON'T GO IN THE KITCHEN!' she yelled from the bathroom. 'OK??'

I quickly left the scene and tiptoed into the living room. 'I'm watching *Peppa Pig* in the living room,' I replied. 'I'm nowhere near the kitchen. Daddy Pig's shirt turned pink, it's hilarious. Come and watch with me.'

I could hear her scrambling to flush the toilet and I yelled at her to wash her hands. Mainly because it's my duty as a mother but also because she'd be touching my damn pastries soon. I heard her and Oliver whispering as they clattered about in the kitchen and then my breakfast was brought to me by Molly on a Disney tray with Oliver following bearing coffee. It was perfect. Molly had a playdate later so I had the house to myself and birthday giftage to look forward to later. GO ME!

12 p.m. I had a really underwhelming birthday wank. It was one of those ones where I only did it out of boredom and because I was lying down anyway, so why not? I wonder if I'll get birthday sex later. Even old people deserve birthday sex.

1.30 p.m. Lucy called me and played 'Birthday Chick' down the phone to me, ignoring Kyle's requests for her to turn that 'noise' down at once.

'What you got planned then?' she asked. I could tell she was dancing along.

'Just a quiet one with my darling family,' I replied. 'This will be my last birthday. I refuse to get any older now.'

'I couldn't decide what to get you, so I've stuck a Debenhams gift card in your desk and you can get it on Thursday.'

'Do you think I should get fillers in my smile lines? They don't seem to be fucking off when I stop smiling.'

'No. Not until you're fifty. Then looking as weird as possible should be your only goal.'

3 p.m. Picked Molly up from her playdate where she threw her arms around me like I'd just returned from Iraq. I know that by Primary Four she'll be avoiding any public affection so

I'm making the most of this while it lasts. She also made a birthday crown because I am the damn birthday queen!

6 p.m. Oliver made a beautiful carbonara for dinner and even bought those little garlic dough ball things I eat too many of when given the chance. Molly gave me some new perfume and Oliver got me a new iPod to replace my broken one (hints dropped and received) and *Dead by Daylight* on the PS4 because I am a child. Apparently I have another gift that I'll get when Molly is in bed. It had better be battery operated.

9:46 p.m. 'She just fell asleep, bless her. I had to read her—'
  'THAT'S REALLY INTERESTING – PRESENTS!'
He stopped and smirked. 'That crown has gone to your head. Molly has created a monster. OK, fine – come with me.'

I jumped up from the couch and followed him through to our bedroom where he made me sit on the bed and close my eyes before he placed something into my hands. It was the sex jar with a piece of paper inside.

Confused, I paused for a moment. 'Sex isn't just for birthdays, Oliver. It's for life.'

'Just read it.'

I unscrewed the lid and pulled out the note. 'If this asks me to lick your—'

MARRY ME

I swear my heart dropped four feet into my shoes. I read the note again.

MARRY ME

I looked at Oliver, who had produced a ring while I was busy having a stroke.

'I love you,' he said earnestly. 'I love us. Let's fucking do this.'

In hindsight, my reaction probably wasn't what he expected, but in my defence, NONE OF THIS IS WHAT I FUCKING EXPECTED.

'Why?!'

He hesitated for a second, still clutching the ring. I couldn't even look at it. It made it too real. 'Why? Because of those reasons I just said.'

'But we're not that couple. We've never been into marriage! I mean, we basically *are* married but without the piece of paper.'

'Well, yes but—'

'YOU KISSED SOMEONE ELSE!'

And there it was. My inability to move the fuck on from this.

He nodded and put the ring back in his pocket.

'I'm trying to fix this. I really am,' he said quietly. 'I thought we were making progress. I thought this might help . . .'

'Is that what this is *really* about?' I replied. 'An attempt to move past what happened? A solution to fix my hurt feelings?'

He sighed. 'It was me asking you to be my wife. To show you that this is it for me. That I don't want anyone else and I never will.'

'Not kissing anyone else is a better alternative.'

'I give up. I fucking give up.'

We both sat in a crushing silence for what felt like forever. I stood up to leave but he grabbed my hand.

'Phoebe. Are we in trouble here?'

Hot tears started to pool in my eyes as he waited for my response. 'Honestly?' I replied. 'I don't know.'

Wednesday September 27th

I called Pam to see if she could fit me in this morning. Thankfully she was free at 11 a.m. She seemed surprised to see me sitting alone when she opened the door.

'Is Oliver on his way?'

'Nope,' I replied, taking a seat, 'just me today.'

She paused. 'I thought we discussed that I don't tend to see clients involved in couple's work individually . . .'

'I know, but . . . well, I'm here now and I need to talk. Please.'

She nodded hesitantly and sat across from me while I initially bawled my eyes out. I felt so stressed I could have vomited on her lovely purple couch but it passed.

I explained to her about Oliver's lie regarding his kissy bastard colleague, about how I'd tried to fuck the frustration out, about how one minute I'd be OK and the next wallowing in self-pity and lastly, about how he'd proposed for all the wrong reasons.

'What makes you think his reasons for proposing were wrong?' she asked, handing me yet another tissue.

'I feel like he was just trying to distract from what happened. I honestly think if he'd never made the mistake in the first place, he wouldn't feel so guilty he'd have to propose!'

'Ah, so you think he did it out of guilt or fear, instead of love?'

'Yes. Maybe. Oh, I don't know. I just know it was never something we planned. We'd never even spoken about it properly.'

She wrote something in her book before closing it over. 'It's interesting how you've reacted to this,' she began. 'For two people who've been together as long as you have – and I don't just mean physically – you seem to have lost all confidence in him surprisingly quickly. You assume the worst. I wonder if perhaps that's because you feel that's what you deserve.'

'I deserve? I don't understand.'

'You've tried to talk through this but you haven't really listened – if you had, you'd be more accepting of his mistakes. You've tried to work through jealousy by proving that you're more sexually capable and dominant than this woman you imagine is your competition.'

'Actually the sex thing was Lucy's idea—'

'And you think that his proposal is to appease you, because why on earth would someone want to marry you otherwise?'

Fucking hell, the truth stung like a bitch. She was absolutely right.

'What I'd suggest is that you decide whether you're actually able to hear and believe what Oliver tells you. Come from a place of love for this man rather than suspicion. If this isn't something you're capable of, you have to let him know. It'll be better in the long term for both of you.'

I left Pam's office with a lot to think about. I also decided never to take Lucy's advice when I'm vulnerable and she's more interested in eating her lunch.

Thursday September 28th

I told both Lucy and Hazel about Oliver's proposal. There's no way I could keep it from them. They're like sniffer dogs when I have a secret; they can smell it a mile off.

'Shame! We could have had a double wedding,' Lucy lamented, only half-kidding. 'But I understand why you said no. I think Oliver still has a lot of making up to do. And what if he does it again – though hopefully he won't – but then you're married and you have to explain to Molly why Auntie Lucy kicked her dad's penis off? No. It was the right move.'

Hazel, on the other hand, saw things a little differently.

'OH. EM. GEE. You should have snatched that ring out of the box! Honestly, Phoebe, he's going to fuck up constantly between now and death, it's no reason not to marry him. Just hope that he doesn't take the rejection too personally. Don't take his name, though – Phoebe Webb – too many Bs.'

Fuck you very much, ladies. That was zero help.

Friday September 29th

Tonight was tough. After Molly went to bed, Oliver and I agreed to sit down and talk. I could see the visible strain on his face as he mentally prepared himself for another possible argument neither of us wanted.

'I'm finding it very hard to trust you,' I admitted. 'You say that it was just a kiss but I know how these things go . . . and

I know you. In order for me to truly deal with everything, I have to know everything.'

He shifted uncomfortably on the couch. 'I didn't sleep with her. That's the absolute God's honest truth.'

'OK.'

'But you're right . . . there was touching.'

I fucking knew it. I took a deep breath. 'Where?'

'Boobs mainly. Also her arse.'

'Did she touch you?'

He cleared his throat. 'I don't understand how this—'

'Oliver . . .'

'She put her hands down my trousers, alright,' he replied. 'She touched my cock, I touched her boobs and her arse OVER her clothes. I swear that was it.'

Finally I believed him, but the thought of them all grabby hands and heavy breathing made my bottom lip wobble.

'See, you're upset now,' he said, gesturing to my imminent sobbing. 'I didn't want that.'

'I am,' I admitted, desperately trying to hold it together. 'But you don't get to pick and choose how I feel about this.' I dabbed my eyes with the sleeve of my jumper. 'How can you see her every day at work and not think about what happened? Do you still fancy her?'

He gave a little laugh. 'Phoebe, I could ask you exactly the same question. How do you see Frank every day and not replay what happened? That cuts me up inside, just as much as me working with Beth does with you.'

'Oh, it's *Beth* now . . .'

'Really?'

'Look, the difference is I didn't cheat on you with Frank

and yes, I do occasionally think about what happened between us, but certainly not in a nostalgic way.' I shuddered. 'Frank reminds me of my life before this one; a life I wasn't happy with. If you think I'm secretly yearning to revisit that, you're wrong. Oliver, I have done nothing to make you distrust me.'

He sighed. 'I know. I just can't shake the thought that one day you'll wake up and realise that you could do better.'

I couldn't help but laugh. 'With Frank?'

'With anyone. Bottom line, Phoebe, I didn't mess around with Bethany because I was bored with us. I messed around because I was bored with me.'

Now his lip was starting to wobble. I placed my hand on his knee, the same hand I'd considered giving him a dead leg with a few minutes ago.

'I do want to marry you,' he said with a sniff. 'I know my timing was shitty but I do. I love you.'

'I love you too,' I replied. 'But yeah. Shitty timing. I'd rather just focus on us as we are now.'

Our talk lasted well into the wee hours of the morning but I got through it. We got through it.

Saturday September 30th

The day after a huge, heart-wrenching talk where tears and snot still reside on the faces of those involved, one of two things normally happens: 1 – They give each other space. 2 – They are lovey-dovey as fuck. Oliver and I were the latter.

We made love in the morning (see – sickening), we fought

to make breakfast for each other, we took Molly to the park and gazed lovingly at her and each other and we snuggled on the couch, frequently touching each other like we were scared the other would disappear if left unchecked. To outsiders it would appear nauseating, but to me, it was glorious. I felt unreservedly wanted.

OCTOBER

Monday October 2nd

I gave Hazel a call from work to catch up but she was in bed with a sore throat, being looked after by Kevin. Apparently they're finally taking her tonsils out soon. I don't even know what the fuck tonsils do, but it's a shame regardless.

After her bath, Molly told me that a boy in her class, Jason, had told her that if she ever wanted to know anything about *Minecraft*, she was to ask him because he had it on PS4 and he was an expert. 'Pfft. Just cos he's a boy he thinks he knows more than me? Mum, he has no idea who he's dealing with. I am going to destroy his world.'

I know she meant his *Minecraft* world but it was still an excellent, Bond-villain-worthy threat.

Wednesday October 4th

Hazel's had her tonsils out. I popped round to see her at lunchtime with a litre of ice cream and some flowers. She was propped up on the couch looking glum.

'Aww! How are you feeling?' I asked. Stupid question really, but it was better than saying 'Damn! You look like shit'.

'Swollen,' she replied. 'And sore. I wasn't too bad yesterday but today my throat feels like it's on fire. The painkillers are awesome, though. I get a good hour of flying high before they start to wear off.'

'Lucy sends her love,' I informed her, handing Kevin the ice cream and flowers. 'And said to let you know that she's paid the deposit on the DJ.'

Hazel smiled. 'She's done well with the whole wedding caper. I think I had three breakdowns while organising my first, AND I threw up into a potted plant an hour before I walked down the aisle. She'll be a champ.'

'You've been a star, though,' I added. 'Honestly, if I had to help her, it would be a disaster . . . Hazel?'

Hazel had fallen asleep. I quietly crept out with a whispered goodbye to Kevin, making a mental note to ask Hazel to save me some of those painkillers. She can be Lucy's wedding planner and also my dealer. It's not a huge ask.

Thursday October 5th

'Sri Lanka. Two whole weeks of sun, beaches and whatever the hell else they do over there. It's our wedding gift from Kyle's parents – much fancier than the honeymoon in Tenerife we were budgeting for.'

I casually started Googling 'visit Sri Lanka'. 'Bloody hell, Lucy, it looks gorgeous. Ooh, you can go on a proper safari. I've always wanted to do that – not like the muddy, bleak safari park we took Molly to last year. Every animal looked utterly depressed that it had ended up in Scotland – even the native ones.'

She opened the link I'd emailed and beamed. 'This is going to be amazing. However, I now need to tell Frank that I'm taking two weeks off. He's going to kill my buzz, isn't he?'

'Of course he will,' I replied. 'But you can handle him. Or you could just change the work calendar and when he notices, insist he already approved it. Then cry until he gives up.'

She laughed. 'Oh, that's much more amusing. Imma do that.'

Tuesday October 10th

I've hardly seen Hazel since she had her tonsils out but she texted me today, informing me that she was feeling much better, mainly thanks to my ice cream.

When I arrived at work, Kelly was in a foul mood as she hadn't been successful in her application to become Queen of Classified Advertising or whatever the job role was.

'They don't even tell you why,' she snarled, slamming her desk drawer shut. 'Sexism, I'd imagine.'

'But Dorothy was our boss for years,' Brian informed her, a grin appearing on his face. Lucy threw him a look that could have killed. A look that said *Don't be THAT fucking guy. She's upset. Just leave it.* He seemed to get the message, leaving at once to make coffee.

'Between us,' Lucy began, walking over to Kelly's desk, '– and you didn't hear this from me – there's talk of budget cuts again and you know how Scotland and Manchester always get hit first. I think there's just no extra money right now; in fact, I'm almost certain.'

This seemed to perk Kelly up a little. 'Really? Yes, that would make more sense. Thanks, Lucy.'

From: Phoebe Henderson
To: Lucy Jacobs
Subject: That was nice

Nice job on the well-meaning bullshit. You did a good thing and Jesus will reward you.

From: Lucy Jacobs
To: Phoebe Henderson
Subject: Re: That was nice

It wasn't bullshit – well, not the budget-cut stuff. I saw a memo on the system. Chances of us getting any new staff, pay rises and even bonuses are slim.

HAPPY TUESDAY!

Oh brilliant. Just brilliant.

Friday October 13th

Right, the schools are off on holiday again. Who the fuck do I complain to? Oliver has taken some time off to watch Molly and we've paid Maggie a big wad of cash to have her on the days where we both have to work. Sometimes I think having a job where I work from home would be ideal, but in reality Molly would constantly interrupt me, I'd work stupid hours and spend most of them in my dressing gown.

To make matters worse, my parents will be here next Thursday and I'll have to entertain them so they don't think I'm a terrible, ungrateful child.

Monday October 16th

From: Lucy Jacobs
To: Phoebe Henderson
Subject: Halloween

I don't know whether to have a Halloween party or not this year. It's close to the wedding now and one party full of ghouls might be enough.

From: Phoebe Henderson
To: Lucy Jacobs
Subject: Re: Halloween

I don't know why you're consulting me on this, considering you ban children from attending and I've only been able to come to one in the last five years, you mean bastard.

I heard her snort from across the office.

From: Lucy Jacobs
To: Phoebe Henderson
Subject: Re: Halloween

Haha! If it wasn't for my Halloween party, you might not have let Oliver knock you up, remember? Just because you make children at my house doesn't mean I'll let you bring them to my fabulous adult party. Besides, Jenny Tyler tried to dook for apples using her tits last year. No child needs to be subjected to that, I'm doing you a favour.

Now I was the one who was snorting. Jenny Tyler was notorious for getting her tits out when pissed. I heard that she did it on the night bus last year and got fined £200. Pretty certain she's done it since though. She's not well.

From: Phoebe Henderson
To: Lucy Jacobs
Subject: Re: Halloween

I think you could do without the stress of a party this year but it's up to you. I shall be taking Molly to her school Halloween disco if you'd rather join me at that?

From: Lucy Jacobs
To: Phoebe Henderson
Subject: Re: Halloween

Are you serious? Halloween is supposed to be fun, shithead. Stop trying to involve me in your life.

Wednesday October 18th

This month's session with Pam was far less snot-covered and stressful than the previous. There's part of me that wonders if she just rolls her eyes whenever she sees our name in her appointment schedule. I would. I'd be all 'OH GOD NOT THESE WHINY LITTLE BITCHES' but then again, I'm not getting paid to listen to us.

For once she wasn't scribbling away in her book. She just listened and nodded and at one point sneezed so unexpectedly it scared the shit out of me.

'I think you've both made excellent progress,' she said. 'You came here to address the sexual concerns in your relationship, but it became apparent that they were hiding deeper issues for both of you, which may never have surfaced had you not taken the first step. You have the tools now to work with each other on your issues. Talking is obviously crucial but don't forget the power of music. And written communication – whether it's using your jar or just leaving a simple note that acknowledges the other person.'

And with that, we left Pam's office and headed home, feeling smug that we hadn't given up on this. Or on us.

Thursday October 19th

My parents arrived at quarter past eleven this morning, exhausted from their flight and ecstatic to see Molly, who to be fair was only interested in hearing about their dog.

It doesn't matter how old I get, my parents coming to see me will always make me anxious. It's like I'm presenting my life for them to judge. I judge myself enough for everyone.

I was really pleased to see them though – they were both looking well. Mum had dyed her hair a darker blonde that suited her and while the remainder of my dad's hair was either still in Canada or had exited his head for good, he looked cheerful and tanned. As I hugged him it struck me that he always smelled like Mum's perfume. Not in the sense that he'd been spraying himself with it, more like she lingered on him. It was comforting.

'We've booked you into the Travelodge up the road from us,' I informed them as we helped wheel their cases to the car. 'I've also arranged for your rental car to be dropped off there tomorrow.'

'When did you become so organised?' Dad laughed, giving me a squeeze. 'Molly, I remember when your mum used to be such a scatterbrain. She was hopeless.'

Why do grandparents do that? Why do they try to make you sound like a dick in front of your kids? I'm quite capable of doing that myself, thanks all the same. Besides, if I was an idiot child, it's their fault.

We dropped them at their hotel and I arranged to see them for dinner later, then headed back to the flat where Oliver was busy not meeting my parents at the airport.

'They get in OK?' he asked, sprawled out on the couch.

I nodded. 'We'll eat with them later. They look good!'

'Remember Molly has Adam's birthday party tomorrow. I'll take her – let you catch up.'

Oliver hates kids' birthday parties but would offer to disembowel himself with a spoon if it meant wriggling out of a family get-together. Still, he had to endure dinner later so I let it slide.

We'd booked a table at a Thai place for six but we still had to wait fifteen minutes for our table, which gave me time to down a double Jack and Coke. When we finally got seated, they handed over presents they'd brought for Molly, including a framed picture of their dog, a plush beaver toy and a couple of t-shirts she feigned interest in before returning to the beaver, which admittedly was pretty cool. It had a hat on.

My parents talked incessantly throughout dinner; they are a very endearing couple to be around. They enjoy listening to each other and they both get overly involved – finishing each other's sentences and finding the other hilarious. I was also thankful that they were mindful of the content of their stories while Molly was around. The same rules don't apply when it's just me. I think Molly sees Oliver's parents as grandparents – they're grey and old and they creak a lot when they move – whereas mine are just slightly older weird people who happen to be my parents.

Friday October 20th

Day Two of the Henderson Invasion. I took Mum and Dad out for lunch while Oliver took Molly to her friend's birthday party. The restaurant was reasonably quiet for a wet, Friday afternoon; I'd have expected chaos during the school holidays.

Dad excused himself to give his neighbour a quick call to check on Daphne while Mum and I were seated at a window table overlooking the pissing wet beer garden.

'Any recommendations?' Mum asked, taking a menu from the holder.

'I always have the fish and chips here,' I replied. 'It's great.'

Mum mumbled something about sustainable haddock and continued browsing the menu, shortly followed by Dad who announced that Daphne was 'well' and *in good spirits*.

What the fuck did he expect to hear? That she'd taken ill with fever and was walking the moors until his return? She's a dog.

'So what's been going on with you then, darling?' Mum asked, rearranging her napkin. 'Any news for us?'

My parents and I have always been able to discuss

anything and they're generally more forthcoming than I am when it comes to matters of love or sex, often making me cringe with their frankness and willingness to say, unfiltered, whatever the fuck comes into their head at any given moment. But I took a leap of faith.

'Oliver proposed,' I informed them, casually looking through the menu. 'On my birthday.' I didn't look up from my menu but was aware of them glancing at each other. 'I said no.'

'Why on earth would you say no?' Mum enquired. 'Oh, let me guess. It's an archaic institution and it's nothing more than a piece of paper.'

Now my eyes were on her. 'Well . . . yes!' I replied. 'We've been together for years. We have Molly. There's no reason to change anything.'

Dad laughed. 'Honestly, Phoebe, I've never met anyone so frightened of change. What are you afraid of? Why would you want everything to stay the same for the rest of your life? That's not living, it's just existing.'

Before I had a chance to reply, the waiter came to take our order, hovering impatiently while Mum tried to decide whether she wanted potatoes or chips with her steak. In a feeble attempt to prove I wasn't scared of change, I ditched my plans for fish and chips and impulsively ordered the Chicken Schnitzel instead. That'll show them.

Once the waiter had scurried off with our order, I picked up the conversation again, stubbornly trying to get my 'if it ain't broke, don't fix it' point across, but a little voice in my head repeatedly reminded me that he was right. I do fear change. I've been in a job I've hated for years. I've had the same hairstyle for as long as I can remember. Apart from the list I created a few years ago to change my sex life, I haven't actively gone out of my way to rock whichever boat I might be in at the time. My life exists around routine, which I thought was for Molly's sake, but now I realise might actually be more for mine.

'He kissed someone else,' I confessed, not caring that the waiter was now placing a dreadful-looking chicken dish in front of me. 'A while ago. We've worked – *are working* – through it . . .'

Mum placed her hand on mine. 'Hmm . . . a kiss isn't the worst thing he could have done.'

'What? He felt her up too!'

She shrugged. 'Oh darling. We all get bored. I've been married to your dad for four hundred years – sometimes these things happen . . .'

I wasn't sure whether she was trying to tell me that she had personal experience in this area or that they'd each been tempted to stray, but she didn't volunteer any further information and I wasn't about to ask for it. I've heard enough about their sex life over the years without bringing new players into it.

'Just be careful you don't dismiss something that could offer even a brief moment of joy. Grab your happiness, darling,' Mum continued. 'It's those moments that make all the bullshit we endure worth it.'

As we sat in silence eating our lunch, it struck me that my parents are actually more level-headed than I give them credit for. Despite their cavalier attitude to life, when I need them to be my parents, they come through for me.

'And you know, if you're struggling to keep the flame alive, you should try Viagra, Phoebe. Your dad and I have been experimenting with it. It's strong stuff.'

Oh fuck right off.

Saturday October 21st

Molly and I were there to say goodbye to my parents this morning as they jumped into their hire car and headed for the ferry to take them to Arran. As usual, Dad asked me if I needed any money and I told him no, but I knew he'd have already transferred some into my online account. I'm nearly forty – he shouldn't be doing that, but will there ever come a point where I stop making sure Molly isn't skint if I can afford to help? Probably not.

I've never understood these really wealthy celebrities who insist they're not leaving their fortunes to their children because their children should make their own money. I don't get that. I would give every penny to Molly if it made her life easier. I guess when you're rich it's easier to be an asshole.

I used to wonder whether I was a disappointment to my parents. I wasn't incredibly successful, wealthy, married and or in any way remarkable. However, after becoming a parent I realised that all they wanted was for me to be happy. And I'm almost there.

Monday October 23rd

October school break is over and if I'm right, the next holiday won't be until Christmas which is encouraging. Also,

HOW THE FUCK IS CHRISTMAS THE NEXT HOLIDAY? I want my year back. Once I have it back I can waste it in a far more organised manner.

Tuesday October 24th

Sarah Ward-Wilson was in my office at lunchtime, waiting for Frank to finish some calls so they could go and stuff their faces, which Frank would expense as a 'client lunch' because he's cheap as fuck. I made sure I was busy on calls to avoid having to listen to her brag or bitch. I did hear her have a conversation about Shellac nails with Kelly that sounded riveting.

Lucy's decided not to do a rehearsal before the wedding as she wants it to be as laid back and informal as possible and also *'It's a total waste of money. I know how to walk a few steps towards someone and then eat a dinner, for God's sake'*.

She handed out invitations to the evening reception to Kelly, Brian and Frank. Pretty little cards with silver writing which sparkled if the light caught them at the right angle. I already had mine as I was a full-day guest/chief bridesmaid, which basically makes me the most important person who ever lived.

Wednesday October 25th

This morning as I dropped Molly off at nursery, I overheard Lord Wilson talking on the phone. I didn't mean to eavesdrop, but, well, I was walking behind her with my ears and she had no idea.

'Well it's still early days but I quite like him. Divorced. Loaded. A bit desperate. You know the type. Works with one of the mums I know from school . . . Pardon? Oh, not friends as such, she's just the only one who hasn't aged horribly after forty.'

My ears started to burn. I AM NOT FORTY.

'Anyway, we'll see how it goes,' she continued, her leather boots causing puddle splashback as she clomped towards her car. 'If anything, it shows that cheating bastard that I'm not hanging around. Just a shame I couldn't have found someone a bit younger. Still, it's nothing serious; he's a useful distraction while I work out my next move.'

I arrived at my car first and watched her walk further up the road, still unaware that I'd overheard her conversation. Climbing into my car, my first instinct was to tell Frank what she'd said. That she'd called him desperate. That he was only a distraction. I felt strangely protective towards him and it was completely disconcerting. However, by the time I arrived at work, I'd come to the decision not to get involved. It was none of my business. For all I knew, Frank could also be using her. When it comes to women, he's not the most earnest man I've ever met. Sarah though – she's really wound me up. What a shifty little fucker she is.

Friday October 27th

Molly insisted on reading her own book tonight and I have to say, I felt rather deflated. Like I'm surplus to requirements now. I wonder if other mothers are totally up their own arse like I am, or whether they just feel happy that they've raised a literate child. Sometimes it feels like every little milestone in Molly's life is a reminder that things will continue to change whether I want them to or not and it happens so quickly.

Sunday October 29th

Tonight Molly informed us that she is the only one in her class and possibly the world who doesn't have a brother or sister to play with. So we've been advised to get her a sibling as soon as possible.

'What do you think about having more kids?' Oliver asked as we lay in bed. 'Seriously, not just for Molly to push around.'

'I haven't thought about it,' I replied. 'Maybe that's quite telling.'

'I have,' he replied. 'Fleeting thoughts. Like whether we'd get another good one or an evil little nosepicker who kills small animals.'

I laughed. 'Aww, our very own serial killer, honey. Nah, I can't imagine having any more. I don't think I want to be doing nappies and sleepless nights in my forties. I'd quite like to have the house to myself again one day. Which means you'll have to move out too.'

He chuckled. 'Do you remember we used to just call her "the baby" because we'd be too tired to remember her name at 3 a.m.?'

'Oliver Webb, stop being broody this instant!'

'Why?'

'Because I'd have to go through childbirth again and that's

not happening,' I replied. 'I'm a fucking coward. I have no idea how women with multiple children do it. Being in labour for fourteen hours before they finally gave me the good drugs was the worst fucking agony I've ever felt in my life. Not to mention the indignity of having to sit and bounce on a giant inflatable ball in the name of pain management.'

Oliver turned to face me, resting his head on his arm. 'What does it actually feel like? Pain-wise?'

I thought for a moment. 'It's hard to describe accurately, but you know when something is so fucking sore, you might vomit? Well, if vaginas could vomit, it would happen then. It genuinely feels like your entire arse region is falling out.'

'Jesus.'

'So yeah. Molly might just have to get a goldfish instead. You too.'

Tuesday October 31st

'You haven't let me know what you want to do for your hen night,' I reminded Lucy. She stopped typing on her keyboard and looked up at me. I waited with bated breath for her list of hedonistic demands, convinced there would be at least one illegal activity involved.

'Oh. Right. God, I hadn't even thought about it. We could go for dinner, I guess?'

'Dinner? Wait . . . is that code for strippers or something? I'm confused.'

'No, it's code for dinner. Actual food. We could get some Chinese – I quite fancy trying that new place near the golf course. Have a couple of drinks, maybe?'

'Who are you and what have you done with my friend?'

She chuckled. 'Honestly, I can't be bothered being hungover, I'm too busy. Just something low key is fine by me.'

'Um ... right then,' I mumbled, starting to walk away. Then I stopped. I wasn't buying it. I swung around and returned to my spot in front of her PC.

'So, is this like one of those things where you pretend you're not bothered, but really you're expecting Grey Goose, half a kilo of cocaine, a guest list and a live sex show?'

'No, but I know now what to plan for your funeral. Thanks.'

I left again and went back to my desk, still puzzled at Lucy's desire for zero debauchery on her hen night. Lucy's coffee breaks are more exhilarating than this plan.

I texted Hazel.

Lucy wants to go for a meal on her hen night. It's the End of Days. Save yourself.

Her reply came swiftly.

A meal? Is that code for strippers?

See? Even Hazel gets it. I finally accepted defeat and booked a table for three on Friday night.

Molly's Halloween disco was held in the gym hall from 6.30 p.m. – 7.30 p.m. and as I'd stupidly volunteered to chaperone, I had to endure Sarah Ward-Wilson, head of the parents' committee, girlfriend of my boss, two-faced telephone-conversation-haver and all round bore bag. Now that I had absolute proof she was a nasty creature, I wanted as little to do with her as possible.

Molly had dressed as a cat (no surprise) and made me also cattify my face for the occasion, which was fine, but of course Lord Wilson turned up as Maleficent, in full fucking costume and make-up. Honestly, there's getting into the spirit of things and then there's just being an absolute try-hard.

I grabbed one of the apple-juice boxes that were stacked high on a trestle table and made my way through the costumed kids towards a free seat at the edge of the hall, hoping to sit and watch Molly have fun in peace. No such luck. I had barely sat down before I was spotted.

'I hear we're going to be wedding chums,' Sarah announced, plonking herself down beside me. 'I have this gorgeous little Moschino dress that's been looking for a place to show itself off. What will you be wearing?'

Your skin as a mask.

'Sorry? What wedding?'

It took me a second to realise she meant Lucy's, then to piece together how on earth she could be attending, but then it dawned on me: Frank would have been invited to the reception with a plus one. Brilliant.

'A bridesmaid dress,' I replied. 'I'm the chief bridesmaid.'

She laughed so loudly, people turned to look!

'What's so funny?!'

She put a hand up, instructing me to wait until she'd finished laughing. Only she wasn't even laughing – it was all fake.

'Oh, it's nothing. Nothing at all,' she finally replied.

'No. Carry on.' I wasn't letting this go.

'Aren't you a little old to be a bridesmaid? No offence, but it's a little strange seeing someone in their forties wearing a dress that should be on a much younger woman.'

I'd had enough. 'Seriously?! You're sitting there dressed as a Disney character and you have the cheek to try and make *me* feel stupid? What the hell is wrong with you? I swear to God, you say one more word and you and your Moschino dress will be going fucking nowhere.'

She looked embarrassed but not beaten. 'My my. I thought Frank was exaggerating when he said you were overly sensitive but apparently not.'

'Oh, Frank knows exactly where my sensitive spots are, sweetheart. Maybe he'll tell you about that one day too.'

I grabbed my juice box from the table and stood up. 'And I'm not in my forties, I'm thirty-nine. This is what thirty-nine looks like when you haven't frozen your face into oblivion, you old trout. Oh, and next time you call someone desperate and a useful distraction, make sure their friend isn't listening behind you.'

As I left she remained quiet, but I could tell she was angry because for the first time in the three years I'd known her, Sarah Ward-Wilson had a frown line.

I spent the remainder of the hour in my car, fuming with her but mainly with myself for letting my secret about Frank slip. He's going to think I did this on purpose.

NOVEMBER

Friday November 3rd

Oliver's doing Movember. This man grows hair like a fucking yeti so I reckon it'll take him two weeks tops to look like Groucho Marx. It's also officially winter now despite it being November. Seasons mean nothing in Scotland. There was a faint shimmer of ice on the pavements when I picked Molly up from nursery and everyone on Facebook has put their heating on. Still, tonight was Lucy's hen night and I wasn't going to let anything spoil it, not even hypothermia.

Still not convinced that we weren't going to end up in a nightclub or prison, I wore my favourite little black dress and killer heels. I slipped some flat shoes into my bag to soothe any sore dancing feet (or in case we needed to flee from the police). Lucy it seemed was steadfast in her meal plan, though, turning up in jeans and a plain red top, face au natural.

Despite the fact The Jasmine Gardens was miles from anywhere, it was a decent restaurant and not as overpriced as the city centre eateries I'd suggested in my bid to lure Lucy out of the suburbs.

'What's Kyle doing tonight?' Hazel asked, looking around at the half-empty restaurant. 'God, this place is quiet.'

'It's quiet because all the fun people are in bars, drinking heavily,' I responded glumly.

'Kyle's out with his friends,' Lucy replied, making a face at me. 'I think they went to The Butterfly and the Pig. He'll be out for hours.'

Even though the waitress who'd been eyeballing us since we walked in hadn't seen us pick up a menu, she still marched over to take our food order. Luckily, I knew what I wanted and that was *time to look at the menu, Sharon*.

'Can you give us a few more minutes?' Hazel asked the impatient server. 'And do you have a wine list?'

'Nope.'

I liked her.

'OK, a bottle of house white is fine. Just whatever, as long as it's not chardonnay.'

When the wine came, we all predictably ordered the same dish we always ordered and raised a glass to Lucy who was already hogging the prawn crackers.

'To Lucy! I hope you and Kyle have a wonderful life together,' Hazel said sincerely. 'We love you loads.'

'Hear, hear,' I seconded. 'May your life be filled with laughter, sex and the desire to babysit for me as often as possible.'

I saw Lucy's bottom lip begin to quiver. 'Oh Jesus, I was kidding! You don't have to babysit.'

'It's not that,' she said, in between wobbles. 'I'm just feeling a little overwhelmed.'

'About the wedding?'

'I don't know,' she admitted. I passed her a napkin to blow her nose. 'It's just, I've spent so long being in charge of my life. What if I can't relinquish that control? I used to go on holiday alone. I used to disappear for weekends without having to inform anyone! I like my own space! I'm scared I'm going to stop being this whole person and just become half of a couple, or worse. That I'll just be this impossible person to live with and Kyle will fuck off and find someone more wife-like.'

Hazel placed her hand on Lucy's arm. 'You'll find a balance. Don't forget that Kyle wants to marry you because of these things. I think he'd find it unnerving if you suddenly stopped being this independent woman he fell in love with.'

'A *wife*, though,' she mumbled. 'It's just so fucking old-fashioned.'

Hazel laughed. 'It's whatever you make it. Stop worrying. I've managed it twice without disappearing back to the fifties.'

Lucy steeled herself and raised her glass, motioning for us to do the same. 'Promise me, ladies, that this won't change. That regardless of how many husbands or children come along – we will always make time for each other.'

'Agreed,' I replied. Hazel looked like she was going to cry now.

Lucy wiped her nose and grinned. 'And promise you'll forget that I suggested going for a Chinese on my hen night when we have dancing and shots available to us. One of you better have some lippy and mascara I can use; we're fucking out of here.'

'Bill, please!' Hazel yelled as I downed my wine and called a cab into town. In a little over a week my best mate would be married, but tonight she belonged to us.

Sunday November 5th

Bonfire Night! Despite the fact it was baltic, we all went to Glasgow Green to see the massive firework display they'd put on. I feel like I'm getting the whole parenting thing right when I do stuff like this. It gives me a sense of calm.

When we got there it was packed with bobble hats and gloved hands holding sparklers as far as the eye could see and Molly got one of those overpriced spinning things that lights up and then breaks by the time you get home. Hazel, Kevin and Grace also attended but we decided just to have our own family time. Just me, Oliver, Molly and several thousands of pounds' worth of dangerous explosives, surrounded by strangers. It was splendid.

Monday November 6th

Oliver's Movember tash is coming along nicely and when I say nicely, I mean he's already starting to look like a sex offender and it's disturbing me. That man can grow facial hair at an alarming rate.

After my little outburst on Halloween, I was expecting Frank to haul me into his office to ask why the hell I'd let slip about us to Sarah, but he didn't say a word. Not even an awkward glance or underhand comment. There's no way she's mentioned it to him. She's obviously scared I'll tell him about her bitchy phone conversation.

Wednesday November 8th

I found another note in the sex jar this morning and I felt a little pang of guilt, given that the last one was a proposal I'd turned down. I haven't been near the jar since. Still, Oliver had obviously left it out for me to read so I obliged.

You might want to shower first.

It didn't take me long to put two and two together. I had bacterial vaginitis a few years back and Oliver commented on the smell while he was going down on me. Now I'm paranoid and prefer to shower before he puts his face anywhere near my foof. Oliver thinks I'm neurotic and I absolutely agree.

I scrunched up the note and threw it in the bin before sending Oliver a quick text.

> I will be thinking about this all day now. Nicely played, you complete shit.

By the time Oliver put Molly to bed, I was already in the shower shaving my bits and by the time he was finished with me, I was back in the shower again, while he stripped the soaking wet sheets off the bed. God, he's talented. Maybe the moustache could stay.

Thursday November 9th

Tonight I walked around for three hours in my bridesmaid's shoes to make sure they were broken in before the big day. Lucy is now regretting not having a rehearsal in case she walks out of time to the music and looks like a prick. So now I'm also worried about this and have been practising slow walking up the hall in high heels and pissing off the neighbours below us.

Friday November 10th

Despite my ninja moves, Sarah Ward-Wilson spotted me in the school car park this morning, pulling up alongside me in her unnecessarily large car. I prepared myself for battle.

'I'd like to apologise if I came across as being mean-spirited at the Halloween disco,' she said, turning off her engine. 'I realise that my sense of humour can be misread at times.'

'OK ...' I replied, waiting for her to yell PSYCHE! and drive her damn Monster Truck over the top of my car. But she seemed sincere.

'And I realise you said what you said out of anger. The easiest way to rile up another woman is to imply that you have intimate knowledge of her boyfriend. I didn't believe for a moment it was true ... well, because you're not Frank's type.'

'You're absolutely right, Sarah. I said what I said to wind you up – I'm absolutely not Frank's type.'

'I knew it.'

'But what you said about Frank was out of order,' I continued. 'Really disingenuous.'

She rolled her eyes. 'Look, the bottom line is, I intend to see a lot more of Frank, so I think it's probably a good idea that we put this behind us and—'

'And please don't tell Frank what I heard you say?' Her motives here were so transparent.

Finally she dropped her pretence. 'He wouldn't believe you anyway, dear,' she replied.

I smiled. It was pointless arguing. This woman was beyond reproach and I was bored. 'You know, you're probably right. Just like you were right about your sense of humour being shite.'

'What? Hang on, I never—'

'See you at the wedding!'

I drove off before she had the chance to respond. What a conniving, wholly unhappy woman she is.

Lucy is staying with Hazel tonight and we're all meeting at the hotel tomorrow to get ready. A woman called Sabine is coming to do our hair and makeup at 9 a.m. and it's our job to make sure Lucy has the best day ever. No pressure then.

Saturday November 11th

2.30 p.m. 'Oh God, my stomach hurts. I might be sick. I might poo myself! Fuck, what if I walk down the aisle shitting myself as I go! I *knew* wearing white was a bad idea. OhGodohGodohGod.'

Lucy had spent months panicking over her wedding and five minutes before the actual ceremony was no different. She stood in front of the full-length mirror, her hand rubbing her stomach over her striking ivory wrap wedding dress. She looked magnificent; like a cross between Florence Welch and Guinevere. I quickly straightened the small flower garland which nestled perfectly on her red curls and smoothed down her dress at the back while her eyes darted between me and Hazel, looking for reassurance.

'Just relax!' Hazel soothed, placing her hand in Lucy's. 'We've got you. There will be no shitting on my watch.'

I saw Lucy's shoulders visibly relax as she exhaled deeply. Taking one last look in the mirror, she said vehemently, 'Right. I'm ready. Here we go, bitches . . .'

3 p.m. We all stood behind the doors at the back of the room. Lucy had stopped panicking, all hair was perfect and no one had lipstick on their teeth. As soon as we heard 'I'm Kissing You' by Des'ree start to play, the doors would open and Hazel and I would start walking. But Des'ree doesn't start playing. The mellow piano chords were nowhere to be heard. What I heard was 'Hold My Hand' by Jess Glynne and what I saw was Lucy grinning.

'Lucy?'

'Change of plan, ladies. Now dance me down the aisle or lose me forever.'

Before we could respond, the doors swung open and Hazel and I were faced with over one hundred guests, all as bemused as we were. Just as I was about to tentatively shuffle forwards, Hazel threw her arms in the air and began leading the charge, so I followed suit. We owned that aisle like we were appearing on Soul Train and when Lucy appeared behind, out-dancing both of us, there wasn't a single person in that room who didn't join in. We danced that woman right down the aisle before entrusting our best mate to the only man we've ever truly approved of.

3.30 p.m. Kyle started crying during his vows. Lucy got dry mouth and her top lip stuck to her teeth and someone in the back of the hall had the loudest hiccups I've ever heard.

3.45 p.m. Lucy Jacobs was now officially Lucy Hamilton and my waterproof mascara was a lying piece of shit.

4.30 p.m. We hung around the function suite drinking champagne and eating canapés while the main area was set for dinner. The pale yellow room buzzed with the guests' excitement over the soft background music. I'm certain Lucy had said there were forty confirmed for the meal and at least one hundred for the evening reception, but looking around it seemed like everyone had shown up at once and 99% were fighting for first place in the Most Hideous Fascinator competition I was secretly judging. The woman with what looked like a lace seagull was currently in first place.

I caught sight of Oliver making his way back from the toilets, occasionally forced to stop and politely introduce himself to the many women who thrust their hands in front of him. He always did look good in a kilt but for some reason today he looked especially delicious. Maybe it was the romance in the air or the joyful feeling in my heart, but I felt like the luckiest woman alive.

6.30 p.m. Dinner was excellent. They'd decided to do a buffet with salmon, lamb and the most delicious mini lobster rolls I've ever had in my life. It was a smart move given that they chose to pay for the entire thing themselves – a full sit-down meal would have been a waste. It was all very informal and from the look on Kyle's mother's face, not quite what she'd hoped for. Kyle's family were quite something. And by 'quite something', I mean 'fucking abominable'. Given that Kyle loves nature and poetry and my best mate, I'd assumed they'd be equally laid back and gentle, but how wrong I was. The dad, James, is a cardiovascular specialist (he told me this five times) and his mum Diana is a dentist with a private clinic in Bearsden. They were loud, condescending and devoid of any discernible humour. From what I could make out over dinner, the rest of the Hamilton clan weren't much better – their chatter mainly focussing on money, their house renovations and whispers on how they'd have organised this wedding very differently. Lucy and Kyle handled it very well but intermittent glances my way from Lucy let me know she was very aware of their bullshit too. You could tell that these people weren't often all in the same place together and that they were definitely one whisky and water away from a punch up.

'Kevin's just off to pick up the girls,' Hazel informed me after they'd cut the cake. 'I've asked Rosie to make sure they're party ready!'

Hazel's niece Rosie had saved the day, agreeing to babysit both Molly and Grace to let us have the day with our friends. Molly had been so excited to come this evening, I feared she might burst.

7.15 p.m. The girls arrived. Molly looked adorable in her pink dress and Grace looked annoyed that she'd been made to wear a dress in the first place. Lucy and Kyle appeared a little later than planned, looking dishevelled. It was obvious they'd been shagging because it's Lucy. She'd shag at her own funeral. Also, Kelly and Brian turned up together. TOGETHER. At first I thought they'd just shared a cab but neither appeared to have brought a plus one. WHAT THE FUCK WAS GOING ON?

7.30 p.m. I just watched my best mate and her husband dance like fools to 'Kiss' by Prince. It was glorious. There was no attempt to be graceful during their first dance, it was balls to the wall, sexy moves from the first beat. Lucy looked so happy, I started crying – my mascara once again ruined – but I didn't care.

We all joined after the first chorus, even the Hamilton clan who by now were ten sheets to the wind but happy with it. Molly and Oliver performed some sweet moves they'd obviously been practising and Lucy, Hazel and I danced like we always did, like everyone was watching.

7.50 p.m. Kelly and Brian were deep in conversation. His hand brushed against hers and she touched his leg. PERVERTS.

8.45 p.m. I'd almost forgotten that Frank had been invited until I saw him stroll in with Sarah Ward-Wilson and her black, satin Moschino dress. Being in the best mood ever, I, Chief Bridesmaid Henderson, graciously said hello and welcomed them before returning to my seat at the table. I would have been happier if they hadn't followed me back and sat down but hey, *nothing* was going to spoil my day.

'She looks wonderful,' Frank said, waving over at Lucy. 'Really super.'

'She does,' Sarah chimed in. 'What a beautiful dress. It's very ... unusual. Frank, why don't I get us some drinks? You and Phoebe can catch up.'

Catch-up with what? I thought; we saw each other at work yesterday. I watched her walk towards the bar and turned to Frank, who was smiling at me. It was kind of creepy. Like a serial killer who knew where the bodies were buried and would never tell.

'What are you so happy about?' I asked, taking a sip of my lukewarm champagne. 'Did someone finally Pimp Your Ride?'

'I don't even know what that means,' he responded. 'But yes, I am happy and I have you to thank.'

'Me? Why? What did I do?'

'Well, without you, I'd never have met such a wonderful woman. She's really something, Phoebe. Between you and me, I think she might be *the one*.'

My heart sank. Not only was he was smitten with this woman, he was thanking me for making it all possible. Frank might not be my favourite person in the world, but I can't bear the thought of anyone being taken for a ride. However, a wedding was not the place to inform him that his girlfriend was an arsehole.

'Blimey, Frank,' I said. 'That escalated quickly. I thought you'd only had a couple of dates. She's still living with her husband. Aren't you jumping the gun a bit?'

'Seven dates to be exact,' he replied, taking off his suit jacket, 'and it's just a temporary arrangement between them. For God's sake, Phoebe, you sound like my mother.'

'No champers left, babe, this will have to do.'

Sarah sat down and placed some prosecco in front of him.

He inspected the glass and shrugged. 'It's fine. We can have something decent at my house, later.'

It was almost like they'd been made for each other in a lab. Perhaps this relationship had more merit than I gave it credit for.

'What's with the disposable cameras?' Frank asked, picking one up. 'How odd.'

'The guests are the photographers,' I replied. 'It's an excellent idea. There's loads of them kicking about. Lucy will get them developed after her honeymoon.'

'Seems silly,' Sarah piped up. 'Everyone has camera phones, why not just use them?'

I sighed. 'Because it's fun, Sarah. And it's easier to keep all of the photos in one place instead of having them emailed in dribs and drabs.'

And with that, Sarah picked up the camera. 'When in Rome,' she said, throwing her head back and taking a selfie of her and Frank. A fucking selfie.

Before I had the chance to address this, I saw Sarah's eyes light up and Frank's face suddenly turn pale.

'Oliver! How lovely to see you! I don't think I've seen you since the kids went into Primary School.'

I felt Oliver reach over my shoulder and grab some water. Damn, this was awkward. 'Nice to see you, Sarah,' he replied. 'And you, Frank.' His chest puffed out and his shoulders broadened. Oh God, he was peacocking. PLEASE KILL ME NOW.

Frank greeted him politely and put his arm around Sarah, almost using her like a human shield.

'Oliver, I must say, I'm quite fond of that moustache,' she commented. 'It makes you look very distinguished.'

Distinguished? It makes him look like a seventies footballer.

Out of the corner of my eye I saw Frank's hand creep up and touch his bare top lip. This was getting painful.

'Shall we dance?' I asked Oliver, my eyes telling him to get me the fuck out of here.

He winked. 'Lead the way.'

We slow-danced beside Kevin and Hazel while Molly, face full of wedding cake, tried on Lucy's garland and danced with Kyle. Oliver and I rarely get to dance and although it initially felt a bit silly, it also felt romantic. It felt old-fashioned. It felt like we were timeless. I felt like any moment I would tread on Oliver's toes and ruin everything.

'I think my work colleagues who hate each other have started shagging,' I said, my head motioning to where they were sitting. 'I did not see that coming. It's too weird.'

Oliver glanced over and smirked. 'Lucy just married a man who shops at Wholefoods. Nothing makes sense anymore.'

'I can't believe she's fucking married. I'm so happy for her.'

'Don't go getting all misty-eyed on me, Henderson. I don't think your mascara will cope a third time.'

'I'm not,' I lied, sniffing. 'I'm just glad her day went so well. She deserved it.'

10 p.m. Someone called Marjory punched a man called Angus and it all kicked off on the dance floor. I managed to avoid being knocked over in the fracas but Marjory accidently pushed Molly and sent her flying across the floor where she bumped her head. I then promptly knocked fuck out of Marjory.

11.25 p.m. The police decided not to take matters any further and Kyle's parents agreed to pay for any damages caused by the Henderson clan. Oliver had taken Molly home in a taxi and Lucy had wrapped some ice in a towel for my aching hand.

'I've never hit anyone in my life! I'm so sorry, Lucy, I saw red.'

She smiled. 'Phoebe, if I'd have been there, Marjory would have gotten more than a busted lip. She deserved it. No one touches our Molly. You're pretty much my hero right now.'

'Did you see Brian and Kelly? TOGETHER?'

She abruptly stopped tending to my wounds. 'What do you mean *together*? I thought they just shared a cab here.'

'I saw physical contact. And flirting. They were definitely sharing more than just a cab.'

'How the fuck am I supposed to relax on honeymoon, knowing that this is happening? You'd better do some serious snooping for me. I'm counting on you.'

When I arrived home at midnight, Molly was already in bed.

'Alright, slugger?' Oliver teased, grinning at me. 'Man, I've never seen someone go down so quickly. She was absolutely hammered, though.'

'Ugh, I'm mortified. Is Molly OK?'

'She's fine. She's fucking overjoyed that you hit that woman. Honestly. She thinks you're the coolest right now.'

I sank on to the couch. 'Oh God, she's going to tell her classmates that Mummy punched someone. I'll need to have a word with her tomorrow.'

Oliver put his arm around me and kissed my sore hand. 'You worry too much. I am also proud of you. You're like a fucking lioness protecting her cub. It was sexy as hell.'

I turned to look at him. 'Are you aroused by this?'

He shook his head. 'Not by this. By you.'

Marjory's face wasn't the only thing that got pounded that night.

Monday November 13th

With Lucy away to Sri Lanka for a fortnight, I already felt lost. Still, I had plenty of free time to secretly study and observe Kelly and Brian and discover whether there were actual romantic shenanigans taking place.

3.45 p.m. Brian made Kelly some tea. THIS NEVER HAPPENS. EVER.

I'm writing this shit down like a detective. I will solve this.

Tuesday November 14th

I could just *ask* Brian and Kelly what the hell is going on but they'd only deny anything and then they'd know I was on to them and be extra sneaky around me. I AM THE ONLY SNEAKY SNEAKER HERE. They have no idea I'm on to them.

4.59 p.m. Brian asked everyone what their plans were for tonight. When Kelly said she was having a friend over, he blushed and rubbed the back of his neck because HE IS CLEARLY THE FRIEND. I am going to make myself an evidence board.

Thursday November 16th

The plot thickens – today Kelly remarked that her love of fudge doughnuts was going to make her fat. Now, normally Brian would respond 'what do you mean, *make* you fat?' and then they'd have a massive row, but TODAY he said *'Don't be silly'*.

DON'T BE SILLY! I'm now convinced. They are doing it.

I sent Lucy a message to get her thoughts on this. I don't give a fuck if she's on her honeymoon, this is important.

Friday November 17th

Text from Lucy at 4 a.m.

OMG THEY ARE SO SHAGGING.

I feel validated in my efforts now.

Saturday November 18th

I received a WhatsApp from Lucy with a photo of her surrounded by mountains, sitting on top of an elephant with her face almost hidden by the floppiest pink sun hat I've ever seen. I laughed and sent her back a picture of the rain-soaked street below us, complete with an overflowing trash bag and dog shit.

Monday November 20th

Oliver decided to go and play footie tonight, his first game in ages. I like it when he goes out and does physical stuff that gets his adrenaline pumping. He's like a sex beast when he comes back. I wish I was more like that; when I do anything physically demanding, I'm ready for the bin.

Tuesday November 21st

Today on Shagging She Wrote, I saw Kelly pass Brian a note and I've spent far too long wondering what it said. My top three guesses are:

Call someone about a work thing.
Phoebe is watching us! LOL!
Are u my boyfriend? y/n

This is getting sad. Hurry up and come back, Lucy, I'm losing the plot.

Wednesday November 22nd

We had a quick parents' evening session at Molly's school tonight to go over how she's doing. Molly came with us, hanging out in the library with her friends while we headed to the main hall.

Her teacher, Mrs Ali, was a very animated woman who waved her arms around when she spoke, a massive mop of jet black hair bobbing in union with her arms.

'Molly is a wonderful child!' she exclaimed, picking Molly's file from the top of the pile. 'This really is going to be a short conversation.'

She began to read down her notes. 'Her reading proficiency is very advanced for her age and she's showing competency in all other areas of the curriculum. She's a very happy child and gets on well with her peers. I'll give you her work jotters to have a look at once we've finished here.'

Oliver and I sat together and looked through her work, giggling at the terrible drawings of us and the things she chose to write about in her news book.

My dad triped over his shoos and then my mum was laughing and he ate her biskit.

'YOU ate my damn KitKat. I knew it!'

'That kid is such a snitch.'

'If we ever fuck up big time, Mrs Ali is going to know about it.'

We collected Molly from the library, telling her what an excellent report she received. We treated her to ice cream on the way home as a reward for all her hard work. She was so proud of herself. 10/10 would do this again.

Thursday November 23rd

Oliver was looking particularly fine this morning. So fine, in fact, I decided to email him and wind him the fuck up. Just like the good old days.

From: Phoebe Henderson

To: Oliver Webb

Subject: Question

Did you put something in my coffee before you left this morning, because I have been on heat ever since. I really want
you to hear me cum. Please let me know when you're available for heavy breathing.

From: Oliver Webb

To: Phoebe Henderson

Subject: Re: Question

Of course you would tell me this when I'm about to head
into a meeting for the rest of the day, because nothing
screams professional like a man with a raging boner.

Can you hold out 'til I get home?

From: Phoebe Henderson

To: Oliver Webb

Subject: Re: Question

This doesn't suit my need for instant gratification but I guess
it'll have to do. Have a great day and please don't be distracted by the attached photo; they're only breasts.

From: Oliver Webb

To: Phoebe Henderson

Subject: Re: Question

Oh fuck you. I'm not opening anything else from you today. Otherwise I'm going to have to disappear into the toilets with this photo like the worst human ever. Now leave me alone.

From: Oliver Webb

To: Phoebe Henderson

Subject: Re: Question

I just noticed your knickers are pulled down around your thighs. You fucking shithead. I'm literally throbbing.

Ten minutes later he called me from inside a cubicle and we had phone sex. Damn, that turned me on.

Friday November 24th

Another photo from Lucy today, sunbathing on the edge of a pier with a drink in one hand, surrounded by the bluest sea I've ever seen in my life. I swear she must have filtered that shit, it was the colour of a raspberry slush puppy.

I started re-reading *The Handmaid's Tale* last night but Oliver distracted me by calling me Ofoliver and asking me if I wanted to play Scrabble. He's such a dick sometimes.

Monday November 27th

Thank God, Lucy is back. The office has been far too quiet and harmonious without her.

'I know I sent you a few pics while I was away but I've uploaded loads to my Instagram, if you want a look.' She smirked. 'I know how much you love Instagram ...'

'Oh I'll look through your photos, no problem, as long as you haven't hashtagged them with every word in the English dictionary.'

'Not *every* word. I'm not a monster. Oh, talking of photos, we got our wedding snaps developed. Some of them are amazing – I'll bring them round. But there does seem to be an awful lot of Frank and that bloody woman ... no one else, just them doing weird selfie pouts. I'm going to stick them up all over his office. Fucking losers.'

Tuesday November 28th

Oliver isn't well and when Oliver isn't well, the entire house must hear about it continuously, on a loop, twenty-four hours a day.

'How can you have the flu?' I asked, rushing to help Molly get ready. 'You got your flu shot at work last week!'

'I think that's what gave me the flu. Can you bring me some tea?'

'Yes. In a minute. I'm just sorting Molly out.'

I swear if that fucker gives me his diseases, I'll scream.

DECEMBER

Friday December 1st

Since Oliver's been sleeping so much during the day with his man-flu, he's now determined that no one else shall sleep at a normal hour.

'You still haven't told me what you want for Christmas.'

I turned on the bedside lamp and saw Oliver's eyes peering at me from over the duvet.

'Are you kidding me? Oliver, if you wake me up at five-thirty to ask me that, ever again, the answer will be "a gun".'

'No, seriously,' he insisted. 'What do you want? It's less than a month away.'

I sat up and rubbed my eyes, catching sight of myself in the wardrobe mirror. Holy crap. I looked like Young Einstein.

'I want a pony, Oliver. I want a pony called SHUT UP, WE'RE BARELY OUT OF FUCKING NOVEMBER,' I replied, my harsh whisper burning the back of my throat. 'And while we're on the subject, are you losing the porn star tash today? You look like a pervert. And not in a good way.'

He rolled over and plumped up his pillow. 'It was for charity, grumpy arse.'

'But no one sponsored you. You just wanted to be Tom Selleck.'

'I think you'll find that every man born before 1980 wants to be Tom Selleck. Anyway, why are you in such a bad mood?'

'Because I'm tired!' I replied. 'I'm tired and I'm frumpy! Look at the state of my hair. Actually, look at the state of YOUR hair.'

He pursed his lips together and turned off the lights. Moments later, I heard him whisper, 'A pony it is, then.'

Haha! HE'S SO ANNOYING.

Monday December 4th

Frank looked rather serious as he started the morning meeting and with good reason.

'I'm sorry to have to tell you that London has decided to close the Scottish office. I'm afraid the way the market is, our little contribution to the newspaper as a whole doesn't justify keeping us open.'

'Just us?' Brian asked, his face turning as pale as mine was. All I could think was, *Fuck. We're all unemployed.*

Frank shook his head. 'No, everyone from editorial to display. I'll be speaking with you all individually to discuss your redundancy packages, along with HR, but this will be your last week. Again, I'm very sorry.'

'But it's fucking Christmas!' Kelly exclaimed. While we had all turned pale, her face was bright red. 'They couldn't have picked a better time?! What are they offering? I mean, Jesus Christ, Frank.'

I felt sorry for Frank. This wasn't his fault. He cleared his throat and told Kelly he'd speak to her first.

We all left the conference room and returned to our desks; well, except Lucy who pulled up a chair and sat beside me.

'Oh fuck,' she said. 'So this is happening. We've just paid for that wedding. Oh fuck.'

I nodded in acknowledgment. 'I'm still paying for my child.'

She started to laugh. We both did because neither of us knew what the fuck else to do. Behind us we could hear Brian on the phone to a recruitment agency. He wasn't wasting a single moment, unlike those of us who were in mild hysterics.

'I'm trained for NOTHING,' I said, my face beginning to ache. 'What the hell am I going to do now? I'm nearly forty! Retrain as a plumber?'

Lucy abruptly stopped laughing. 'Wait. We're not going to be working together anymore. Oh God, we're going to have to go to interviews and pretend we take this shit seriously.'

Yep. After a decade working for *The Post* I was going to have to start all over again, doing the same shit with people that weren't Lucy. Suddenly it wasn't so funny.

Tuesday December 5th

After my meeting with Frank yesterday afternoon, I discussed everything with Oliver, who was a fucking champ.

'So I'll get a month's salary for every year I worked there. That should keep us going while I look for something else.'

'Shit,' he said, cuddling me. 'You OK?'

'I think so. It's just a bit of a shock. I wanted to leave there, of course, I just wanted to do it on my own terms. Kelly walked out yesterday, telling Frank if he expected her to lift another finger, he was sorely mistaken. I admire that.'

I lay down and rested my head on his lap while he stroked my hair. 'I could probably get another sales job but my heart is telling me that this redundancy is actually a kick up the arse to find out what else I'm capable of.'

'You could be right,' he agreed.

'But what if I'm not capable of anything else?'

He stopped stroking my hair. 'Seriously? You're the brightest, funniest person I know. You can do whatever you want. I earn enough to support us for the moment; we'll worry when we have to worry. At least take the rest of the month to slow down and think about your next move.'

I've never been a woman who needed saving but right now this man was offering himself up as my safety net. I clasped his hand tightly. 'I love you, Oliver. Thank you for not panicking, too.'

He smiled. 'Whatever happens, happens – good, bad – I'm here regardless.'

And at that moment I decided to listen to my mother for once. I was going to grab my happiness.

Friday December 8th

Today I left *The Post*, carrying a small box of stolen stationery and the elephant mug Lucy had brought me back from Sri Lanka. Only Lucy, Frank and I had turned up, with both Brian and Kelly vanishing earlier in the week for pastures new. I never did find out if they were shagging.

Once outside, I said my goodbyes to Frank while I waited for Lucy to lock up. When he wasn't hovering over my desk, he looked smaller.

'What are your plans now?' I asked him. 'Anything lined up?'

He shrugged. 'I'm fifty-one. Maybe I could retrain as a plumber?'

'Jesus, Frank, do you eavesdrop on EVERYONE?'

He laughed. 'I wasn't eavesdropping, you were just never very good at being quiet. Sarah will be here to pick me up soon. I've had to hand back the company car. She was very supportive when I told her my situation. Not many women would be.'

'You have a very low opinion of many women then,' I replied.

'Possibly,' he smirked. 'You know, I'm glad we got to work together again. Despite your annoying demeanour, I have a lot of time for you, Phoebe.'

'You complete me, Frank.'

'Oh fuck off.'

We had a brief hug then Lucy appeared and did the same, telling Frank to be good, like she was ET and he was a young Drew Barrymore. As we left him standing on the pavement waiting for his ride, I suddenly had the horrible feeling that Sarah Ward-Wilson wouldn't be picking him up any time soon. If ever.

Thursday December 14th

I got a call from Hazel this afternoon, while I was extremely busy watching Judge Judy repeats on YouTube. I love her – she hates people more than I do.

'So Kevin had an idea,' she said, excitedly.

'Amazing! Was it his first?'

'Shut up, smartass. Listen, we are renting a little farm-house over Christmas. It's just on the outskirts of Glasgow. We went there last year. It's very peaceful and very cosy.'

'OK . . .'

'And we feel shitty that our friends might have a crappier Christmas than we will. So why don't you all come?'

'All of us?' I counted quickly in my head. 'That's eight people. Is there enough room?'

'There should be. And if there isn't, we'll just improvise. Say you'll come, it'll be our gift to you.'

'That's so kind! But I'd hate to impose. Have you asked Lu—'

'Oh, she's already packing.'

'Haha! OK then. I'll talk to Oliver but it's a provisional FUCK YES.'

She whooped right into my ear. 'Oh God, it'll be just like our New Year get-together. Only with children. And less hard-core boozing. But still, YAY!'

I HAVE THE BEST FRIENDS EVER.

Friday December 15th

Of course Oliver agreed to going away for Christmas, he was just as thrilled about it as I was.

'But wait! That means we'll miss our neighbours' Christmas party,' he said sadly. 'You sure about this?'

'What? The party we hear every second of, even though we're never invited? You betcha.'

Oliver laughed. 'I hope this year they get arrested for their terrible taste in music. A man can only hear "Stay Another Day" so many times before he snaps.'

I sniggered. 'They've also been playing "7 Years" on a loop for months. That's the kind of motive no jury would convict.'

Molly, on the other hand, was concerned that Santa wouldn't know we've gone away and she'll wake up with no presents.

'I'll email him,' I reassured her. 'Give him the new address.'

'Santa has email?'

'Of course he does. He's very modern. I'm pretty sure he also has Instagram but it's on private.'

She bought it. I'm the best liar ever.

Sunday December 17th

I finished my book last night and now I am in need of new reading material, so I cornered Oliver in the kitchen, armed with a list of authors I love and which books of theirs I haven't read yet. Subtle, but I think he took the hint.

Friday December 22nd

Molly finished early today for her Christmas holidays, proudly carrying a small selection box that her teacher had given her. On the way home I stopped at the shop to buy dinner and we bumped into Sarah Ward-Wilson, struggling to keep her four children in check while she loaded up her car.

Of course, the moment she saw me, the fake smile appeared in a flash.

'Oh hello, Phoebe. I was so sorry to hear about you losing your job . . . and during the festive period. How awful.'

Who the fuck says *festive period*? Fuck off, Dickens.

'It's fine actually,' I replied, collecting my trolley. 'We're all heading off for Christmas anyway. We'll still have a wonderful time. How's Frank?'

She looked at her feet. 'Well, Frank and I – we had a lovely time but he just wasn't the man for me. And well, I have the kids to think of and—'

'You dumped him because he got made redundant. Didn't you?'

'NO! Not exactly. Look, we're selling the house and I can't be expected to support everyone on what my ex-husband gives me, now can I?'

'Ex-husband?'

She nodded. 'He's started divorce proceedings.'

I started to laugh. 'You stupid woman. You know how much Frank is worth, right? How much his father left him in the will?'

She looked confused. 'What will?'

'Oh. He didn't tell you? Smart move on his part.'

'Phoebe, what on earth are you talking about?' I could see her getting more anxious by the second.

'Let's just say that Frank didn't need to work. In fact, Frank doesn't need to work ever again. Big mistake, Sarah.'

I immediately saw her brain kick into action. How much was he worth? What should she say when she called him, telling him she'd been too hasty?

'And I'll be texting him shortly, telling him to expect your call. And to ignore it, you gold-digging little worm.'

I left her fuming beside her car while I took Molly inside.

'Is your boss really rich?' Molly asked me.

'No idea, sweetheart,' I replied, grabbing a bag of apples. 'I just made that up. But what I do know is that he's worth more than that horrible woman.'

Saturday December 23rd

We all met up this afternoon to make our holiday arrangements: who'd be driving who, who'd be bringing what and most importantly, how we'd sneak in the kids' Christmas presents unseen because Santa was definitely still a thing.

'Kyle and I will bring them in our car,' Lucy offered. 'They won't be seen there. Just bring them over to mine before we leave tomorrow.'

Hazel put a little tick beside the first item on her list. 'Great. Now, we'll need three days' worth of food. I think everyone should spend £50 max and that includes some cheap wine and beer. I already have the turkey, so someone else can bring the veg and dessert.'

'We'll do the pudding,' Oliver replied. 'Don't ask Phoebe to bring the veg, our New Year potatoes were repulsive.'

Oliver kept Molly busy while I carried her Christmas presents to the car later that evening, before picking up Grace's gifts from Hazel's and dropping them all off at Lucy's house. Kyle helped me transfer them to his car so I could sneak home before Molly started asking where I was.

We leave at lunchtime tomorrow. I'm so freakin' excited,

it's ridiculous. This year has been a hard one but somehow this makes it all disappear.

Sunday December 24th

2 p.m. After battling with the sat-nav, we were the last to arrive at the farmhouse, pulling up beside Hazel's people carrier. I caught sight of Kevin carrying some boxes into a side door and yelled to let everyone know we were here. We hadn't all been together like this for five whole years and I could hardly contain my excitement, which mainly seemed to be trying to escape through my bladder.

From the outside the house looked pretty unremarkable. It was a long, purpose-built, grey-brick bungalow sitting alone in a field with the main farmhouse about half a mile away in the distance, looking far more inviting than ours. However, inside it was like a Tardis. A vast kitchen area with dining table, three double en-suite bedrooms, a main bathroom, a living room with huge patio windows and a kid's room set up with a television, bean bags and bunkbeds. It was modern, clean and all ours for three whole days.

3 p.m. Bedrooms chosen and cases unpacked, we all sat down for coffee in the kitchen, remarking on how marvellous everything was and how clever Kevin was for finding this place. Oliver set up the PS4 for the kids. We were all so well-behaved. It wouldn't last.

11.45 p.m. We'd gone through three bottles of wine, two boxes of Pringles and some mint Matchmakers while we arranged everyone's presents under our makeshift Christmas tree (a coat stand with tinsel wrapped around). The kids were fast asleep in their bunkbeds as we all sat around finishing our wine and making each other laugh. Every single one of us wondered if we could get a quick shag in that night without everyone else hearing.

12.50 a.m. Lucy and Kyle failed. Spot the amateurs who don't have kids.

Monday December 25th

When Molly and Grace got up at stupid o'clock this morning, they found all their presents laid out in the living room and their shrieks of delight made us all crawl from our beds to join in.

Kevin Bluetoothed his Christmas playlist to the speaker while Hazel and I made tea and toast for those who had an appetite at six-thirty in the morning. As I waited for the bread to pop up, I looked outside into the still-dark morning; snow had been falling heavily overnight and lay perfectly untouched. It's remarkable how the sight of something so cold can make you feel so warm inside.

After the violent shredding inflicted upon the kids' presents, we all started opening our own. My gift to Oliver was a pair of sold-out tickets to see The Prodigy next year, some terrible musical socks and the *Peaky Blinders* box set. He bought me the new Mhairi McFarlane novel and a gorgeous leather bag (must thank Lucy). Attached to the bag was a tiny pony on a keyring.

'You got me a pony!'

He winked. 'What? Did you think I'd forget?'

'This is the best Christmas EVER.'

3 p.m. We're done eating. I don't think we will ever be able to eat again. I literally crawled from the table like a wounded soldier to the living room where I claimed my position on the couch and refused to move until Boxing Day.

4 p.m. Oliver found chocolate. Damn him. I ate it.

5.30 p.m. The girls decided to play *Minecraft* while the adults all remained in a bloated position, hoping for death or a second wind.

7 p.m. Since our gatherings would not be complete without dancing, we all took turns playing the DJ, choosing our favourite tunes. Who knew that Kevin was such a fan of Taylor Swift? Lucy even encouraged Kyle to put on 'Africa' by Toto, despite her hatred of the song.

'How can you hate this song?' Oliver asked. 'It's phenomenal.'

'EXACTLY!' Kyle exclaimed, high-fiving Oliver.

Those boys were bonding hard.

7.30 p.m. 'I would like to dedicate this next song to Phoebe, the love of my life. Well, until Molly came along, but she still ranks in my top two.'

I chuckled, while everyone else made *aww*ing sounds, as he chose the next song on Kevin's Spotify. The opening chords of 'Danger! High Voltage' began blaring out. He looked over and smiled at me. It was a smile that made me realise that the song he'd chosen all those months ago in Pam's office to describe how he felt about me hadn't changed. Despite everything, Oliver still felt the same. And as he pulled me in to dance with him, I realised that while he felt the same, something in me had changed.

All those years wasted, longing for romantic gestures and lightning bolts, waiting for the perfect moment – why the fuck did I assume they would happen *to* me? Why couldn't I be the one who made them happen? I AM THE HERO I NEED. The only grand gesture that mattered was the one I was about to make.

I pulled away from Oliver, announcing that I'd be right back, and made my way to the kitchen. What was I doing? How would I do this? If I was going to make a fool of myself, it had to be romantic. It had to be amazing.

It had to be eighties John Cusack holding a boombox outside a window amazing.

But this wasn't the eighties and I didn't own or have access to a boombox. What the fuck was I going to do? Sneak out and hold my Samsung phone above my head outside the patio windows? I'd die of fucking exposure before anyone knew I was even out there.

I needed it to be loud enough to make him investigate. I needed him to hear the song and to know why I was playing it. I needed his heart to skip a fucking beat, like he'd made mine do so many times before. I also needed to do this before someone wondered where I was.

I grabbed my car keys from the table and snuck out the

side door, wishing I'd chosen to do this in summer. My bare feet crunched into the snow as I sprinted over to the car, unlocking the doors as I ran. Fuck me, it was chilly, but my adrenalin had taken over. Starting the car, I plugged my iPod into the radio and quickly logged into Spotify; I put on 'Sweet Disposition', the song he knows defines how I feel about love. How I feel about him.

I rolled down all the windows and pressed play, letting the song drift out into the night. I was excited, I was scared and I was fucking freezing. I turned on the heaters and rubbed my arms, hoping he'd appear soon. But as the song played to an audience of me, I realised that the house's double glazing, combined with their music, meant that no one could hear a fucking thing outside. I didn't even have my phone to slyly alert Lucy to my whereabouts. This plan was going to shit.

So I did what any frustrated person in my situation would do: I put my foot on the gas. I had lost my damn mind. A foot's worth of snow meant that I didn't get very far but I wheel-spun impressively, flashing the lights on full-beam and honking the horn. In fact I didn't just honk the horn, I blasted that horn so loudly that I'm pretty sure I gave every animal on that farm a heart attack and I kept blasting until several faces appeared at the windows, wondering what the hell was going on.

As Oliver stepped out into the night, I slid the car to a halt and stopped the music, accidentally dropping my iPod under my seat. He peered into the driver's side.

'Phoebe? What the fuck are—'

'Wait,' I demanded, scrambling to pick up my music player. 'Just WAIT!!'

By this time, everyone had gathered outside and I was pretty sure that the owners of the house would be on their way. Oh fucking hell, why am I so shite at everything?

'Go back inside!' I yelled to everyone but no one moved. I could see Molly and Grace pointing at me from the kitchen window.

'Um, what is happening here?' I heard Lucy ask as again I insisted everyone go back indoors.

'I am trying to do a THING HERE,' I insisted, shooing them from the driver's window. 'Please. Just go back in.'

Confused, they all turned and made their way back inside. I knew that I had fucked this up royally but I could either carry on and look foolish and romantic or abandon the plan and look foolish and certifiable. There was no turning back. I pressed play on my song.

As the music began to play for the second time, it didn't take long for Oliver to come back outside, laughing as he crunched through the snow. I got out of the car to meet him.

'You and this song . . .' he said, grinning. 'What exactly is going on here, Henderson? Have you lost your mind?'

'I'm grabbing my damn happiness,' I replied firmly, watching everyone else pile out of the house again, including Molly. Oh God. My audience was now up to seven. Lucy yelled something about getting her coat and pissed off back inside. I took a deep breath.

'I fucking love you!' I announced loudly. Molly covered her ears. 'So very much. In fact, I think I've fallen in love with you all over again. I'm not making sense, I know, but this whole mess is my way of saying that the answer is *yes*, Oliver Webb. I will marry the shit out of you.'

I heard Hazel give a little muffled gasp.

Oliver rubbed his brow and took a step back from me.

'Hang on. So now you're saying yes? After saying no?'

'Yes. Exactly.' He wasn't moving any closer to me. I glanced over at Hazel who gently shrugged in confusion. I turned back to meet his gaze. 'Oliver?'

He bowed his head. 'Phoebe, this isn't right. It doesn't feel right. You turned me down, remember? God, why are you doing this now?'

'But I – I thought . . . I mean I hoped—'

'I haven't just been biding my time, waiting for you to change your mind, for fuck's sake! And now you do this in front of our friends? In front of our daughter?'

'Oliver, I was just—'

And then I noticed the smirk on his face.

'You're fucking with me, aren't you?'

'Yep.'

'Oh, God, Oliver!' I cried out, whacking him on the arm. 'You bastard! My heart! My poor heart! And my poor frozen feet!'

He took my face in his hands and kissed me gently before lifting me out of the snow. I heard Molly and Grace make *ewww* noises in the background.

'I would have waited forever for you to change your mind,' he said. 'There was no other option.'

'WHAT THE FUCK IS HAPPENING? I AM FREEZING!'

We both turned to see a pair of Lucy eyes glaring at us from behind a parka that was zipped up over her face. Bizarrely, I didn't feel the cold anymore.

Oliver started to carry me back towards the house. 'Nice

jacket, Lucy,' I said nonchalantly. 'Maybe you can wear it to our wedding.'

Even from behind that parka, Lucy's shriek could be heard for miles around.

Tuesday December 26th

We had to get the farmer to tow us out this afternoon after I'd managed to wedge our car in between two piles of hard snow. Embarrassing but totally worth it. Molly spent the entire journey home talking about being a flower girl and how excited she was to tell everyone at school. Oliver, however, was less than eager to tell his parents.

'I'm not telling them,' he said, pacing our bedroom floor. 'Not now . . . maybe never.'

'Oliver, you have to tell your parents we're engaged! If you don't, Molly will let it slip.'

He paused to consider this. 'It's fine. I'll pay her not to. She responds well to money.'

I grabbed his arm and pulled him back on to the bed with me. 'Oliver, you're overreacting. They'll be thrilled with the news.'

'You don't understand. Your parents were normal about it.'

'Normal?' I replied. 'They said "well done" and then told me that Daphne was pregnant. A dog stole my thunder. That's not normal.'

'Mine will be thrilled, sure. They'll be so thrilled they'll start planning shit the moment we tell them. Before we've even finished the phone call, they'll be inviting their friends and suggesting priests and chapels in Dublin. Then they'll get upset when they find out you haven't even been baptised!'

'But, I don't want to get married in a church!'

'Me neither. Let's just pack a bag and go to Gretna,' he suggested. 'Me, you and Molly.'

I laughed. 'Run away with me in twenty-nine days, after we've filled out our official forms and they've had time to process them.'

He grinned. 'You've already looked into this, I see.'

'Haha! For Lucy.'

'So we'll go to Vegas and get Elvis to marry us.'

'Not in a million years.'

'New York?'

'As fabulous as that sounds, you seem to be forgetting that I'm out of work. Planes cost money and it still doesn't address the problem that you will have to tell your parents. It'll be fine. I promise!'

Wednesday December 27th

It was not fine. Louise is willing to overlook my non-Catholic persuasion but favours a June wedding in Dublin. Also their local community centre is perfect for our reception and she'll start making enquiries this week. I tried to distract her by telling her that Daphne the dog was pregnant, but she'd already put the phone down to go and find her mammy's wedding band in the drawer.

'I told you,' Oliver said, shaking his head. 'She's like an unstoppable force.'

I flopped down on to the couch and sighed. 'I saw all the crap Lucy had to put up with and I can't be arsed with any of it. I don't want the big dress and the big venue and the big breakdown which occurs halfway through the planning. I don't want to have to compromise to keep everyone else happy and I don't want to drag this shit out for years either. I just want us.'

'Fuck it,' he mumbled under his breath before opening up his laptop. 'Pass me my wallet, will you?'

Saturday December 30th

From the moment Oliver booked the flights and hotel on Wednesday, it's been a bit of a blur. Unlike Lucy who spent months planning her perfect day, we've been rushing to apply for a wedding license online, hunting for appropriate ID, finding out when City Hall was open over the holidays, and of course breaking the news to my parents. They couldn't have been happier.

'Oh darling, that's wonderful!' Mum gushed. 'How exciting – married in New York!'

I heard Dad yelling his approval in the background followed by a faint bark from the dog. 'Thanks, Mum,' I replied. 'We're spending a week there so we'll have lots of photos . . . Listen, I'm sorry we're not having a big family wedding but—'

'That's not important,' she said. 'We have you for the rest of our lives – this day is for you and Oliver.'

It was great to have their support but I had no doubt they'd be happy either way. They also offered to pay for our hotel for the week we were staying; a gesture we gratefully accepted.

My friends, of course, were disappointed that they wouldn't be there, but they took the news well when I had them over for lunch.

'Are you fucking kidding me?' Lucy asked, looking at Hazel in disbelief. 'I would never have gotten married without you there. This is entirely selfish behaviour.'

'Aw, don't be like that,' I pleaded. 'I feel terrible enough. We'll all get together when we get back, I promise.'

Hazel was far more diplomatic with her disappointment but I could tell it was there. Although I never imagined getting married in the first place, the reality of now doing it without my friends' involvement made me more than a little sad. I think it's the first major thing Lucy and Hazel haven't been involved with since I met them. Christ, they drove me to hospital when I went into labour at Lucy's house during dinner; Hazel calmly navigating traffic while Lucy called Oliver and told me repeatedly to '*fucking breeeaatthheee*'.

I know Oliver would have liked his sister to be there, but there's no way she'd have kept quiet to the rest of his family, and having them guilt-call us every ten minutes wasn't an appealing thought.

Still, this time next week it'll be all over and I'll be a married woman. Haha! Holy shit!

Sunday December 31st

New Year's Eve began with the sound of a snoring Irishman and the tired grumps of an equally-exhausted, soon-to-be flower-girl who'd just spent nearly fifteen hours travelling from Glasgow, including a three-hour stopover in London. I was too excited to sleep. Not only was I getting married, but I'd never been to New York. To be honest, I wasn't sure which prospect excited me more.

I sat back in my seat, staring at the small television screen without paying attention to the in-flight movie. I envied Oliver's ability to pass out – my brain was swarming. The plan was to turn up at the City Clerk's Office on Tuesday after the holiday to get our license, then return on Thursday to wait in line to get hitched. We'd need a witness but apparently getting one there was easy enough. Oliver had packed his best suit to wear for the ceremony but I still had to buy dresses for Molly and me. Nothing too outrageous or expensive but something I felt special in. Also, was I going to change my name? We gave Molly Oliver's surname when she was born but Hazel was right – Phoebe Webb has too many B sounds. Phoebe Henderson-Webb? Do I want a double-barrelled name? Do I want Oliver's name at all?

My thought train came to a halt when the captain announced that we'd be landing at Newark shortly. As I leant across Molly and looked out of the window, my stomach back-flipped with excitement. God, this was thrilling. This time last year I was buying ugly potatoes and enjoying a sexless relationship, now here I was, flying over New Jersey on my way to get married! Was that the Manhattan skyline in the distance? I nudged Oliver to wake him up.

I felt his hand press on my leg as he peered over me to catch a glimpse of the view, waiting for him to marvel with me at the skyline before it disappeared. I wanted us to have a little moment while Molly slept.

'Wow . . . is that IKEA down there?'

Moment denied.

'This all feels very surreal,' I said quietly, trying not to wake Molly up. 'You ready to get hitched, Webb? You ready to be an actual husband?'

'Definitely,' he replied. 'Though soon you'll be a Webb too. Wife Webb!'

'I still haven't decided what my wife name will be, thank you very much. You could always take my name – Husband Henderson has a nice ring to it.'

'I like Webb,' he responded, grinning. 'It reminds me of Spiderman.'

Oliver took my hand in his and held it while we sat silently for a moment, contemplating what lay ahead. Well, I was; for all I know Oliver might have been thinking about IKEA. 'It was nice of your parents to pay for our hotel this week,' he mused. 'They transferred the money to me straight away. £2000. More than our hotel actually cost.'

'Brilliant!' I replied. 'Looks like we have some extra spending money! Let's buy me some shoes.'

'Actually, it's already gone,' Oliver confessed. 'I wanted to help some friends out. Don't be mad.'

'Oliver, you gave someone part of our wedding fund without telling me?!' I snarled as quietly as possible. 'Who the hell needed the money?'

'Lucy did,' he replied. 'Oh, and Hazel. I split it between them. It was the right thing to do.'

'*My* Lucy and Hazel? I don't understand.'

'I thought they might like to come and see us get married,' he replied. 'Turns out I was right. They arrive on Wednesday.'

'You're lying.'

'Not this time.'

I gave a loud squeal and pounced on Oliver, kissing his sneaky little face. 'I can't believe you did that! I love you! Oh my God, my friends are coming to my wedding! This is literally the best thing you have ever done in your entire life.'

Passengers in the middle aisle were beginning to stare, along with the cabin crew, but I didn't care because only one thing mattered: Oliver Webb had just pulled off the greatest grand gesture of all time.

Acknowledgements

Huge thank you to everyone involved with this book. My brilliant and patient agent Kerry Glencorse, Kathryn Taussig, Emily Yau and Alainna Hadjigeorgiou, Celine Kelly and the entire Quercus crew – you're all amazing! I also want to thank my mum, dad and sister for being as supportive as ever – I love you all.

To those who have kept me sane and laughing, especially Nicola, Em (please write more – you're hugely talented and lovely) and Faye, I'm eternally grateful.

Finally, I'd like to thank my funny, smart, beautiful daughter Olivia for putting up with me. I love you a disgusting amount.